This gift
provided by:
The Seattle Public Library Foundation

A MATTER OF DEATH AND LIFE

Also by Simon R. Green

The Ishmael Jones mysteries

THE DARK SIDE OF THE ROAD *
DEAD MAN WALKING *
VERY IMPORTANT CORPSES *
DEATH SHALL COME *
INTO THE THINNEST OF AIR *
MURDER IN THE DARK *
TILL SUDDEN DEATH DO US PART *
NIGHT TRAIN TO MURDER *
THE HOUSE ON WIDOWS HILL *
BURIED MEMORIES *

The Gideon Sable series

THE BEST THING YOU CAN STEAL *

The Secret History series

PROPERTY OF A LADY FAIRE
FROM A DROOD TO A KILL
DR DOA
MOONBREAKER
NIGHT FALL

The Nightside series

JUST ANOTHER JUDGEMENT DAY
THE GOOD, THE BAD, AND THE UNCANNY
A HARD DAY'S KNIGHT
THE BRIDE WORE BLACK LEATHER

** available from Severn House*

A MATTER OF DEATH AND LIFE

Simon R. Green

SEVERN
HOUSE

First world edition published in Great Britain and the USA in 2022
by Severn House, an imprint of Canongate Books Ltd,
14 High Street, Edinburgh EH1 1TE.

Trade paperback edition first published in Great Britain and the USA in 2023
by Severn House, an imprint of Canongate Books Ltd.

severnhouse.com

British Library Cataloguing-in-Publication Data
A CIP catalogue record for this title is available from the British Library.

ISBN-13: 978-0-7278-9129-7 (cased)
ISBN-13: 978-1-4483-0839-2 (trade paper)
ISBN-13: 978-1-4483-0838-5 (e-book)

All Severn House titles are printed on acid-free paper.

Typeset by Palimpsest Book Production Ltd.,
Falkirk, Stirlingshire, Scotland.
Printed and bound in Great Britain by
TJ Books, Padstow, Cornwall.

There is a world beneath the world. Where treasures can be found, although they're nearly always guarded by monsters, and you can make all your dreams come true if you have the nerve to stand your ground and bet it all on one roll of the dice.

The world beneath the world. The underworld of crime.

My name is Gideon Sable, these days.

I specialize in stealing the kind of things that can't normally be stolen – like a ghost's clothes, a unicorn's urine or a radio that plays all the hit singles famous singers never got around to recording. I dress in black and white because it's a style thing. I'm handsome enough to run most cons and fleet enough of foot to avoid the consequences. I like to think of myself as a modern-day Robin Hood, because I only steal from the bad guys. To make them pay for the pain they cause others.

There used to be another Gideon Sable, but he disappeared, so I stole his identity and reputation. Now I'm the legendary master thief, rogue operator and criminal mastermind. Your last chance for revenge and a little quiet justice.

I have my own crew to help me get things done.

Annie Anybody, the woman who can change her persona at the drop of a wig. Lex Talon, also known as the Damned, the scariest agent for the Good, ever – because when you know you're damned to Hell for all eternity, you can do anything. And Johnny Wilde, also known as the Wild Card, who can see behind the curtains of reality and occasionally pops backstage to rearrange things.

Together, we broke into the greatest treasure vault of all time and brought down Fredric Hammer, the worst man in the world . . . and ever since I've been considering what to do for an encore. It's not as if there's any shortage of things worth stealing or people who need showing the error of their ways, but it had to be something worthy of our time and talents.

I had no idea that the whole matter was about to be taken out of my hands. Fortunately, I always have a plan.

ONE
The Gallery of Ghosts

There are those who say London's Soho isn't the weird adventure playground it used to be, but that's only because most people don't know where to look. Soho is where you go when you think you've seen and done it all, because the strangest part of London can always surprise you. Street lamps glow a dull yellow in the early hours of the morning, like light that has spoiled and gone off, and there are shadows everywhere, because some sins can only flourish in the dark. The streets are full of predators and prey, the working girls all have smiles like sharks, and every bad idea you ever had can be found loitering on one street corner or another.

On this particular early morning, everyone was giving me plenty of room as I strode through some of the darkest back streets and alleyways. Because I was mad as hell and didn't care who knew it. The most precious thing in my life had been stolen from me, and I was heading for the Gallery of Ghosts, that legendary exhibition of the world's strangest photographs, with revenge and retribution on my mind.

Collectors, historians and connoisseurs of the weird and unnatural have always been ready to pay the gallery's exorbitant entrance fee, to see something they know they shouldn't want to and something they'll never be able to forget. There was a time when people believed a camera stole your soul when it took your photo, but some cameras take other things, too. There's a reason it's called the Gallery of Ghosts.

I finally came to a quiet cul-de-sac where the street lamps were reminders of a bygone age. All black iron and ornate stylings, their light was so hazy that shadows formed dark pools between the lamps, like sinkholes in the world. The buildings were just dark shapes, with no lights at any of the windows, slumped together like drowsing animals, waiting for their prey to come within reach. Ample warning that this was not an area to be entered lightly, because the phrase 'urban jungle' isn't always a metaphor.

I picked out one particular door and stopped a cautious distance away. It was just a blank slab of dark-stained wood in a crumbling brick wall. No sign and no name plate; either you knew what the Gallery of Ghosts had to offer or you had no business being there. I looked the place over carefully, and once I'd assured myself there were no obvious guards or surveillance cameras, I walked up to the door and took out my special skeleton key. The one that can open absolutely anything. I showed the key to the lock and it shrugged resignedly, because it isn't only love that looks down its nose at locksmiths. The door unlocked itself in a sulky sort of way and swung silently back. I put the key away and slipped quietly inside, and the door shut itself behind me.

I was braced for an unfriendly reception, but there were no guards and no guard dogs – nothing but a long, dimly lit passageway without a door or a turning, as though someone wanted to make it clear that now you'd committed yourself, there was no turning back. The way before me seemed perfectly open and straightforward, but I knew a nightingale floor when I saw one. Each slender wooden board had been carefully arranged and fitted so it would sing out loudly the moment anyone stepped on it. The perfect hidden alarm system. But I've been around. I studied the layout carefully and then walked steadily forward, cautiously placing my feet on opposing boards so they cancelled each other out. The floor remained entirely silent as I made my way down the corridor, and I couldn't help but grin.

For every security system, there is an equal and opposite trick of the trade.

Still no surveillance cameras or hidden viewing ports. I've been a professional thief long enough that I can always spot the telltale signs. It was as though the gallery owner expected people to find their way in and didn't care, because he had a use for them. The best kind of trap is always the one you walk into willingly. I didn't let the thought slow me down. The owner of the gallery should have known better than to steal from me.

Sebastian Hargrave, the Thief of Time. The man who imprisoned people inside photographs. Whose collection was a horror show and a celebration of suffering. I hadn't just come to the Gallery of Ghosts to take back what was mine; I was there to organize a jailbreak.

There was another locked door at the end of the corridor, but it didn't even try to give me a hard time. The old-fashioned mechanism surrendered to my skeleton key with little more than a sniff and a shrug, and just like that I was inside.

I hadn't been sure what to expect; I'd never been rich or well-connected enough to receive an invitation. Those lucky souls who had been allowed access to the Gallery of Ghosts did so on the strict understanding that they couldn't talk about what they saw, on pain of never being admitted again. So no one ever said anything, because some pleasures were simply too exquisite to risk losing. But instead of some tastefully illuminated museum, with carefully mounted displays of the photographer's art, I found myself facing white plasterboard walls covered with dozens of photos, framed in cheap wooden surrounds and crammed so close together they were practically overlapping.

I moved slowly forward into enemy territory. The corridor stretched away before me, branching suddenly this way and that to form an intricate maze. Everywhere I looked, there were scenes and portraits, proud vistas and amazing sights, and all manner of faces staring out at the world with silently screaming eyes. The fluorescent tubes overhead provided a stark impersonal light, as though determined that not one detail of this circus of horrors would go unappreciated.

Sebastian Hargrave was proud of his prisoners.

I hurried through the endless passageways, taking turns at random, checking each photo but always moving on. I had to find what I was looking for, before Sebastian discovered he had a fox in his henhouse.

The Camera of Dr Caligari first appeared in 1921. A strange mixture of obscure scientific principles and black magic rituals, it was supposed to capture photos of the dead. Spirit portraits from séances were good business at the time, providing comfort for families who'd lost loved ones in the Great War. But instead of the recently and tragically departed, Caligari's camera captured strange and shocking glimpses of other worlds and different realities. That would have been profitable enough, but when the camera's owners experimented, they discovered that under the right conditions it could also physically remove people from this world and freeze them in a stolen moment of Time, in any number of other worlds.

Caligari's camera quickly acquired a reputation among the cognoscenti, and the photos it took became increasingly expensive collector's items. Often improved and updated, the camera passed through many hands, more often than not prised from the cold, dead fingers of an owner reluctant to give it up. Until finally an obscure paparazzo figured out how to make serious money from what the camera could do. Why sell the photos when people could be persuaded to pay to see them again and again in the greatest and most exclusive portrait gallery of all time?

One photo showed a city where every building had been carved from a single piece of bone, and insects the size of people, or perhaps people who moved like insects, crawled up the outsides of the buildings. Another photo showed a flock of white whales, flying over an endless desert like living dirigibles. In a New York where all the skyscrapers were wrapped in ivy, lizards in smart city suits walked briskly through the financial district. Pterodactyls flapped around a broken Eiffel Tower, dropping bloody bits of people into viciously thorned nests to feed their young. A pack of werewolves in Nazi uniforms pursued a fleeing figure across the moonlit snow. And a young Queen Elizabeth smiled at the camera to show off her pointed vampire teeth.

All the worlds of if and maybe, to show that God not only rolls the dice but takes side bets as well.

In the end, though, it was the ordinary everyday faces that offended me the most. All the men and women ripped out of their lives and trapped in a still image, forever. A photographic menagerie, a prison of images, where there was no end to the prisoners' suffering. I couldn't stop to help. I had to keep moving. But even though the eyes didn't move to follow me as I passed, I knew they knew I was there.

Finally, I stopped in front of a photograph showing a young woman in the middle of a dark forest, standing alone and at bay. The clearing was full of shimmering moonlight, pressing against the surrounding trees as though it was all that was holding them back. The whole wood had been warped and twisted by some unseen malignant force, and gnarled branches reached out toward the young woman like crooked arms with angry fingers. It was a forest from a fairy tale . . . the dark original versions, before they were cleaned up for children.

The woman had a sharp face and long red hair, and she was wearing a black leather catsuit. She wasn't flinching or falling back from the reaching branches; she stood her ground with raised fists and glared right back at them, ready to lash out at any that got too close. But the branches were pressing forward from every side, possessed of a terrible strength and an endless hunger, and I knew I had to get her out of there before something really bad happened. Just because the moment was frozen, it didn't mean it couldn't change.

I smiled at the woman in the photograph. My love and my partner in crime, Annie Anybody. The woman who can take on any identity, changing her personality to fit the situation. The Thief of Time had taken her from me with his damned camera, and he really should have known better.

I studied the scene before me – Annie lost and alone in the dark heart of the forest – and tried not to feel as if it was my fault. I couldn't be with her all the time, because she wouldn't let me. She insisted on being her own woman, whoever that happened to be. And most of the time I trusted Annie to look after herself. But Sebastian Hargrave had got to her – perhaps as a way of getting to me – and all I could do was hope she wouldn't be too mad at me for coming to rescue her.

I took out my skeleton key and pressed it against the surface of the photo. I could feel the surface tension, the pressure holding me out, the barrier between worlds. I turned the key slowly, unlocking the forces that held Annie prisoner in the forest, and the barrier collapsed. Suddenly, I was looking through a window into the world beyond. The smell of trees and growing things billowed out into the corridor, quickly overridden by a stench of mulch and decay, of dead things rotting down into the forest floor. The photograph's wooden frame flexed and stretched, as though it was breathing.

I put more pressure on the key, and it sank into the photo. The forest air was uncomfortably warm, like the unhealthy heat of a fever room. I palmed the key and forced my arm deeper into the photograph. I stretched out my hand, and Annie slowly turned her head to look at me. A slow recognition formed in her eyes

. . . and the beginning of hope. The branches strained further into the clearing, desperate to get to Annie. I yelled her name, and she reached out to me. I grabbed her hand and hauled her out of the dark forest and back into the world.

She burst out of the photo like a swimmer from the depths and landed heavily in front of me. I dragged her away from the photo, just as a thicket of gnarled branches shot out after her, hunting for the prey that had escaped them, only to be cut in half, as my skeleton key locked up the photo again and the interface between the worlds shut down. The amputated branches fell twitching and clutching to the gallery floor. Cut off from the dark forest, they quickly became still as the unnatural life went out of them. Annie kicked the nearest ones away from her, with a mixture of anger and disgust. And then she turned to me and hugged me tightly, and I held her as though I'd never let her go.

'I knew you'd find me,' she said quietly.

I looked over her black leather shoulder at the dark and brooding forest in the photo. Nothing was moving, but the trees still looked hungry and cheated. The severed ends of branches were still clawing at the other side of the photo, fighting to get through. After a while, Annie let go of me. She stepped back and looked at me steadily, in control of herself again. She still kept hold of my hand.

'Talk to me, Gideon. How the hell did I end up in that forest?'

'You're in the Gallery of Ghosts,' I said. 'The Thief of Time made an exhibition of you. I thought I'd better remind him that I have a prior claim. Welcome back to the world, Annie.'

'Call me Emma,' she said. And then she stopped and looked at me sharply. 'How did you know I was being held here?'

'I found your note,' I said. 'Saying you were taking Emma out for a spin. That was three days ago. When you didn't answer your phone, I got worried. I checked out Emma's usual haunts, but no one had seen any sign of you. So I used my special compass, the one that only ever points to what I need, and it took me to Old Harry's Place. I asked Harry where you were, and he told me.'

'How did he know?' said Emma.

'Because Harry knows everything,' I said.

'What did he want in return?' said Emma.

'A future favour.'

She winced. 'That's going to be expensive.'

'You're worth it,' I said.

Emma realized she was still holding my hand and let go. Because she always has to stand on her own two feet. She shrugged defensively.

'You let your guard down for just one moment . . .'

She looked around, taking her time, to make it clear she wasn't at all flustered. She scowled at the reaching branches inside the photo, and then her frown deepened as she took in all the other prisoners, in all the other worlds.

'So . . . this is the Gallery of Ghosts. I never really understood what Sebastian gets out of it. There must be safer ways to make money, ways that wouldn't leave so many enemies baying for his blood.'

'Whenever Sebastian removes someone from Time and Space,' I said, 'he stops their existence short of where it should have gone. He can then absorb all that potential – all the years these people should have had, everything they could have been and done – and use it to live forever.'

'That's just nasty,' said Emma. 'Why haven't we done something about him before this?'

'We've been busy,' I said. 'But taking you was the last straw. That brought Sebastian right to the top of my to-do list.'

'Tell me you have a plan.'

I had to smile. 'You know me, Emma. I always have a plan.'

And then we both looked round sharply as a freezing wind came howling down the passageway. The bitter cold hit us like a fist in the face.

'Where is that coming from?' said Emma.

'A photo I passed earlier,' I said. 'Nazi werewolves in a winter setting. It would appear someone knows we're here and has opened a window between the worlds.'

'Nazi werewolves?' said Emma.

'I know,' I said. 'It is rather piling bad on top of bad.'

Emma squared her black leather shoulders. 'We'd better take them down before we go any further. We don't want a pack of wolves sneaking up behind us while we're going after Sebastian.'

'I'm a thief,' I said. 'Not a fighter.'

'Good thing I'm here, then, isn't it?' said Emma. And then

she looked at me. 'What were you planning to do, once you caught up with Sebastian?'

I smiled coldly. 'Take his photos.'

I led the way back down the passageway. Emma strode along beside me, a warrior in black leathers with mayhem in her eyes. Clothes really do make the woman. The wind had died away, but the corridor was still getting steadily colder. Our breath steamed thickly on the air before us, and my bare face smarted from the bitter chill. We walked into winter, with cold hearts and colder intentions.

I recognized the photograph on the wall long before we reached it. The surface was bulging out into the corridor like a soap bubble under pressure. As we drew nearer, a pair of clawed and grey-furred hands suddenly grasped the wooden frame from the inside, and a grinning wolf's head thrust out into the light. The narrowed eyes were piss-yellow, crafty and feral. The werewolf sniffed at the air, then surged out of the photo and dropped into the passageway. It stood upright, though its back was bent and its head thrust forward; it was huge and powerful, sleek and vicious. The Nazi uniform had been torn apart by its transformation, and tufts of thick grey fur thrust through the rents. More of its kind came bursting out of the photo, leaping into the passageway one after another, until a whole pack of humanoid wolves in ragged Nazi uniforms were crouching before us, their long muzzles packed full of jagged teeth.

The air was heavy with a rank and musky odour: the stink of beasts with murder on their minds. The werewolves swayed back and forth as they studied Emma and me, grey lips pulled back in savage grins, clawed hands flexing eagerly. One of the wolves growled and the others joined in, filling the corridor with the sound of hate and hunger.

'I've never liked werewolves,' Emma said briskly. 'They stink the place out and shed all over your furniture. Leave this to me, Gideon. I am just in the mood to beat the crap out of something deserving.'

'You're not really a fighter,' I said cautiously.

'I am when I'm Emma,' she said.

She strode down the passageway, heading straight for the wolves without any sense of hesitation or mercy. They stopped grinning and glanced at each other uncertainly. Emma quickly picked out the alpha wolf and ran straight at him. He reared up threateningly, and she grabbed two big handfuls of his chest hair and shook him hard. The werewolf howled miserably and then broke off as she kneed him savagely in the groin. She let go of the wolf as he bowed forward over his pain, and then punched him viciously on the back of the neck. The werewolf collapsed to lie sprawling on the floor, like a rug that had taken a good beating.

The other wolves barely had time to react before Emma had dived in and among them. She picked one werewolf up and slammed him against a wall, hard enough to make all the photos shake and rattle. As she threw the stunned wolf to one side, another darted forward, only to be met by a swiftly rising knee under the chin that slammed its teeth together and rattled its brain. She raged among the remaining werewolves, striking them down with solid punches and elegant kicks, terrorizing the entire pack and making it look easy.

I stood back and let Emma get on with it, because she'd never forgive me if I didn't. But I was still ready to guard her back if she needed it, and let her be mad at me later. I might not be much of a fighter, but I do have certain advantages.

Unfortunately, no matter how hard Emma hit the werewolves, they always got up again. Whatever damage she did to them healed immediately, and they came back angrier and more determined. She was fast, but they learned quickly. Fanged mouths snapped shut where an arm or a leg had been just a moment before, getting closer every time. Clawed hands left deepening scratch marks on her black leather. She went from winning to too close to losing in a matter of moments, and Emma had no choice but to back off. She quickly retreated down the corridor to stand with me. The werewolves grinned nastily and padded unhurriedly forward.

'I suppose it's too much to hope,' said Emma, just a bit breathlessly, 'that you might have something silver and impressively destructive about your person?'

'That wasn't part of my plan,' I said. 'But you know me: I always bring something useful to the party.'

I took out my skeleton key, pointed it at the werewolves and turned it on the air, unlocking the change mechanism inside them.

Just like that, the wolves were gone, replaced by a group of very surprised men in ragged Nazi uniforms that didn't fit them any more.

Emma stared at them, and then turned to look at me. 'Why didn't you do that before?'

'You looked like you were enjoying yourself,' I said. 'Are you still in a hitting mood?'

'I've got my second wind,' said Emma. 'Are you ready to get involved this time?'

'Of course,' I said.

I might not be a fighter, but no one gets away with threatening my Emma.

We left battered and unconscious Nazis scattered the length of the corridor, and when it was all done, Emma and I leaned on each other for a while as we got our breathing back under control. There's a lot to be said for healthy exercise, but it does take it out of you. When I felt up to it, I moved over to stand before the photo the werewolves had escaped from. Emma moved in beside me.

'Why are you frowning, Gideon?'

I raised a steady finger and pointed out a distant figure striding across the winter snows toward us.

'The last time I looked, the werewolves were chasing someone,' I said. 'But I don't think that's him.'

The figure crossed the intervening distance impossibly quickly, and Emma and I backed away. A dark shape emerged unhurriedly from the photo, long limbs uncurling slowly ahead of the rest of him. He dropped lightly to the floor, straightened up and smiled brightly, his eyes full of an unpleasant mockery.

'What the hell is that?' said Emma, just to make it clear she wasn't the least bit impressed.

'Allow me to present the Thief of Time himself,' I said. 'Sebastian Hargrave – ringmaster, gaoler and scumbag manager of the Gallery of Ghosts.'

Sebastian was abnormally tall and spindly, with a shaven head and the narrow face of an ascetic. He wore a long black robe like a priest, and his face and hands were so pale he looked like a black-and-white photograph of himself. He held himself with an absolute arrogance, lord and master of his own private kingdom. He barely glanced at Emma, before fixing me with a cold sardonic look.

'Welcome to my extravaganza of marvels, my grand parade of spectacle and sorrows. I'm so glad you could make it, Gideon Sable and Annie Anybody.' His voice was soft and sibilant, like a snake that had taken elocution lessons. 'I was alerted the moment you entered my gallery, because every image on display here is mine to command. I can look out of every photo and watch through the eyes of all my possessions. I hope you've had time to enjoy and admire all my very special photographs. They're not just my pride and joy, my treasure and my obsession; sometimes they're bait, to lure in special trophies like you.'

'So basically you're just a long-legged spider, luring flies into your web,' said Emma.

'The spider traps flies because it's hungry,' I said. 'What is it you do with your victims, Sebastian?'

His smile widened, but there was still no humour in it. 'I don't just store my stolen lives; I savour them.'

Emma glared at him. 'If I ever find out you tried to savour me, I will hit you so hard every photo in your gallery will laugh out loud.'

He still didn't even glance in her direction. Just kept on grinning at me, like a man with all the trump cards tucked up his sleeve. I smiled easily back at him, while my mind raced, trying to see the shape of the trap we'd been lured into.

'You shouldn't have stolen so many people, Seb,' I said. 'You must have known someone would come to make you pay.'

'Is there such a thing as too much immortality?' said Sebastian. 'All the lives here have their own unique flavour. Even poor deluded wannabes like Gideon Sable, who stole another man's life, and Annie Anybody, who's content to be anyone other than herself. Special people make for special photographs, and then their particular qualities become mine – forever.'

He laughed softly, enjoying the disapproval in our faces. 'All their triumphs and secrets, their hidden shames and longings – a never-ending carnival of pleasures.' He gestured grandly around him. 'So many lives and so little time to get to know them. But the energies stored in these photographs will make sure I live long enough to enjoy all of them, eventually.'

He cocked his head to one side, as though measuring us for the perfect frame.

'The two of you together will make a splendid portrait. I shall enjoy showing you off to my visitors and wallowing in your lives.'

'Do you honestly think I'd let you take our photo?' I said.

Sebastian giggled suddenly, his eyes full of happy malice.

'Do you really think I'd let a professional thief anywhere near the Camera of Doctor Caligari?'

But everyone has their tell, their own little reveal, and I didn't miss the way one of his hands moved towards a hidden pocket in his robe. I made a mental note of its location, even as Sebastian giggled again.

'Look at you, standing there like you're the heroes of this story. You're in my world now, and I have everything I need to put you in your place.'

He snapped his fingers commandingly, and at the other end of the corridor the photo of Emma's dark forest bulged outwards. Its frame heaved and strained, and suddenly gnarled branches shot out into the passageway. They hit the opposite wall so hard they flattened and rebounded, and then curled viciously in the confined space, searching the air for the prey that got away.

Sebastian drew their attention with a polite cough, and all the branches whipped round to point in our direction. Sebastian indicated Emma and me with an easy gesture, and then had to jump backwards and press himself against a wall as the branches came flying down the narrow passageway, churning and roiling as they spilled endlessly out of the opened photo. Emma and I were already sprinting down the corridor, but the branches caught us before we reached the first turning. They whipped around us, enveloping us in unnaturally flexible branches, and then they closed abruptly, in coils so tight we couldn't fight them. They lifted us off our feet and dragged us helplessly back down the passageway, to the world of the dark forest. And what was waiting for us there.

Emma and I fought the branches with everything we had, but the coils were crushing the breath out of us, with all the strength of the malignant trees. They'd been cheated of their prey once, and I could tell they had plans for us. And yet I didn't think Sebastian would actually let the forest have us. He'd wait till we were back in the photograph and facing the horrors of the wood, and then he'd shut it down, leaving us pinned to an awful moment in Time, like mounted butterflies.

A salutary lesson for all those who came to visit the Gallery of Ghosts. Of what happened to people who dared to defy Sebastian Hargrave, the Thief of Time.

That thought was enough to galvanize me to a greater effort – if only because I couldn't stand the thought of Sebastian being acclaimed as a greater thief than me. I forced one hand inside my jacket, and a sudden relief ran through me. Sebastian wasn't the only one who dealt in frozen moments. I hit the button on my own ace in the hole, and Time crashed to a halt.

Of all the marvellous devices bequeathed to me by the original Gideon Sable, the time pen has always been the most useful. The moment it was activated, I existed outside of Time, caught between one moment and the next, between the tick and tock of reality itself. All sound stopped, and the light darkened to a sullen crimson. There wasn't any air to breathe, and I had to fight against the resistance of a frozen world.

The branches were held motionless in mid-air. Sebastian Hargrave stood completely still, like one of his own photos. I tried to wriggle out of the branches holding me, but the frozen moment had made them stiff and inflexible. I stopped to think my way out of the trap, and then suddenly Time slammed back into motion, and Sebastian laughed happily.

'I know all your tricks, Gideon! The poor souls imprisoned in my photos can't hide anything from me. I hear all their slow sad thoughts as I stroll through my gallery . . . all their little secrets and hard-won knowledge. So I know everything there is to know about anyone worth knowing. And with the captive energies of a thousand lost lives to drawn on, in this place, in my own private domain, Time and Space do what I tell them.'

The branches dragged Emma and me down the passageway, back to the dark forest. And although we fought them furiously, we couldn't even slow them down. Emma looked at the photo looming up ahead and turned her head to glare at me.

'Do something!'

'I am,' I said. 'I'm thinking.'

'Think faster!'

Sebastian's laughter filled the passageway, but I'd stopped even trying to fight. I waited until we were almost on top of the photograph. Its wooden frames stretched and bowed hungrily, as the dark forest readied itself to welcome us. I hung on till the very last moment and then thrust one arm between the branches, stabbed the bulging surface of the photo with my time pen and hit the button.

The pen sank halfway into the world beyond the photo and then stopped abruptly. A terrible pressure closed around my hand, crushing it with vicious force, but I wouldn't let go of the pen. Wild energies ran up and down the surface of the photograph as the two conflicting Time powers fought each other, and then the frame exploded as the pen short-circuited the set-up.

The forest photograph snapped shut, like a slamming door. The branches were cut off again and fell limply away from me and Emma. We fought our way free, leaving the severed ends to curl and die on the floor. Sebastian turned to run. I chased after him and threw him to the floor. We struggled, but he quickly broke free. He lurched to his feet and started to stumble away, but I didn't go after him. I'd already taken what I wanted from his hidden pocket.

I'd only just got to my feet when all the photographs on all the walls blew out like a series of firecrackers. Their seals were broken, and the photos had no choice but to release what they contained. Sebastian cried out in horror as the cascade failure raced through his gallery, and dozens of men and women erupted out of the frames on the walls, fighting their way out into the world. They staggered back and forth in the narrow passageway, clutching at each other to prove they were real again; laughing and sobbing in shock and relief. A babble of voices filled the gallery, demanding answers, but I kept my gaze fixed on Sebastian Hargrave.

His face was full of a slowly dawning horror. With his Gallery of Ghosts destroyed, his connection to all the stolen lives had been cut off. He seemed to recede into the distance without moving, fading out of reality, and then his silently screaming face was staring out of every photo on every plasterboard wall. Thousands of images of Sebastian Hargrave, trapped in a thousand different hells, forever. Because supernature abhors a vacuum, too, and all sins must be paid for.

I grinned at Emma and gestured proudly at the returned crowd.

'Welcome to my jailbreak.'

'Show off,' said Emma.

The floor began to shake. Great cracks raced jaggedly across the plasterboard walls, while the fluorescent lights swung madly, sending shadows flying in all directions. The gallery was giving up the ghost and falling apart. I pulled the time pen out of the shattered photo, grabbed Emma by the hand and hurried down the corridor, yelling for everyone to follow us. They weren't sure what was happening, but they were happy to follow anyone who sounded as if he had a plan.

We all took turns trampling the unconscious ex-werewolves underfoot.

I retraced my path through the maze and then led everyone across the nightingale floor to the exit. The bare boards cried out piteously under the weight of so many uncaring feet. I threw the door open and fell back to let the victims leave first. Emma stood with me, watching the prisoners rush to freedom.

'Why are we staying?' she asked with commendable calm.

'In case some of the bad things I saw in some of those photos have also got out and are coming after us. I didn't come all this way to release all these people, just to have them jumped on at the last moment.'

'Fair enough,' said Emma.

It took a while for everyone to leave. I hadn't realized just how many people the Thief of Time had photographed. But nothing else emerged from the gallery to follow them. Emma looked at me thoughtfully.

'You risked the time pen, your most precious asset, to save me.'

'I can always steal another asset,' I said. 'There's only one Annie Anybody.'

When the last of the gallery's prisoners had departed into the night, Emma and I stepped out on to the street, laughing happily. And the group of men who'd been waiting for us threw bags over our heads and bundled us into a waiting black limousine. And as we were driven away at speed, all I could think was *You let your guard down for just one moment . . .*

TWO
Unfinished Business

I had no idea what was going on or where we were going. Sitting in the back of a limousine with a nasty-smelling bag over my head, I couldn't be sure of anything. I only knew that Emma and I could be in real danger, and since ignorance of the situation just made things worse, I made myself sit calmly and think. I could feel Emma wedged in beside me, her whole body stiff with tension. I pressed my arm against hers, and she pressed back. Neither of us said anything. The men crowded into the back of the limousine with us were clearly professional hard men, and almost certainly not inclined to put up with anything that might be interpreted as a challenge.

It did seem to me that there was room for optimism in our situation. We hadn't been handcuffed, drugged or knocked unconscious. Which suggested someone wanted us delivered undamaged, if possible. And while we might be surrounded by large muscular types, I still had an ace up my sleeve: the time pen. I raised my hand slowly to scratch at my chest and then slipped it inside my jacket. One quick push of the button, and Time crashed to a halt inside the limousine.

I pulled the bag off my head and looked quickly around. I only had as long as I could hold my breath to decide what I was going to do. There were three large muscular types crammed into the back seat with Emma and me, all of them frozen in place. It shouldn't be that difficult to clamber over them to the car door, grab Emma and jump. But what would momentum do to us, once we were outside the moving car and I was forced to restart Time? And even if Emma and I did survive the fall, how far would we get before they turned the car around and came after us? And on top of all that, I wanted to know why we'd been abducted . . . I put the bag back over my head, put the pen back in my pocket and allowed Time to start up again.

I let my hand fall naturally back from my jacket and did some more thinking. How had the kidnappers known to find Emma and me at the Gallery of Ghosts? I hadn't known I was going there until a few hours before. They must have been following me for some time, and I hadn't seen or heard anything. I've been a professional thief, rogue and chancer long enough that I can usually tell when someone is dogging my heels. Which meant these hard men had to be real professionals. Given there'd been no real violence, that suggested whoever was behind this needed me and Emma to perform some task for them.

I grinned inside my bag. I had a lot of experience when it came to turning the tables on people who thought they had me at their mercy. If the kidnapper wanted something from me, that gave me the advantage. They could make whatever threats they liked, but at the end of the day they'd have to agree to some kind of arrangement. And I've always been really good at driving a hard bargain.

Some time later, the limousine finally eased to a halt, and Emma and I were hustled out of the car with professional roughness. The bags were whipped off our heads, and after a certain amount of blinking at the returned light, I finally got a good look at where we'd been brought. And my first thought was *Oh hell, not again.*

Judi Rifkin lived in a large brooding manor house on the edge of the city, in the middle of extensive open grounds. She'd had all the vegetation dug up and removed, so any intruder would have nothing to use as cover. The grey and dusty grounds stretched far and away into the distance, empty and lifeless like the surface of the moon. The perfect setting to match Judi's cold heart. Even her house had been built to impress and designed to intimidate. Its grim and characterless exterior suggested a fortress, rather than a home.

Judi was the former wife of Fredric Hammer. There was a time when they had been the world's most successful collectors of the weird and unnatural, their reputation second to none. And then Fredric decided he didn't want to share any more. He divorced Judi and used every legal and underhand trick there was to make sure she got nothing. Now all she cared about was getting revenge on her despised ex. I'd been here once before with Annie, when Judi hired me and my crew to break into Hammer's secret vault and steal his most treasured possession – a time television, on which you could view every event in history – just to upset him. Since we never actually delivered the television, Judi probably had a great many unpleasant things she wanted to say to us.

The hard men urged Emma and me forward, but kept their hands off us as long as we kept moving. I appreciated the professional courtesy, but still made a mental note to arrange some kind of future payback. You can't let people push you around, or no one will respect you. And sometimes respect is all you have to keep the flies off.

The massive front door opened on its own as we approached, and Emma and I stepped through into a lobby packed with armed guards and the kind of full-body scanner you usually only find at airports. We passed through without setting off any alarms (because the kind of useful devices I carry can't be detected by most technology) and were quickly hustled through a series of high-ceilinged chambers and wide-open rooms. The same paintings and statues were still in place from our last visit, all of them extremely rare and valuable . . . but there was no sense of theme or personal taste. For Judi, it was all about scoring points over Hammer. I often thought she only acquired things to make sure he couldn't have them.

Security cameras kept a close watch on us from every nook and cranny, whirring quietly as they turned to follow us. They perched on top of shelves and peered over the shoulders of statues, their cold red eyes as unblinking as carrion crows contemplating the soon-to-be-dead. Because no one stole from Judi Rifkin and lived to boast of it.

We were finally ushered into an elegant and very private drawing room, where Judi Rifkin was sitting on an ornate medieval throne, suitably elevated so she could look down on everyone else. Stiff-backed, with her head held proudly erect, Judi was a painfully thin, grey-haired presence in a wraparound robe. She had been pretty once, but time and loss and bitterness had scoured all beauty away, leaving nothing but bones and wrinkles. Her cold eyes missed nothing, and her wide slash of a mouth clamped down on all emotions to make sure none of them escaped. She had to have been in her late seventies the last time I saw her, but she looked a lot older now, and a great deal more fragile, as though her obsession had finally caught up with her and was burning her up from the inside. She hit me with her hardest stare, to make clear how much trouble I was in, and I smiled politely back at her.

'Nice to see you again, Judi. Really, though, there was no need to go to this much trouble.'

'You owe me,' she said flatly.

I gave her my best casual shrug. 'We did break into Fredric's vault, but the situation turned out to be a bit more complicated than we expected.'

Judi dismissed that with a curt sniff and turned her gaze to Emma, standing tall and proud in her long red wig and black leather catsuit.

'Am I ever going to see what you really look like, Annie?'

'Not if I can help it,' Emma said easily.

Judi almost smiled, then remembered she was mad. Her gaze became cool and businesslike, and she sat carefully back in her throne so she could look down her nose at both of us.

'I have another job for you. And no, you don't get to decline.'

'The time television was quite definitely destroyed when Fredric surprised us inside his vault,' I said.

'I don't care,' said Judi. 'I don't want that any more. I've moved on.'

I wasn't sure I believed her, but I nodded in an understanding sort of way.

'I need your special talents again, for a very special job,' said Judi. 'You get me what I want now, and I will call it quits and leave you in peace.'

Emma and I didn't need to glance at each other. We both knew better than to believe anything Judi was promising, but we had enough sense to act as though we did. Judi suddenly remembered that the hard men were still in the room with us, and dismissed them with a slow gesture from an arthritic hand.

'Leave us. But don't go far; I may have other uses for you.'

One of the hard men cleared his throat in a carefully respectful way.

'Are you sure that's entirely wise? Gideon Sable and Annie Anybody have reputations for being professionally sneaky and surprisingly dangerous.'

Judi glared at him. 'There is no one more dangerous in this room than me. And yes, that includes you.'

The hard man didn't have an answer to that, so he just gathered up the other hard men with a glance and led them out of the drawing room. Judi waited till the door had closed behind them, and then smiled at me in an almost flirtatious way.

'You know better than to try anything, don't you, Gideon?'

I had no doubt Emma and I had been covered by hidden weapons systems ever since we entered the house. The kind that could reduce any threat to a discreet pile of dust, small enough to be removed with a dustpan and brush. Judi hadn't survived this long by taking any chances. So I just smiled easily back at her and waited for her to continue.

'I have grown old,' Judi said bluntly, 'while that bastard ex-husband of mine had his youth restored when he made himself immortal. I'm damned if I'll die while he's still ahead of the game. Although I have to admit, I am baffled by his current behaviour. Selling off his treasures so he can give the money to good causes . . . Either he's finally lost his mind or it's all part of some devious scheme to make me drop my guard. And that is never going to happen.'

I was quietly relieved that she hadn't discovered the truth: that her hated ex-husband was dead and gone, his body possessed by my old friend the Ghost. I did wonder if I should tell her. She might be pleased to learn that Fredric's soul had been forced out of his body and sent screaming down to Hell. It could give her peace and a chance at closure. Then again, it might not. Judi's hatred of her ex was all she had to keep her going. She could see his death as cheating her out of revenge. I wouldn't put it past her to summon his soul back and reinstate it in his body, just so she could go on hating him. I realized Judi had started speaking again, and made myself concentrate.

'I have decided that it isn't enough simply to keep acquiring precious items before Fredric can,' she said. 'I must become young and immortal, just like him, so my revenge can never end . . .' She fixed me with a harsh and implacable stare. 'And for that, I need the Masque of Ra.'

Emma and I didn't say anything, and we still didn't look at each other, but Judi must have seen something in our faces. She arranged her old bones a little more comfortably on her throne and smiled knowingly.

'You were both involved in an attempt to steal the masque, years ago. But my ex got to it first, destroying your lives and reputations in the process. You had to completely reinvent yourselves, just to survive. Bring me the Masque of Ra, and you can have your revenge on Fredric and put some unfinished business to rest at last.'

'Put up sufficient money, and you have a deal,' I said, keeping my voice carefully even. 'I'll put a new crew together and get it done.'

Judi looked at me suspiciously. She hadn't expected it to be so easy.

'You've already proved how easily you can find us,' I said steadily. 'If stealing the Masque of Ra will get you off our backs, that makes it a good deal. So, what do you know about the masque?'

Judi settled herself comfortably on her throne. She loved to lecture people about all the weird stuff she knew that other people didn't.

'The ancient Egyptians put a lot of thought into the idea of immortality. They mapped their afterlife in great detail and invested a lot of time and effort in preparing their dead bodies so they had a better chance of reaching it. But for some, living for ever in the next world wasn't enough. The Pharaoh Khuffu worked thousands of slaves to death building his pyramid, but the pyramid itself wasn't important. It was the deaths that mattered. The Masque of Ra absorbed all the slaves' souls as they died, and as long as the pharaoh owned the masque, he could draw on those stored souls and live thousands of lifetimes.'

Emma and I glanced at each other, remembering Sebastian Hargrave and his Gallery of Ghosts. Judi was so caught up in her story she just kept going.

'No one seems to know who actually created the Masque of Ra, or how it was able to do what it did. History from that time is very spotty. But it seems that Khuffu's priests really didn't like the idea of a pharaoh who would never die, because that would undermine their authority. So they stole the masque and hid it away in a secret chamber inside Khuffu's pyramid.

'The pharaoh went insane with rage and spent the rest of his life and most of his empire's resources trying to find it. But he never did. He finally died, was mummified and laid to rest in his pyramid – so he could spend eternity lying next to the prize he'd spent his whole life searching for. Never upset priests; their sense of humour isn't like anyone else's.

'The masque wasn't rediscovered until the 1970s, when a prog rock band called Odin's Other Eye decided to record a song inside Khuffu's pyramid. For the atmosphere, the mystical vibe and the publicity. While searching for just the right chamber to record in, they stumbled across the secret hiding place of the Masque of Ra.

'There are those who say all of this was arranged by the group's manager, one Albertus Myers, a man with an extensive background in the occult, who was believed to be personally responsible for the band's amazing success.'

I nodded quickly. 'I've heard of him. He disappeared into a mirror in the early eighties.'

'What matters,' Judi said heavily, 'is that he sold on the Masque of Ra almost immediately. Since then, the masque has passed through many hands, leaving a trail of murder and mayhem in its wake. Its reputation has risen and fallen, as such things do, and it is currently on open display in the lobby of the ancient Egyptian-themed Khuffu Casino in Las Vegas.

'It is possible that the current owner, on old-time mobster called Saul Montressor, doesn't known what he has. Or perhaps he's showing it off in public just to demonstrate how powerful he is. The masque could be his way of saying *Don't mess with me*.'

'Isn't he worried it might be stolen?' I said carefully.

'The masque is protected,' said Judi. 'Of course, that hasn't stopped some people from trying.'

'What happened to them?' said Emma.

'No one knows,' said Judi. 'And no one wants to talk about it, because what happens in Vegas stays in Vegas.'

'You're really not selling this job,' I said.

Judi's smile was openly mocking. 'If it was easy, everyone would be doing it. But you will do this for me, won't you?'

'Yes,' I said.

'Because it's unfinished business,' said Emma.

'Get me the masque,' Judi said briskly. 'Refuse, and you die.

Keep the masque for yourselves, and you die. Get caught by Saul Montressor, and you die. But if you can pull this off, and personally deliver the masque into my hands . . . I will give you the five million pounds I promised you for the time television. And then we'll finally be quits. Won't that be nice?'

Yeah, right, I thought. Judi Rifkin had never been one to forgive a slight. The moment she didn't need us any more, she would take her revenge on Emma and me, for daring to fail her the last time. Or at least she'd try. The day I couldn't think rings around someone like Judi Rifkin, they might as well start nailing down the coffin lid.

'I will not be funding this operation,' Judi said briskly. 'Because I can't risk Saul Montressor discovering any connection between us. I'm not ready to fight an open war with that man. But I will provide you with a means of getting to Las Vegas unnoticed, so Saul won't know you're coming. Assembling a crew is down to you. I don't need to know the details, because I don't care. Just get me the masque – whatever it takes.'

'Why that particular mystic artefact?' I said. 'It's not like there's any shortage of unnatural short cuts to immortality. And a lot of them come with better reputations than the Masque of Ra. I would have thought it had been largely discredited these days.'

'Saul Montressor bankrolled Fredric and me, back when we were first starting out as collectors,' said Judi. 'In return for a percentage, obviously. But when our marriage broke up, Saul sided with Fredric. And overnight I was left out in the cold, with no money and no protection. I thought Saul was my friend . . . but he went with Fredric, because that was where the money was. So I will avenge myself on Saul by taking the Masque of Ra and by denying him his chance at immortality.'

Her every word was soaked in rage and hatred. A reminder that this much-reduced old lady could still be extremely dangerous. And that there really is no fury like a woman scorned.

'We'll get it for you,' I said.

Judi looked at me thoughtfully. 'I saw something in your face when I said Saul's name. What did he do to you?'

'Some years ago he came to London, looking to buy a casino,' I said. 'But no one would sell to him, because everyone knew a threat to the status quo when they saw one. So Saul decided to show the locals just how dangerous he could be. He set his sights on a particular casino, owned and run by the Ashanti brothers, Robert and Doug. They were friends of mine. When they refused to sell, Saul blew the place up. Killed a lot of people, including Robert and Doug.

'After that, everyone closed ranks, and suddenly Saul's people started turning up dead. Eventually, he gave up and went home. I couldn't touch him; he had money and power and connections, and I was smaller then. But now . . . I'm ready. The Masque of Ra isn't my only piece of unfinished business.' I looked at her steadily. 'But you already knew all of that, didn't you?'

Judi leaned back in her throne and tried to arrange herself a little more comfortably. 'I hear things. And I have always believed in hiring properly motivated people.'

'Do you really think that the masque is everything it's supposed to be?' I asked carefully. 'We can get it for you, but I can't guarantee it will make you immortal.'

'I trust my sources,' said Judi. 'And they say the masque doesn't just let you live for ever; it also makes you young and powerful. Just what I need to take on my dear ex-husband.'

'Anything else we need to know?' I said.

Judi's smile widened. 'I have an informant among Saul's people. He reached out to me and put this whole thing in motion. Big Bill Buxton, resident stand-up comic at the Khuffu Casino and a very old friend of Saul's.

'Or at least he was, until Saul decided to make himself young and immortal and leave his old friend behind. Bill sees that as a betrayal, which is why he's turned against Saul. Once you get to Las Vegas, he's ready to tell you everything you need to know about the casino's security system. In return for you taking the masque and forcing Saul to grow old with Bill.'

She produced a thick folder from down the side of her throne and handed it to me. Her heavily veined hand trembled noticeably, but neither of us mentioned it. 'This contains all the information he's provided so far. On the casino, on Saul and on his family.'

She sank down in her throne, looking suddenly older and worn out. She dismissed Emma and me with a slow gesture, but I didn't move.

'Why not put your own team together?' I said. 'You have all kinds of people working for you.'

'Why put myself at risk when I can use you?' Judi said shortly.

'If you get caught, they'll just put it down to your old grudge against Saul.'

I thought about it, taking my time. I was happy enough to steal the masque and humiliate Saul, but I had no intention of handing it over to Judi. The moment I did, she'd kill me, and everyone with me. Which meant I had a lot of hard thinking to do. I smiled at Judi.

'We'll do it. Piece of cake.'

'I like cake,' said Emma.

We left Judi sitting on her throne, dreaming bitter dreams of vengeance.

THREE

Who's Who and What's What

The hard men drove us back into London and didn't speak a single word between them until one finally stirred himself to ask where they could drop us off. I said Old Harry's Place, and the atmosphere in the limousine became suddenly very tense.

'Is there a problem?' Emma said sweetly.

The hard men looked at each other, all of them hoping someone else would go first. In the end, it was the driver who spoke, without once taking his eyes off the road.

'Everyone in our line of work has at least heard of Harry and his Place. It's not somewhere I would choose to go.'

'It's not like I'm asking you to drive into bandit country,' I said. 'The natives might get a little restless on occasion, but they're not going to ambush you.'

'There are stories about Old Harry's Place,' said the driver, and all his fellow hard men nodded. 'They say it's where you go to sell your soul, or someone else's.'

'There are a lot of stories about Harry,' I said. 'But he's always done right by me.'

'Then maybe the old lady isn't crazy after all, choosing you to take on the Montressors,' said the driver.

* * *

And so we ended up driving through the shadowy depths of Soho, where the streets have no name because the locals don't want anyone knowing where they live. We passed shops selling things people aren't supposed to want, clubs where lost princesses can dance till their shoes fill with blood, and the more dubious establishments where love and heart's ease can be had for knock-down prices, and only slightly shop-soiled.

The night market, where the wages of sin are endlessly negotiable.

The limousine finally eased to a halt outside Old Harry's Place, and the hard men bundled Emma and me out on to the street. We had barely regained our balance before the limousine was racing down the street and taking the nearest corner on two squealing tyres. I took a quick look around, but it all seemed very quiet and utterly deserted. There was no sense of a watching eye anywhere, so I felt free to give Old Harry's Place my full attention.

Everyone's heard about those marvellous magical shops that sell wonders and treasures and all the stuff that dreams of avarice are made of. Those odd little establishments, tucked away in dark corners, which aren't always there when you go back to look for them. Old Harry's Place is always there and always open. It's a pawn shop, ready to buy or sell anything you ever desired. Including all the special little items you've dreamed of your entire life; all those that plague your nightmares and haunt you in the early hours.

'Why did you want to come back here?' said Emma. 'You already owe Harry more than is healthy.'

'Because Harry knows things,' I said. 'And we're going to need some help with the heavy lifting on this one.'

'Harry isn't noted for being generous with his time or his favours,' Emma said carefully.

'I know,' I said. 'But needs must, when the devil's vindictive ex-wife has you by the unmentionables.'

'Tell me we're only doing this so we never have to think about the Masque of Ra again,' said Emma. 'Tell me we're going to stick it to Judi Rifkin. Tell me you've got a plan.'

I grinned at her. 'I've always got a plan.'

'But is it a good one?' said Emma.

I looked thoughtfully at the window of Old Harry's Place. It was full of an impenetrable darkness, so deep it could contain anything. The darkness at the edge of the world, where light runs out. I always think of it as a test of character. If you haven't got what it takes to stare into the darkness and dare it to look back, you really shouldn't be contemplating doing business with Old Harry. Emma moved in beside me, considered the endless dark and sniffed loudly.

'Typical of Harry. Too mean even to provide a reflection.'

I turned to the door, which was doing its best to appear ordinary. The small flickering neon sign set above it said simply *Buyer Beware*. But when I tried the door handle, it refused to turn, and I realized with something of a shock that the door was locked. I turned to Emma, who appeared equally taken aback. She shouldered me out of the way and rattled the door hard, to no effect.

'But . . . Old Harry's Place is always open!' said Emma. 'That's the point!' She stopped abruptly and glared at me. 'Have you done something to upset him?'

'I'm pretty sure Harry would have made it very clear to me if I had,' I said.

'I am not being locked out,' Emma said firmly. 'Use your shoulder. Or your skeleton key. How dare Harry not be open to us!'

'We don't know that it's just us,' I said carefully. 'So I think I'm going to try being polite – until I've got a better idea of what's going on.'

'And if that doesn't work?'

'There's got to be somewhere around here that would sell us a sledgehammer.'

I knocked courteously on the closed door, and a face rose up out of the dark wood. It was fashioned along human lines, but too perfect to be real, and the eyes held something of the infinite. Like a god manifesting in its church to make sure everyone was behaving themselves. The mouth opened, and when it spoke, the voice sounded as though it had crossed immeasurable distances to make itself heard.

'Old Harry's Place is closed. All deals are concluded, all business completed, and any unfulfilled desires you might still have are therefore your own problem. No refunds, no apologies, no second chances. Now, go bother someone else or I'll turn you into a pillar of salt.'

I met the simulacrum's gaze unflinchingly. Never give the supernatural an inch, or it'll walk all over you.

'Cut the crap,' I said. 'I'm Gideon Sable.'

'Well, why didn't you say so?' the face said grumpily. 'You're the one he's been waiting for. Get your arse inside, before someone gets a good look at you and thinks we're going downmarket.'

The face disappeared back into the wood, scowling all the way. The door unlocked itself and swung slowly back.

'Well, it does seem that we're expected,' said Emma. 'Is that good or bad?'

'Knowing Harry, probably both,' I said.

I strolled into the shop, doing my best to look as if I was just there to browse and sneer at things, while Emma stuck close behind, so she could use me as a human shield if necessary.

The shop was empty. Normally, Old Harry's Place was packed from wall to wall with endless shelves and stacks and display cases, crammed full of things that fell off the back of reality. Maps of countries that history has never heard of, medals from shadow wars that no one wants to remember, crates full of all the teddy bears mothers threw away. Wishing rings and haunted tuxedos, a false face guaranteed to steal anyone's heart, and a book full of all the addresses you wish you'd had when you were a teenager. Wondrous things, expensive things and more than a few downright dangerous things, peering out from rows of shelves that seemed to go on for ever. There are stories about people who'd gone into those stacks exploring and never came out again. Of course, there are all kinds of stories about Old Harry's Place.

But I had never once heard of anyone who'd walked in and found nothing but a lot of empty space, like a church no one attends any more. Bare light bulbs cast an almost apologetic light, and the shadows were very still and ordinary. The long counter behind which Harry always sat, perched gnomically on his high chair, was deserted. Even the great stuffed bear that stood by the door and occasionally acted as bouncer was conspicuous by its absence.

'Must have been one hell of a closing-down sale,' said Emma.

'But I was here only a few hours ago!' I said. 'And the shop looked just like it always did. Harry was checking out a new consignment of possessed laptops, and I got dive-bombed by a bunch of flower fairies out of their minds on electric pollen. Just another night at Old Harry's Place. There's no way he could have emptied his shop out this quickly.'

'Except this is Harry we're talking about,' said Emma. 'And you know what they say . . .'

'That no one knows anything for sure when it comes to Harry,' I said.

Emma nodded slowly. 'Could something have happened to him?'

'Things don't happen to Harry,' I said. 'He happens to other people.'

I took a look behind the counter, but even the high chair was gone, along with the specially blessed metal gloves Harry used to handle particularly hazardous items. It felt strange, standing on that side of the counter. Like walking backstage after a magic show, when the magician has gone home and taken all his tricks with him. I came back out and rejoined Emma, and we stood together in the middle of the deserted shop, staring around like children abandoned in a haunted house.

'Where could he have gone?' said Emma.

I shrugged. 'It's not like we have any real idea of where he came from.'

While there are a great many stories about the true nature of Old Harry's Place, there are even more about the man himself. Some say he's a demon let out of Hell to tempt people into giving up their souls in return for the wonders he has to offer. Others have been known to claim that he's immortal, and he and his shop have always been around in one form or another, tricking people into giving up things that matter, in return for things that really don't. And some say he's the front man for a really strange alien invasion, buying up our culture one crooked deal at a time. There are lots of stories about Harry, all of them contradictory. Most of us think Harry makes them up himself, to keep us guessing.

I went to the rear of the shop and called his name. My voice fell flatly on the quiet, because now that all the shelves were gone, the shop was merely shop-sized. Walking through the rows and rows of shelves used to feel like travelling through a forest. I had journeyed into those depths myself on more than one occasion, and they went so far back I half expected to come out in Narnia. I called again, adding my name, but there was still no response. Emma came forward to join me.

'Could he be hiding somewhere?'

'There's nowhere left to hide,' I said. 'And I can't believe he'd just walk away. Not while I still owe him a favour. Harry has always believed in balancing his books – often in weird, innovative and appallingly punitive ways.'

'Quite right,' said Harry.

Emma and I spun round, and there he was, standing serenely in the middle of his empty shop, smiling his usual *I know all manner of things that you don't* smile. A large square man with a large square face, Harry was a thoughtful presence in a dark suit that looked as if it could use a good dusting. He peered cheerfully over the granny glasses perched on the end of his nose, and I glared right back at him.

'What is going on here, Harry?'

'And hello to you, too, Gideon,' Harry said mildly. 'And to you, Ms Anybody.'

'Call me Emma.'

'Why not?' said Harry. 'I'm afraid the cupboard is bare, just at the moment, because I'm leaving. My time is up, my sentence is over, my exile is at an end and I must return to be King of the Cats, whichever answer suits you best. What matters is, I'm going home.'

'Where is that?' said Emma. 'And what happened to all your stock?'

'Home is where the hearts are,' said Harry. 'And I packed all my possessions into a single suitcase by sitting on the lid really hard. They say you can't take it with you, but who listens to them anyway?'

'Why do you have to go?' I said.

'Family business,' said Harry. 'You know how it is. If I don't get back soon, they'll start eating each other.'

And then he just stood there and smiled, defying us to question him further, because we all knew he wasn't going to provide any answers that would satisfy us. So I just nodded calmly and plunged into an explanation of my new heist. Harry listened carefully, nodding in all the right places, and actually raised an eyebrow when I mentioned the Masque of Ra.

'That old thing? I didn't know it was still around. You do know that . . .'

'Yes,' I said quickly. 'I do know that.'

'What do you know?' Emma said immediately, staring at me suspiciously. 'Is there something about the masque that you're not telling me?'

'Let's just say there's less to it than meets the eye,' I said. I kept my gaze fixed on Harry, half afraid he might disappear again if I didn't. 'Has anyone ever tried to sell you the masque, Harry?'

'I have no interest in that particular item,' said Harry.

'Could you supply me with a copy?' I said. 'Good enough to fool even the most sophisticated gaze?'

'Funny you should ask,' said Harry. 'Someone did ask me to make them one, ages ago, but they never came back to collect it. I'm sure I could dig it out before I have to leave.'

I gave him a hard look. He wasn't usually this obliging. And he hadn't mentioned a price, which was always worrying. I pressed on.

'What can you tell us about Saul Montressor and his family?'

'Lots and lots,' Harry said cheerfully. 'Including many fascinating details concerning his recently acquired supernatural security.'

'Do you think you could find the time to share some of that information before you disappear over the horizon?' I said.

He smiled. 'I may be retiring, but business is still business. I'm sure I don't need to tell you that intelligence of that nature comes with a very hefty price tag, including a percentage of all profits. Or . . . you could just pay off the favour you owe me. By agreeing to take over this shop after I have departed for greener skies and darker pastures.'

Emma and I looked at each other, and then back at Harry.

'Just when I think the day can't get any weirder,' I said. 'Why would you want me to do that?'

'Because I have to leave the shop to someone,' said Harry.

I pursed my lips as I thought about it. 'This isn't just a shop, is it?'

'Got it in one,' said Harry.

'Then what is it?' said Emma.

'That's for you to decide,' said Harry.

'All right,' I said. 'I'm game.'

'Just like that?' said Emma. 'Don't you want to at least lift the bonnet and check out its teeth first?'

'We don't have the time to debate it,' I said. 'We need to know what Harry knows.'

Emma folded her arms firmly and stuck out her chin. 'You should still have consulted me before accepting. This affects both of us, and I am not a shopkeeper.'

'Neither am I,' I said. 'So we'll just have to think of something else to do with it.' I turned back to Harry. 'I provisionally agree to take over the shop . . . in return for everything you can tell me about Saul Montressor, his family and his casino's security.'

'You have a deal,' said Harry. 'Of course, I don't actually know much myself. But I know a talking mirror that does.'

He moved over to the nearest wall and turned around a tall standing mirror I would have sworn wasn't there a moment before. Harry shifted it into position to face us, grunting loudly to make it clear how much effort he was putting into helping us, and then stood back and gestured proudly at the mirror. Emma and I moved over to join him. The mirror's reflection didn't show either of us, just Harry dressed as a clown, complete with long shoes, baggy clothes and full makeup. He was holding an axe, whose head was thickly stained with dried blood. Harry sighed.

'Please play nicely, Sidney. We are not at home to Mr Smart Alec.'

'But we are at home to Mr Smug Bastard,' said the mirror in a loud, grating voice. The clown disappeared, replaced by a reflection that showed only the empty shop. 'I do not need to be left facing the wall like a naughty child!'

'Some days, it's the only way to shut him up,' Harry confided regretfully. 'All the talking mirrors in all the worlds, and I had to get stuck with one that thinks it's got a sense of humour.'

The mirror sniggered loudly and showed us a reflection of Harry dressed as a pantomime demon, complete with horns and a pitchfork and sagging crimson tights.

'Oh, come on,' said Harry. 'I'm not that bad a boss.'

'Don't want to play any more,' the mirror said sulkily. 'You're going off and leaving me.'

'You couldn't survive where I'm going,' said Harry. 'But I am leaving you in good hands. This nice gentleman and lady will be taking over.'

The mirror sighed heavily. 'After all the trouble I went to, breaking you in as my boss, and now I have to start again. Still, life with Gideon Sable and Annie Anybody does promise to be interesting . . . And I do like the leather suit, girlie.'

'I will wash your mouth out by smearing soap all over you,' Emma said coldly.

'How do you know I wouldn't like that?' said the mirror suggestively.

'I could leave you facing the wall all day,' I said sternly.

'Bully!' said the mirror.

'Tell Gideon and Emma everything you know about the Montressor family,' Harry said firmly.

'You're no fun,' said the mirror. It showed us a view of a graveyard at midnight, with moonlight shimmering on the headstones. 'This is what happens to people who cross the Montressors, because they are old-school bad guys. The only reason they don't use concrete overshoes is because Las Vegas is in the middle of a desert. And for an extreme case, they'd probably use them anyway and drop you in a swimming pool.'

'Show us the patriarch,' said Harry. 'Saul Montressor.'

The graveyard disappeared, replaced by a close-up view of a large hulking figure in his late seventies. He looked as if he had been dangerous and could be again, if needed. He had a harsh face, a bald head and pitiless eyes. He wore an expensive suit with style and assurance, as though he had extensive experience of all the good things in life. And was perfectly ready to kill anyone who tried to take them away from him. I stared at him for a long moment.

'All these years, and he hasn't changed a bit,' I said finally. 'He still looks like a complete bastard.'

'A mobster from a long line of mobsters,' Harry said easily. 'Right back to when Bugsy Siegal and his pals first put Vegas on the map, as the very best place to throw away your life's savings. But now you are looking at a man who has achieved a great many things, only to wonder, *Is that it?*'

'And what has he decided?' said Emma.

'Faced with advancing age, Saul is having to make some difficult decisions,' said the mirror. 'Should he risk using the Masque of Ra, if he can find the right activating ritual, in the hope of becoming young and immortal . . . Or play it safe and sell it on for a ton of money? And like King Lear . . . he has to decide what to do about his children. Who will succeed him and take over his empire? Which of them is worthy? Are any of them?'

Saul's image disappeared, replaced by a middle-aged man with a flushed face and flat black hair, a sour gaze and an unconvincing smile. He was doing his best to appear dangerous, but the best he could manage was a sleazy sort of menace. He dressed well enough, but style was beyond him. He gave the impression that whatever authority he had would always be second-hand.

'This is Frank Montressor, the good son,' the mirror said chattily. 'In his forties, because all of Saul's children arrived late in his life. He was always far too busy to give his children the attention they needed, so he hired a succession of other people to do it for him. Which goes a long way to explaining why they turned out such a mess. Frank went into the family business to impress his father, and ended up second in command of the Khuffu Casino. But Saul still doesn't respect him, because his son didn't have to fight for things the way he did. He's always second-guessing Frank and shouting at him in front of people.'

'How does Frank feel about that?' said Emma.

'Guess,' said the mirror.

Frank's image disappeared, replaced by a somewhat younger man. Tall and lean, dark-haired and dark-eyed, he had a fierce and hungry look. He dressed casually and glared out of the mirror as though he was at war with the world.

'Tony Montressor is the younger son, in his late thirties,' said the mirror. 'He ran away from home to be a famous artist, but when that didn't pan out, he had to come crawling back and beg his father for a job. Despite all that, Saul respects Tony much more than Frank, for at least having the guts to try to be his own man. He put Tony in charge of casino security, and Tony surprised everyone by being good at it. Perhaps because, unlike his elder brother, he has some experience of the outside world. And, just possibly, because he is his father's son, after all.'

Another abrupt change, as Tony was replaced by a short, plump woman. She wore her dark hair in bangs that didn't suit her, over a face best described as determined. She wore a smart outfit with sullen indifference and watched the world with blunt distrust, as though just waiting to see what it would hit her with next.

'Joyce Montressor,' said the mirror. 'Youngest child, in her early thirties. She never wanted any part of her father's business, but couldn't decide what she did want. Joyce only went to work for her father until something better came along, but all these years later she's still there. Feeling trapped and frustrated, as much by her own indecision as her father's authority. He lets her run the showbusiness side of the casino, because she can do less damage there. Joyce is secretly in a relationship with the casino's resident singer, the lovely Adelaide. They go to great lengths to keep it from Saul because he wouldn't approve.'

Joyce was replaced by a tall, statuesque blonde in a long gown of silver sequins. Glamorous, in a professional kind of way, she faced the world with a practised smile that was probably quite convincing from a distance.

'Adelaide has a good voice,' said the mirror. 'Too good for where she is, but Saul pays her enough to keep her around.' The singer disappeared, leaving an empty reflection. The mirror yawned loudly. 'And there you have all the major players. Any questions?'

'What about Saul's wife?' said Emma. 'The mother of his children.'

'Dana Montressor died four years ago,' said the mirror. 'An ex-showgirl, who never even pretended to marry Saul for love. She got very interested in drinking as she got older – that, and putting Saul down in public.'

'How did she die?' I said.

'Car crash,' said the mirror. 'Nothing obviously suspicious, given the way they all drive in Las Vegas, but there was still a lot of talk, just because she was Saul's drunken, nagging wife.'

I looked at Harry. 'How does your mirror know all this stuff?'

'Because Sidney can see out of any mirror,' said Harry. 'And he loves to gossip. You didn't think I kept him around for his personality, did you?'

'I heard that!' the mirror said loudly.

'Saul Montressor has blood on his hands,' said Harry, ignoring the mirror. 'Figuratively and literally. Not so sure about the family. There are a lot of rumours, but no one's ever proved anything; if there are bodies, no one knows where they're buried.'

'I know where Robert and Doug are buried,' I said. 'Or at least what was left of them.'

'Don't let your emotions get in the way on this one, Gideon,' said Harry. 'Or the Montressors will eat you alive.'

'This heist is all about the masque,' I said steadily. 'The chance to destroy Saul is just a bonus.'

'Don't underestimate his children,' said Harry. 'None of those apples fell far from the tree. And while they're always fighting and feuding in private, they might band together against an outside threat.'

'I have always been a great believer in divide and conquer,' I said. 'The best cons are always based around setting your enemies at each other's throats.'

'That's a bit cold-blooded, isn't it, Gideon?' said Emma.

'Fight fire with fire,' I said. 'And hide all the extinguishers.'

The mirror cleared its throat, just a little self-consciously, and a new figure appeared in the reflection.

'And now it's time for the comic relief. I give you the Khuffu Casino's very own resident funny man . . . Big Bill Buxton!'

A large butterball of a man, Bill had a sweaty face and a bald head, and was well into his seventies. He wore a sloppy Hawaiian shirt over smartly pressed shorts and was grinning determinedly off into the distance, as though willing an audience to laugh.

'He never uses new material because he doesn't trust it,' said the mirror. 'Anyone else would have been kicked out long ago, but Saul and Bill go way back. Saul sees his old friend as a good-luck charm, and Bill is happy to still be working. It helps that he's been around so long he knows everything about everyone.'

'Including what really happened to Saul's wife?' said Emma.

'Wouldn't surprise me,' said the mirror.

'Judi Rifkin's inside man,' I said, studying Big Bill thoughtfully. 'She did provide us with a good reason as to why he might betray his old friend, but I think I'll take that with a pinch or two of salt, until I can talk to the man in person.'

'Would you care for a virtual guided tour of the casino?' the mirror said grandly.

I looked at it thoughtfully. 'Don't they have protections in place to keep out remote viewers like you?'

'There is no one like me,' the mirror said haughtily.

The reflection suddenly showed a massive pyramid, garish

beyond belief and surrounded by spotlights stabbing up into the Vegas night sky. Along with a massive, paved patio, rows of dancing fountains and more neon stylings than the eye could comfortably accommodate. The view shifted to the interior, where everything had been designed to resemble Hollywood's idea of ancient Egypt. Even I could tell that historical accuracy wasn't getting much of a look in. The staff went bare-chested – the women as well as the men – and wore brightly exotic costumes from some of the more inventive mummy movies.

'The look is down to Saul,' said the mirror. 'Not because he's a fan, but because he wanted to provide a proper setting for the Masque of Ra.'

The view switched to the main lobby, where the masque was on open display. It had been positioned halfway up a simple stone column, next to a large sign detailing its history and legend. It looked just as I remembered: a stylized human face hammered out of pure gold. It should have looked beautiful, but there was something subtly inhuman about the lines of the face. As though it was just a mask for something else to look through.

A large sarcophagus stood next to the podium, with its lid off to reveal the bandaged mummy within. None of the crowds hurrying through the lobby paid much attention to the masque or the mummy. They were there to gamble, not sightsee. But now and again someone would stop and turn their head to look at the masque, almost as though their gaze had been drawn to it against their will. And then they would come to themselves again, with a start and a shudder, and hurry on.

'Is that a real mummy?' said Emma.

'Of course,' said Harry. 'You are looking at the actual preserved remains of the Pharaoh Khuffu himself, removed from his pyramid and transported to Vegas on Saul's orders, to keep the masque company.'

'I suppose there are stories about the mummy, too?' I said.

'What do you think?' said the mirror. 'The casino has to shut down for a few hours in the early morning, for a bit of a clean-up and some necessary maintenance. And that's when the mummy is supposed to come lurching out of its sarcophagus and roam the lobby, to guard the masque. Most people think Saul made that up, for the publicity. But . . . you never know.'

'I thought you knew everything?' said Emma.

'I can't watch everywhere,' the mirror said sulkily. 'And I get bored very easily.'

'Are we sure Saul knows what the masque can do?' I said.

'He talks about the legend a lot,' said the mirror.

'Then why hasn't he already used it to make himself immortal?' said Emma.

'Because there are some really unpleasant stories about what the masque has done to people in the past, when they didn't get the activating ritual exactly right,' said the mirror. 'But a man of his age, so unsure as to whether any of his children are worthy to succeed him, must be thinking hard about being young and immortal.'

'If his family found out about that,' said Emma, 'they might decide to force Saul into retirement, before he can use the masque and rob them of their inheritance.'

'But such an attempt could be the last straw that persuades Saul to try the masque,' I said.

'If anyone knows what Saul is planning, it will be Big Bill,' said Harry.

'We'll talk to him,' I said.

'Would you care to see a few more mugshots?' said the mirror.

'I think I've seen enough new faces for one day,' said Emma.

'Oh, be a sport!' said the mirror. 'These are really interesting scumbags. Saul has put together his own supernatural crew to guard the casino and the masque.'

'Go ahead,' I said resignedly. 'But keep it brief or I'll heckle you.'

The mirror showed us a sharp-faced man in a pinstripe suit and a string tie. He had a gaunt face and a rat-like gaze.

'Double Down Dan,' said the mirror. 'He has the power of bilocation – the ability to be in more than one place at the same time.'

Next up was a hugely overweight man in a white suit, with a pale face and colourless hair. He drifted along like a ghost, staring straight ahead.

'Soulful Sam,' said the mirror. 'A defrocked priest who can look at anyone and know what sins they're guilty of. And then use that knowledge against them.'

'That could be tricky for our crew,' said Emma.

'We'll just have to concentrate on our lesser sins,' I said. 'To take his mind off the greater ones. Though if he takes a good look at the Damned, it might blow his head right off his shoulders.'

The ex-priest was replaced by a tall, well-built woman in a tuxedo, her entire face hidden behind a white silk mask with no eyeholes, just dark stylized images of eyes. Simply standing there, she looked dangerous enough to raise the hackles on the back of my neck. There was a power in this woman . . .

'The Enchanted Enforcer,' said the mirror. 'Saul's very own personal assassin. She has the Evil Eye; one look is all it takes, and suddenly you are an ex-problem.'

'Rumour or fact?' I said.

'Thirty-two confirmed kills,' said the mirror. 'Nine of them inside the casino. But that's not all that makes her interesting.'

The woman reached up and took off the silk mask, revealing the singer Adelaide.

'And that is why Saul keeps her around,' the mirror said smugly.

'Does Joyce know?' said Emma.

'Oh, yes,' said the mirror. 'Apparently, it adds a little spice to the relationship. And they say I'm weird . . .'

The Enchanted Enforcer disappeared, leaving just a reflection of Harry, Emma and me.

'That's it!' the mirror said loudly. 'I need to recharge my batteries, so I am going to have a nice little nap now. Feel free to chat among yourselves, but keep the noise down.'

The mirror's reflection faded away to nothing, and it began to snore softly.

'Help me turn Sidney to the wall,' said Harry. 'It helps him sleep. He's not as young as he used to be.'

We carefully manoeuvred the mirror into place, and then Harry led us back to the middle of his empty shop.

'Any chance you could take that mirror with you when you go?' I said. 'It has far too much character for its own good.'

'I'm sure you'll find Sidney very useful,' Harry said firmly.

'Is he all you're leaving us?' said Emma.

'Every owner has to build up their own stock, according to their own interests and intentions,' said Harry. 'That's the point.'

'Assuming we make it back from Vegas alive,' I said. 'And that we survive handing the masque over to Judi Rifkin.'

'I have every faith in you,' said Harry. 'But I'll hang around a while, just to make sure.'

He gestured at the front door, and it swung silently open. Emma and I took the hint and left the shop. The moment we were out on the pavement, I grabbed Emma by the arm and hustled her off down the street.

'What's the hurry?' said Emma.

'That mirror fell asleep a little too conveniently for me,' I said. 'I'll feel easier when we've put some distance between us and the shop.'

'But if he can see all the way to Vegas . . .'

'Let's see how he does with a moving target.'

'Do you really want to run Old Harry's Place?' said Emma.

'It is tempting,' I said. 'But let's pull off the heist first. And for that we need to put the band back together.'

'Including the Ghost?' said Emma.

'No,' I said. 'He's happy being alive again and doing good with Hammer's fortune. Why spoil his fun? But the Damned and the Wild Card should be in their element in Las Vegas. I have another person in mind, to make up the numbers.'

'Who do we start with?'

'The Damned,' I said. 'Because if we can get Lex to go along, convincing the others will seem easy.'

FOUR

Rogues of a Feather

When a man knows, beyond any shadow of a doubt, that he is damned for all eternity, then that man can do anything. Lex Talon chose to become a servant for the Good, just to piss off Hell one last time. And so he became the most terrifying servant of the Good that the Good has ever known – and no, the Good didn't get a say in the matter. The Damned tracks down the really bad guys, the ones the law can't or won't touch, and dispenses his own personal idea of justice.

The Damned has mellowed somewhat of late. His time as a

member of my crew, when we broke into the legendary treasure vault of Fredric Hammer, gave Lex a taste for company and helped him remember what it was like to have friends. He might even be taking his first steps toward some kind of redemption. But in this, as in so many other matters, the Damned goes his own way.

After leaving Old Harry's Place, I stole a car that someone had parked illegally in a disabled parking space, and then Emma and I returned to the less than fashionable part of London where we share a nicely anonymous house. Emma felt the need to change her clothes and become somebody else. Partly because a redhead in a black leather catsuit does tend to stand out and be noticed once the sun is up, but mostly because being Emma was enough to tire anyone out.

We'd barely crossed the threshold before Annie was striding off to the back rooms where she maintains the extensive wardrobe of clothes, wigs and makeup that allows her to be any person she chooses. She closed the door firmly behind her, because no magician wants you to see how the trick is performed. Or possibly because no cook ever wants you to see what goes into the sausages. While she was changing into someone more comfortable, I turned out my pockets and checked I had everything I was going to need for where we were going. I've always been a great believer in being prepared, and since I am a professional thief, I have no problem with what might technically be called cheating.

I moved unhurriedly around the room, browsing through my collection of odd and unusual items, all of them designed to tilt the odds in my favour and keep them that way, even if I had to bend the rules until they changed shape. In the end, I settled for the usual old reliables. Too many options can get you killed while you're still making up your mind.

Eventually, Annie came back into the living room, looking so completely different that for a moment I wondered whether someone else had got into the house. Annie was now a businesswoman in a smart suit, with flat sensible shoes, heavy-framed spectacles and understated makeup, topped off with long black hair. The kind of young woman you can always find striding through the financial district in the early morning hours, on her way to have a power breakfast with someone far more important than you'll ever be. And woe betide any mere mortal who dares to get in her way.

'I am Alice,' she said in a brisk, clipped accent. 'Someone in the City, a mover and a shaker in the markets, with a razor-sharp mind and no discernible conscience. Applaud now and get it over with.'

I considered her thoughtfully. 'You think we're going to need someone without a conscience?'

'We're going after the Damned, aren't we? Show him anything that even looks like a weakness and he'll walk right over you.'

'The man has mellowed,' I said reproachfully. 'Comparatively speaking.'

Alice sniffed. 'I'll believe that when I see him not killing a whole bunch of people for reasons that only make sense to him. Anyway, if we're going to have to drag him out of that deserted Underground station he calls home, I want an outfit that won't show the dirt and the grime.'

'Lex doesn't live down there any more,' I said. 'Hasn't for some time.'

Alice raised an elegantly painted eyebrow. 'Really? I always thought it would take a whole case of dynamite to shift him out of there.'

'Admittedly, the man has taken being anti-social to a whole new level,' I said, 'and that station was as far as he could go without actually leaving the world behind him . . . but a number of very cautious visitors have reported finding the old place completely deserted.'

'Who would want to go looking for the Damned?' said Alice.

I smiled. 'People like us, who want something from him. Lex has been spotted out and about in London, and walking up and down in it. Apparently, he's searching for something.'

'How do you know all this?' said Alice.

'People tell me things.'

Alice frowned. 'Why is it they talk to you and never to me?'

'Because I'm always ready to listen,' I said. 'And because I'm always me.'

Alice shrugged, dismissing the point as irrelevant. 'How are we going to find Lex? Put an ad in the evening paper? *Excessively violent psychopath seeks similar*?'

'I thought we'd go ask Madam Osiris.'

Alice winced. 'Oh, not her. There must be somebody else we can ask.'

'Osiris sees many things that are hidden,' I said solemnly.

'Just part of what makes her such a complete pain in the arse,' said Alice.

'You'll notice I'm not arguing. But if anyone can find the Damned when he doesn't want to be found, it's her.'

Alice nodded reluctantly. 'But, Gideon . . . Osiris sees the future, as well as the present. So you be very careful what you ask her.'

'She probably already knows we're coming,' I said. 'And what we need to know. So she should have the answer waiting for us. I'm more concerned with how much she's going to charge.'

Alice looked at me sharply. 'Hold hard and slam on the brakes. Why can't you just use your special compass to find Lex? The one that always points the way to what you need?'

'I already tried it,' I said. 'And it pointed to Madam Osiris.'

Alice shook her head. 'Sometimes it seems like the whole world is conspiring against us.'

We took the Underground to Tottenham Court Road, because it was quicker than trying to drive through the midday traffic. The pavements were packed with people, and the hustle and bustle of the city was well underway. Emma and I strode casually along, just part of the crowd, and no one paid us any attention at all. It was well into the afternoon before we ended up at a small newsagent's, more a cubicle than a shop, tucked in between two much more prosperous establishments. Almost as though the newsagent wanted to be overlooked.

I led the way in, and Alice stuck close beside me, glaring suspiciously at everything. The crowded shelves offered not just the latest papers and magazines but all the usual bits and pieces you might need in a hurry. And if you knew the glum-faced Sikh behind the counter well enough, you could ask him for any number of unusual items.

'Hello, Omar,' I said cheerfully. 'How's business?'

'Hanging on by my fingernails, like always,' he said sourly. 'There is no room left for the small businessman. What can I get you, Gideon, that you couldn't steal from somewhere else?

And I'll thank you to keep both of your hands in plain sight all the time you're in my establishment.'

'Relax,' I said. 'We're just here to see Madam Osiris.'

'Oh, her. She's in,' said Omar. 'She's always in. Go straight up. I'm sure she'll see you.'

He laughed uproariously at his little joke and gestured to the door tucked away at the back of the shop. Alice and I had to squeeze behind the counter to get to it, and Omar smiled for the first time.

'Always good to see you, Annie. When are you going to leave this low-life pilferer of insufficiently protected trifles and take a proper interest in a fine, upstanding businessman?'

She just kept going, ignoring him with glacial calm. I quickly opened the back door and waved for her to go first. Alice pushed past me and I mouthed, *She's in character* to Omar. He nodded understandingly, and I closed the door firmly behind me. It took a moment for our eyes to adjust to the dim light, so that we could make out the handwritten sign at the foot of the stairs. *Madam Osiris. Sees all, knows all, tells most of it for the right price. Fortunes told, prophecies averted, fates and dooms diverted. No refunds.*

Alice sniffed loudly. 'She might have done her research. Osiris is a man's name.'

'I doubt most of the clients she gets would realize that,' I said.

I led the way up the narrow stairs, treading as lightly as possible on the threadbare carpeting. The wallpaper was so old and faded it was hard to make out what the original pattern might have been. There was a strong smell of rising damp and unsuccessful home cooking. I stopped before the door at the top of the stairs and raised a hand to knock. Before my hand could even start to descend, a voice came booming through from the other side.

'Hello, Gideon! Hello, Alice! Come on in; I've been expecting you.'

Alice scowled. 'Now, that is just showing off.'

I opened the door and the hinges creaked loudly with professional vigour. Madam Osiris put a lot of work into maintaining the proper ambience for her workplace. Alice and I stuck close together as we entered the single room. As much to present a unified front in the face of a potential threat as anything else.

The consulting room was kept deliberately gloomy, with heavy drapes covering the only window, and was cluttered with all manner of mystic bits and bobs; Madam Osiris believed in making an effort and giving the punters their money's worth.

For much the same reason a doctor keeps a skeleton in their surgery, a Baron Samedi scarecrow stood in one corner, dressed in an immaculate tuxedo and a top hat tilted at a jaunty angle. A row of Hands of Glory had been arranged on top of a battered chest of drawers. The severed hands stood upright, their fingertips fashioned into lit candles. The blue flames stood up perfectly straight, untroubled by even a breath of air. A large map of the starry heavens covered most of one wall, showing all thirteen signs of the Zodiac. And a glowing crystal ball stood proudly displayed on a small circular table. A ring of old Norse runes had been carved into the tabletop, forming a protective barrier around the crystal ball.

I read the runes and was pretty sure they didn't mean what Madam Osiris thought they did. At least, I hoped not.

Madam Osiris was sitting on a slightly elevated chair on the other side of the table, so she could stare over the crystal ball at her customers while its glow lit her face from below in a suitably eerie manner. A small red glimmer marked the dark cheroot tucked into one corner of her mouth, but my eyes were drawn to her most distinctive feature. Two soft yellow orbs filled her eye sockets, from where she'd had had her own eyes removed and replaced with small glowing crystal balls.

Osiris was dressed like a gypsy seer from some old Hollywood movie, wrapped in traditional robes and topped off with a silk turban. A handsome woman of a certain age, she looked as if she could still punch her weight. Her bare muscular arms were covered in cheap plastic bangles that clattered noisily every time she moved. She had a lean face, with a hooked nose and a knowing smile, although her features were almost buried under industrial-strength makeup. The outfit had been carefully chosen to project the right image, but it was always the glowing crystal eyes that caught everyone's attention. Just as Osiris intended.

No one knew how or why she acquired her new eyes. Most people were too scared to ask. I heard Osiris got them from Old Harry's Place, but then I hear that about a lot of things. The eyes glowed steadily with their own inner light, but it only took a moment to realize they didn't move in their sockets, so that Osiris had to turn her head slightly as she looked from me to Alice and back again.

'Gideon Sable,' she said in a warm, vibrant voice that did its best to seem welcoming and intimidating at the same time. 'Inheritor of another man's legend. And Annie Anybody, currently Alice – always more comfortable in someone else's skin. Sit down and make yourselves at home. I can't abide people who tower over me.'

Alice and I sat down on the uncomfortable visitors' chairs. I studied Osiris carefully over the glowing crystal ball, and it seemed to me she had come down in the world since her glory days. She used to be impressive, but now she had to settle for making a good impression. She leaned forward, the light from the crystal ball leaping over her face, and fixed me with a steady smile.

'Cross my palm with silver, dearie, and I shall reveal all the wonders of the world. Or, at least, as many as you can cope with.'

I produced a silver bullet and dropped it into her waiting palm. The long bony fingers closed over it immediately, and Osiris chuckled softly.

'You always did have style, Gideon.'

'Good to see you again, Osiris,' I said. 'You're looking very yourself.'

She made the silver bullet disappear with a supple movement of her hand and then leaned back in her chair, giving me her best mysterious smile.

'It's about time you got here. I've been waiting for hours. The eyes are good for predestination, but the fine-tuning drives me crazy.'

'I'm glad you were able to fit us in,' I said smoothly. 'Keeping busy, are you?'

Osiris scowled fiercely. 'No so as you'd notice. It gets very quiet, once the tourist season is over.'

'Well,' I said. 'If you will insist on telling people the truth, instead of what they want to hear . . .'

'I have my pride,' Osiris said haughtily. 'I see what will be and what must be, in detail and with warnings. If all they want is words of comfort and their hand held, let them read their horoscopes. I am a professional.'

'How did you know to address me as Alice?' Alice said loudly. 'I didn't even know I was going to put her on until a few hours ago.'

Osiris smiled smugly. 'It's my job to know things like that.'

Alice smiled at her sweetly. 'How are you when it comes to picking winning lottery numbers?'

Osiris's smile shut off as though someone had hit a switch. 'You would not believe the number of people who come tramping up those stairs, asking for just that. If I could see how to win the jackpot, do they really think I'd be living in a dump like this? The lottery company employs some very powerful specialists to keep out people like me.'

'So what do you tell these poor deluded seekers after fortune?' I said.

'I just give them the first numbers that come into my head, and then warn them they must have faith or it won't work. So if the numbers don't come up, it's their fault, not mine.' She sniffed loudly. 'I'm no good with the horses, either. I swear a horse would rather get hit in the head by a meteorite than win a race for me.' She turned her head to look at me directly. 'I know why you're here.'

'I should hope so,' I said.

'You want to find the Damned – contrary to all good sense and survival instincts.'

'Can you see where he is?' said Alice.

'Of course!' said Osiris. 'Lex is very good at concealing his whereabouts, thanks to those silver bracelets that used to be angels' halos, and most people are perfectly happy to let him stay hidden, because they very sensibly don't want to do anything that might upset him. Fortunately for you, there's not much in this world that can hide from these eyes.'

'So where is he?' I said patiently. 'Right now?'

'That will cost you,' said Osiris.

'Don't get greedy,' I said. 'I'm on a budget.'

'Oh, this will cost you a lot more than money,' said Osiris.

I had to raise an eyebrow. 'You've changed your tune. I've

never known you to kick hard cash out of bed. What do you want instead?'

'A favour,' Osiris said steadily. 'For old times' sake. I want your word that you will get Lex Talon to swear he'll never hurt me.'

'You think he might?' I said.

'Let's just say I have seen a possible future event, involving him and me, that I would much prefer to avoid.'

'A possible *future* event?' said Alice, pouncing on the word. 'So what's to come isn't actually set in stone?'

'It had better not be,' said Osiris.

I looked at her thoughtfully. 'Why would Lex want to hurt you? Normally, he only goes after really big-time villains, the serious sinners. I wouldn't have thought you qualified.'

'We could end up in a situation where I would have no choice but to tell him something about himself that he really wouldn't want to hear,' Osiris said steadily. 'But I'm relying on you, Gideon, to make sure that never happens.'

'All right,' I said. 'I'll get him to promise.'

'I knew you were going to say that,' said Osiris.

'You trust Gideon to keep his word?' said Alice.

'Of course!' said Osiris. 'He and I go way back, to when we were both very different people.' She smiled sweetly at Alice. 'Didn't he ever mention that?'

Alice glared at me. 'No. He didn't.'

Osiris leaned back in her chair, drew heavily on her cheroot and blew a perfect square smoke ring over my shoulder. And then she sat and stared at nothing for some time.

'Aren't you going to consult your crystal ball?' Alice said finally.

'That's just for show,' said Osiris. 'I can see anyone through these eyes. Lex Talon is currently consulting with a rogue angel in a semi-detached house in Islington.'

Alice and I took a moment to look at each other before giving Madam Osiris our full attention.

'Yes, I can give you the exact address,' she said calmly.

'What's a rogue angel?' said Alice.

'One who has taken to walking the Earth without permission,' I said. I looked narrowly at Osiris. 'Which kind are we talking about? From Above or Below?'

'Once they've decided to go rogue, does it really make a difference?' said Osiris.

'Can you tell me anything about this particular angel?' I said.

'It has taken on a human form,' said Osiris. 'Which means its power is somewhat diminished. But it's still sufficiently powerful and scary that most people have enough sense not to go anywhere near it. But then . . . Lex hasn't been what you'd call sane for some time now, has he?'

'You know Lex?' said Alice.

'Oh, we go way back,' said Osiris.

Alice glared at her. 'You have a history with him, too?'

Madam Osiris smiled airily. 'I got around, back in the day. If I could have seen the future then, seen what would happen if I didn't mend my ways . . . I would probably have done it all anyway. Because I was having such a good time.'

'What does Lex want with this rogue angel?' I said.

'He's talking to her right now,' said Osiris. 'But don't ask me what about. I can barely bring myself to look at the angel, even with these eyes; the spiritual glare is too blinding. But you'd better get to Lex fast. It's just possible that he's bitten off more than he can digest this time.'

Alice looked at me. 'Lex has history when it comes to angels. And not a good one.'

I just nodded, not wanting to discuss Lex's secrets in front of Madam Osiris. Who didn't know nearly as much as she liked to imply.

Lex damned himself when he killed two angels who had taken on human form, so he could steal their halos and give them to Fredric Hammer, in return for Hammer bringing Lex's wife back from the dead. Hammer cheated him, of course. But why would Lex go after a rogue angel? Could it be connected to his original sin? And did I really want to get caught between the Damned and a rogue angel? I considered the possible crossfire, and a chill ran through me. But . . . I needed Lex if I was going to get my hands on the Masque of Ra.

I finally nodded to Osiris, and she pushed a card across the table, with the address in Islington already written on it. Alice made me show it to her before I put it away.

'What would a rogue angel be doing in a nice, quiet area like that?' she asked, not unreasonably.

Osiris just smiled. 'Being human.'

Alice scowled. 'What does that mean?'

'You'll find out,' said Osiris.

I cut in quickly before Alice could say something unfortunate.

'Time we were leaving. I think we've learned all we need to.'

'Not quite,' said Osiris as Alice and I were getting to our feet. I looked at her inquiringly.

'Before you go, Gideon,' said Osiris, 'feel free to help yourself to one of my spare eyes.'

She gestured at the chest of drawers under the Hands of Glory. I looked at it for a long moment and then moved over and pulled open the top drawer. Dozens of crystal eyeballs stared back at me from small wooden boxes lined with cotton wool. None of them were glowing, but they all had a certain presence.

'Take one,' said Osiris. 'You're going to need it.'

'Is that prophecy?' I said, not taking my eyes off the eyes.

'No,' said Osiris. 'Just a lifetime's experience.'

I chose a crystal eye at random and reached out to pick it up. And then I pulled my hand back and looked suspiciously at Osiris.

'You're not usually this generous,' I said accusingly.

'I really need that promise from Lex,' said Osiris. 'And you're the only one who can get it for me. I can trust you to do that, can't I, Gideon?'

'All these years we've known each other,' I said, 'and you can ask me that?'

'It's a harsh world,' said Osiris.

I reached for the eyeball, bracing myself in case it turned out to feel soft and yielding, like a real eye. But of course it was just crystal, smooth and solid. I hefted it in the palm of my hand and looked back at Osiris.

'How do I use it? I am not removing one of my own eyes . . .'

'Just hold the crystal up and look through it,' said Osiris. 'And all the secrets of the world will be revealed to you.'

I hesitated, thinking of Johnny Wilde. How seeing the true nature of existence had driven him out of his mind and into somewhere far more interesting and upsetting. Osiris shook her head.

'Just concentrate on what you need to see.'

I carefully tucked the eye away in an inner pocket. Alice looked thoughtfully at Osiris.

'What did you want to see that made you give up your own eyes?'

'What's real, and what isn't,' said Madam Osiris. 'And trust me . . . you're much better off not knowing.'

I started to say something, but she was already leaning back in her chair, her face no longer illuminated by the glowing crystal ball. All that was left was the red gleam of her cheroot and the soft yellow glow of her eyes, shining unrelentingly out of the gloom.

As we hurried down the back steps, Alice gave me a hard look.

'For old times' sake?'

'Not all my secrets are mine to share,' I said. 'I don't talk about Osiris's past, any more than I talk about yours.'

Alice thought about that and nodded.

'What do you think Lex wants with the rogue angel? He hasn't gone back to stealing halos, has he?'

'I wouldn't have thought so,' I said. 'Not after what happened the last time. Maybe he thinks he can make some kind of deal, to save himself from Hell.'

Alice looked at me sharply. 'You think that's possible?'

'No,' I said. 'So we'd better get there fast, before Lex commits himself to something really unwise.'

We had to take a train and a taxi, so it was late afternoon by the time we got to where we were going. The address in Islington turned out to be an entirely average semi-detached property, in one of those streets where nothing out of the ordinary every happens. Alice and I stood well back and looked the place over carefully. There were none of the usual signs of Lex at his work. No screams, no pools of blood, no piled-up bodies. A quick glance up and down the street confirmed that there was no one else out and about.

'Where is everybody?' said Alice. 'Are they all hiding because they know something bad has come to their nice little world?'

'More likely they're all out at work,' I said.

'It's still far too quiet for my liking,' Alice said stubbornly. 'Could we have got here too late?'

'I think if Lex had gone head to head with a rogue angel, we'd be looking at some serious property damage,' I said.

'Why don't you check out the situation with your new eye?'

'Let's try the straightforward approach first,' I said carefully. 'And see where that gets us. I don't think I'm ready to look at an angel without its spiritual clothes on.'

I led the way up the path to the front door, carefully ignoring the garden gnome fishing in a pond, and rang the bell. After an only slightly tense pause, the door was opened by a pleasant middle-aged woman in baggy clothes and an apron, with big, fluffy slippers and curlers in her hair. She smiled at us sweetly.

'Hello, there! You must be Gideon and Alice. So glad you've finally arrived. I'm Ethel Makepeace, rogue angel and old dear by appointment.'

Alice blinked at Ethel and then turned to me. 'What do you want to bet that Osiris knew about this and chose not to warn us?'

'Is that who's been trying to get a peek at me?' said Ethel. 'I was sure I could sense someone hovering. But this is very definitely where the two of you are supposed to be, so in you come. I've just put the kettle on.'

'How did you know we were coming?' said Alice. 'Angelic second sight?'

'More like third and fourth sight,' said the rogue angel. 'I gave up a lot to be human, and I do miss my wings, but I am still what I am.' She stepped back from the door and beckoned us in. 'I'm so glad Lex has found some chums to pall around with. He's a great one for brooding, and it's not good for him. Or anyone he bumps into afterwards.'

I stepped past her into the hallway, and Alice hurried in after me, sticking so close she was almost inside my clothes with me. Ethel closed the door and then led us down the hall into an entirely ordinary kitchen. Where Lax Talon was sitting at the table, drinking tea. A large and brutal figure, he was wearing scuffed black motorcycle leathers, with the jacket left hanging open to show off his hairy torso. Two silver bands glowed at his wrists: all that remained of the halos he'd cut off the heads of the angels he killed. One from Above, one from Below; made human as part of an ancient compact, so they could appreciate exactly what Heaven and Hell were fighting over. Jesus's idea, from when he visited Britain with his uncle, Joseph of Arimathea.

The things you learn in my line of work.

I would have said Lex looked out of place in such an ordinary setting, but it was difficult to think of anywhere he might fit in. He had a face that looked as if it had been chipped out of stone, and a gaze that could stare through mountains and leave a hole big enough for a train to pass through. Lex had killed a great many people in his time as an agent of the Good, and it showed. He looked coldly at me and Alice.

'What are you doing here?'

'We were worried about you,' I said smoothly. 'And . . . I'm putting the old crew back together, if you're interested.'

He smiled briefly. 'A new heist? Must be something very special, and very well guarded, if you think you need me.'

'I'm hoping you want in,' I said. 'It'll be good for you.'

I made a point of meeting his gaze steadily, just to remind him that I was always going to be the boss of my crew. If my composure impressed him, he hid it well.

'I knew you were on your way,' he said. 'Ethel told me.'

'Far too much predestination going on around this heist,' said Alice.

Lex's mouth quirked again. 'I like your new look. Very businesslike.'

'The name is Alice.'

He nodded. 'Suits you.'

'Sit down, sit down, the pair of you,' Ethel said cheerfully, gesturing at the two chairs opposite Lex. Alice and I sat down, just a little cautiously, keeping a wary eye on Lex. I liked to think we were friends, but the rage that burned constantly inside the Damned was rarely far from the surface; when it boiled over, he would lash out at anyone, just because they were there. Ethel bustled around the kitchen, organizing tea.

'Would you like some cake?' she said cheerfully as she hovered over the kettle. 'I've got Madeira, ginger and chocolate. All of it home-made, none of that shop-bought nonsense.'

'Try some; it's really good,' said Lex, just a bit unexpectedly.

'Maybe later,' I said politely. 'We have a lot to talk about.'

'Don't mind me, dear,' said Ethel. 'You can talk perfectly freely, because I already know most things and I don't care. Or at least, not enough to intervene. It's very liberating, being only human. You have no idea how busy being an angel is.'

She set delicate china cups down in front of Alice and me, poured the tea and then made a *help yourself* gesture to a milk jug with flowers painted on it and a chunky glass bowl full of sugar lumps. She sat down beside Lex and smiled happily round the table. Encouraging us to feel at home and chat about whatever was on our minds. I didn't trust any of it, partly because I don't trust most people anyway, just on principle, but mostly because I was having a hard time accepting that this little old lady really was an angel in human clothing. Still, when in doubt, grab the bull by the horns and punch it between the eyes until it behaves.

'What kind of angel were you?' I said bluntly. 'From Above or Below?'

Ethel laughed cheerfully. 'I just love human euphemisms. All the ways you find to talk about things without actually talking about them. But it really doesn't matter any more, because since I retired from being an angel, I am no longer a part of the War.'

'What made you want to be human?' said Alice.

'I was given human form as part of the compact,' said Ethel. 'You do know about that? Yes, I thought you did. Well, once the meeting was over and nothing had changed, as usual, I decided I didn't want to go back. I loved being human and wouldn't give it up.'

'Why?' I said. 'What's so special about being us?'

'An angel is just Heaven or Hell's will, given shape and form to carry out their work in the world of men,' said Ethel. 'Just a part of the celestial machinery. As a human, I'm an actual separate person!'

'But what do you plan to do, now you're human?' said Alice.

Ethel looked at her blankly. 'I don't have to do anything. That's the point. I just want to be me.'

'How long are you planning on staying?' I said.

'As long as this body lasts,' said Ethel. 'I suppose I could stay on after that, by possessing another body, but that's what the old me would have done. I'm someone else now.'

'Aren't you afraid Heaven or Hell will send another angel after you?' said Alice.

'Why should they?' said Alice. 'All they have to do is wait. Time is nothing in the face of eternity.'

I gave up on Ethel and turned to Lex. 'Why did you come here?'

'I hoped Ethel might have some answers to my situation,' he said slowly, staring into his cup so he wouldn't have to look at me. 'I couldn't talk to any other angel, not after what I did, but I thought a rogue might be more sympathetic. I had to know . . . if there was anything I could do, to stop being damned.'

He broke off, and Ethel patted his hand comfortingly.

'How did you know where to find Ethel?' said Alice.

'People tell me things,' said Lex. 'Whether they want to or not.'

I looked at him steadily. 'Did you by any chance leave a trail of bodies behind you, pointing the way here?'

'Well,' said Lex, 'not *dead* bodies.'

'You are mellowing,' said Alice.

'Not a word I would have used,' said Lex, but he managed a small smile for her.

Ethel shook her head and tut-tutted. 'Bad boy . . .'

'That's rather the point,' Lex said solemnly. 'Are you sure you have no words of wisdom for me?'

'I already told you,' said Ethel. 'God has mercy. You can be forgiven.'

Lex looked down into his tea again. 'I didn't just kill two angels. I killed a young woman. One of Hammer's people. After he betrayed me, I went to kill him, and he pushed her in between us to buy him time to escape. I killed her, without hesitating or caring, just because she was in the way. There hasn't been a night since that I haven't dreamed of that moment and then waked to wish I could change it. But I can't. Even if I serve the Good all the rest of my life, she'll still be dead. Of course God would forgive me. That's what he does. *I* don't forgive me.'

'That's human arrogance,' said Ethel. 'Nothing I can help you with there.'

'Excuse me,' said Alice. 'But can I just ask: what happened to the other angel that was made human at the same time as you? Any chance they might be coming here?'

Ethel shook her curlered head firmly. 'He went running straight back home to tell on me. That's angels for you.'

Lex finished his tea, draining the dregs noisily, and looked at me. 'What's the heist this time? What are we after?'

'The Masque of Ra,' I said.

'Never heard of it,' said Lex. 'Just tell me: are we also sticking it to the bad guys?'

'A whole family of them,' I said.

'Then I'm in.'

'Hold it,' said Ethel.

Something in her voice snapped all our heads round to look at her. She had her head cocked slightly to one side, as though she was listening. There was a pause, and then Ethel smiled slowly.

'Company's coming.'

The front door bell rang. Ethel just sat where she was. The bell rang again.

'Aren't you going to answer that?' I said.

'No,' said Ethel.

'Who is it?' said Alice.

'Another bad boy,' said Ethel.

Everyone except Ethel looked round sharply as we heard the front door slam open, followed by the sound of heavy footsteps heading toward the kitchen. Lex was quickly on his feet, glaring at the closed door. Alice and I got up, too. Ethel blew on her tea to cool it, entirely unperturbed.

The kitchen door burst open, and a tall, saturnine gentleman burst into the kitchen. He smiled at each of us in turn, in a smug and self-satisfied way, like a landlord who'd come to tell us he was raising the rent. He was wearing a priest's robe, complete with dog collar, and a large inverted silver crucifix hanging on a chain around his neck. He looked extremely sinister, and his wicked smile was a work of art. Because he'd put a lot of thought into making the right first impression. He nodded briskly to all of us.

'Well, hello! What a fascinating gathering of the weird and uncanny to find in a cosy little suburban kitchen! Sorry to interrupt you at your tea, but I'm here on business. Do I need to introduce myself?'

'Probably a good idea,' said Alice. 'I like to know who I'm about to hit with a kitchen table and then trample all over.' She stopped and glanced at me apologetically. 'Sorry, that's Emma talking. She's hard to throw off. Do you know this poser?'

'Unfortunately, yes,' I said. 'This is Jeremiah Skinner, the Dark Pope of London Town. Self-appointed, of course.'

'Oh, don't let's bother with titles,' said the man in black, smiling happily. 'Call me Jerry. Everybody does.'

'No, they don't,' I said. 'They have a whole bunch of very descriptive terms for you, most of which I wouldn't care to use in front of an angel.'

'Ex, dear,' said Ethel.

Jerry fixed his gaze on her, and his grin broadened. 'So my little army of spies and informers was right on the money. A rogue angel, arrayed in human flesh. How utterly thrilling!'

'If he was any more theatrical, he'd be carrying a spear at Stratford,' said Alice. 'Who or what is this, Gideon?'

'Jerry appeared during your retirement from the scene,' I said. 'He specializes in crimes of a religious nature. He steals precious relics (from any religion – he's an equal-opportunity offender) and then threatens to destroy them unless their Church pays him protection money. He deals in possessions and curses, and dark nights of the soul – causing, not curing. And he kills religious leaders, to order. Not that he ever gets his own hands dirty; he has a small army of gutter scum to do that for him. Some say it's all about defying God to do something to stop him and thus prove His existence.'

'Not a bit of it,' Jerry said briskly. 'I'm just in it for the money. Lots and lots of lovely money.'

'Then what about the rumour that you trade in stolen souls?' I said.

'All part of the image,' said Jerry. 'And anyway, it's not like the original owners were doing anything useful with them.' He bounced up and down on his toes and rubbed his hands together eagerly. 'It is good to be recognized and have one's hard work appreciated. I put a lot of effort into creating this persona. The supernatural crimes field is so crowded these days, it's getting more and more difficult to stand out.' He nodded familiarly to me. 'You'd know all about that. At least I didn't steal my name and legend from a better man.'

'Dark Pope, my bony Protestant arse,' said Alice. 'You're just another chancer, trying to force your way into the big leagues. What do you want here? We were having a nice little chat before you barged in.'

'Well,' said Jerry, 'I'm certainly not here for you, little miss Who Am I Today? In fact, I did wonder whether I should send my people in ahead of me, so they could throw all of you time-wasters out, and I could deal with the rogue angel in private. But I'm just a big fan at heart, and I did so want to meet some of the few real celebrities in our little field.'

'You have people outside?' said Lex. He nodded slowly. 'Something to look forward to.'

Jerry shot him an uncertain glance and then flashed his sinister smile again. 'I decided it would make more of an impression if I did this myself. When word gets around that I not only tracked you here but faced all of you down personally, that will do wonders for my reputation. These days, it's all about the image and the brand. So, Gideon and Alice and Lex . . . I'm afraid you're all going to have to die, because I can't have any witnesses to what I'm going to do to the rogue angel. Nothing personal, you understand. Just business.'

Alice looked at me. 'Could he do that?'

'Possibly,' I said. 'He has no power of his own, but he has stolen some very powerful bits and pieces along the way.'

'Oh, I have,' Jerry said gleefully. 'You would not believe the kind of things that fall off the back of a religion if you hit it hard enough. More than enough to deal with the likes of you.' He fixed his gaze on Lex. 'You inspired me, you know; you really did. So I thought I'd come here, take the rogue's halo and make my own spiritual armour out of it. When you've outraged as many devout believers as I have, you feel the need for some heavy-duty protection.'

'You want to be damned?' said Lex.

'Not necessarily,' Jerry said airily. 'There are always deals to be made, by people with the guts to go after them. Especially if you're negotiating from a position of power.'

'You're a fool,' said Lex. 'And I think I've been patient with you long enough.' He nodded to Ethel. 'Sorry about the mess I'm about to make of your kitchen.'

'Go right ahead,' said Ethel. 'I stopped listening to him ages ago.'

'Well, that's just rude,' said Jerry.

Lex started forward, only to stop abruptly as a gun suddenly appeared in Jerry's hand: a gleaming steel revolver with ivory-inlaid handles. Lex stared at the gun, and Jerry almost wriggled with pleasure.

'Yes, I thought you'd recognize it! The legendary Iscariot Device that fires bullets made from the thirty pieces of silver paid to Judas to betray the Christ. The only weapon that can kill an angel – and the very same gun you used to damn yourself.'

'I gave that to Harry,' said Lex. 'To keep it safe.'

'No,' said Jerry, who couldn't have been more pleased with himself unless he was twins, 'you pawned it to Old Harry. And when you never went back to redeem it, he quite naturally put it up for sale. Well, for auction, actually. You would not believe how much it cost me to see off the competition. Who knew so many people wanted to kill angels? But now the Iscariot Device is mine! I'm assured it can punch right through your very special armour, Lex. And it will certainly kill your friends. Or . . . you could all get down on your knees and behave yourselves, while I kill this frankly ridiculous old bag that's supposed to be an angel and take her halo for myself.'

'Why would you let us live?' I said.

'Gideon . . .' murmured Alice.

'So you can tell everybody all about it, of course,' said Jerry. 'I'm a great believer in free publicity. So back off, Lex; there's a good boy. Unless you want to watch your friends die.'

Lex moved back a few steps, not taking his eyes off the gun. Jerry grinned and winked at me.

'You know, to be brutally honest with myself, which I rarely am, I wasn't entirely certain that would work. And yet it seems the rumours are true! The Damned has been tamed by his need for friends. How the mighty have fallen . . . But I think I've indulged myself long enough; it's time to get down to business.' His smile went cold as he turned it on Ethel. 'I want your halo. Right now. So hand it over, or I'll shoot you down and cut it off your head, the same way Lex did.'

'You have the Magdalene Blade?' Ethel asked politely. 'The knife that can cut through anything?'

'Well, no,' said Jerry. 'I have to admit, I couldn't afford the knife as well as the gun. Even Dark Popes don't have limitless resources. Judi Rifkin got the Magdalene Blade, curse the woman. But no matter! I was able to acquire something just as good.'

His left hand was suddenly holding a large, straight razor, with the blade slung open.

'Behold – the original Occam's Razor!'

We all looked at it for a moment.

'It's just a razor,' I said. 'There's nothing special about it.'

Jerry scowled at me, almost pouting in his anger.

'Yes, well, you would say that, wouldn't you? Harry gave me a special provenance, guaranteeing this particular blade is everything it's supposed to be!'

'I'm starting to see Harry's fingerprints all over this business,' I said.

Jerry sneered at me and turned his full attention on Ethel, who was still sitting calmly in her chair.

'Give me the halo. Now.'

'I gave that up when I decided to stay human,' she said.

'You expect me to believe that?' said Jerry.

She looked at him reproachfully. 'Angels don't lie.'

Jerry scowled hard as he thought about it. 'Even if I did believe you, and I'm pretty certain that I don't, I didn't come all this way for nothing. I mean, walking away empty-handed at this point would be bad for my reputation, and very bad for business. So . . . I'm afraid I am going to kill all of you, after all, and then I'll flay the angel's corpse with my razor and wear her skin as my armour. That should make the right impression.'

Lex surged forward and punched Jerry between the eyes. Jerry cried out, dropped the gun and the razor, and staggered backwards. Lex kicked the gun away, while I grabbed the razor and broke the blade in two, just to be on the safe side. I nodded to Jerry, who had slammed up against the far wall, and was holding his nose with one hand while he stared reproachfully at Lex with watering eyes.

'Occam's Razor, my arse; Harry saw you coming,' I said. 'What does it say over his front door? *Buyer Beware*.'

Jerry took his hand away from his nose and thrust it out – and just like that he was holding the Iscariot Device again. He aimed it at Lex and laughed loudly.

'You can't keep this gun from its master's hand. It was made to kill angels, and it wants to!'

'But I'm not an angel,' said Lex. He smiled slowly. 'Far from it.'

His armour flowed over him, covering him from head to toe like a second skin made of blinding light and terrible darkness. Spiritual armour, made from the halos of two very different angels. The light was like looking into the sun, and the dark was a hole in the world. The Damned was protected by the forces of Heaven and Hell.

Everyone in the room flinched from the armour, including Ethel.

Alice and I got out of the way, to give the Damned room to operate. All the colour had dropped out of Jerry's face, and his eyes were full of a slowly dawning horror. The Damned took a step forward, and Jerry opened fire. The Damned ducked under the bullet and was upon Jerry in a moment, slapping the gun out of his hand. It went skidding away across the floor. The Damned gripped Jerry by the throat and lifted him into the air. Jerry's eyes bulged as he fought for air and scrabbled helplessly at the Damned's armoured wrist with both hands. His feet kicked helplessly above the floor, as the life went out of him.

And then Ethel pushed her empty teacup away from her and rose to her feet.

'Don't kill him, Lex.'

The Damned slowly turned his featureless face to look at her and then at me. Because sometimes he relied on me to be human for him. I thought about everything Jerry and his people had done, all the lives they'd destroyed and the suffering they'd caused . . . And then I thought about the kind of attention Jerry's death might bring, just when I didn't want to be noticed. I sighed quietly and shook my head.

'He's not worthy of you, Lex. Dying at your hand would be his greatest achievement. Just kick his nasty arse and let him go. No one will believe in the Dark Pope after that.'

The Damned opened his armoured hand, and Jerry dropped to the floor. He just sat there, crying and gasping for breath. Lex's armour flowed back into the silver bands at his wrists, leaving him revealed to the world again. He looked coldly at Jerry.

'Don't ever bother this lady again. Or my friends. Or anyone I know. Because if you do, I will show you what *or else* really means.'

He turned to Ethel, and Jerry thrust out his hand again. The Iscariot Device flew back into his grasp. Jerry brought it to bear on Lex's unarmoured form and pulled the trigger. But Ethel had already raised her hand. The silver bullet slammed to a halt in mid-air, well short of its target. We all stood very still, because none of us had ever witnessed a miracle before.

'That's quite enough of that,' said Ethel in the tone of a schoolteacher who'd put up with quite enough bad behaviour for one day. 'I do try to see the good in people, but you would try the patience of a saint, Jerry. And I should know; I've bumped into enough of them in my time. When I think of all the damage you've done, I can't see a single good reason to give you another chance. You've made a lot of enemies in your time, Jerry, and now I am one of them.'

She snapped her fingers, and Jerry wasn't there any more. He was just gone, and the Iscariot Device with him. The silver bullet dropped out of the air to rattle harmlessly on the kitchen table. We all stared at Ethel, who stared calmly back.

'What did you do to him?' I said.

'I sent him away,' said Ethel.

'Where?' said Alice.

'Somewhere he won't be coming back from,' said Ethel. 'Don't look so upset; right now he's meeting a lot of old friends. Or at least people with good reason to remember him.'

She sat down at the table and picked up her cup. It was suddenly full of tea again. Alice moved in beside me and gripped my arm with both hands. Lex looked thoughtfully at Ethel, as though he'd never seen her before.

'At least now we know what kind of angel you used to be,' I said.

Ethel smiled at me sweetly. 'Do you, dear?'

'I thought you'd given up being an angel?' said Lex.

'I chose to be human,' said Ethel. 'But I haven't forgotten where I came from. Now, I think it's time all of you were leaving. *Countdown* will be starting soon, and I never miss it. So . . . off you go! And please feel free never to come here again.'

FIVE

The Ways of the World

Outside, the streetlights had come on, as if rather more time had passed in Ethel's house than I could account for. The street was still empty, but all around us shadows were gathering as though they had a purpose. A cold wind stirred the branches on the trees and sent leaves scurrying along the pavement. I shivered, and not from the cold. I could feel the presence of unseen eyes and the weight of a considering gaze. From someone determined to be left alone.

Alice looked at Lex. 'If that was a retired angel, how were you able to kill two real ones?'

'I caught them by surprise,' said Lex. 'Word has probably got around since then.'

'Is Ethel scary because of what she used to be?' I said. 'Or because she's trying to be human?'

'You always did worry about the strangest things, Gideon,' said Lex. 'Let her play at being human. She'll get tired of it soon enough and go home.'

'And then we can all breathe more easily,' said Alice.

Lex turned his back on the rogue angel's house and gave me his full attention. 'Tell me about the heist.'

I filled him in on the Masque of Ra, Judi Rifkin and the Montressors as quickly as I could. When I was done, he just nodded.

'Vegas. Could be fun. Are we picking up the Wild Card and the Ghost, as well?'

'Not the Ghost,' I said. 'He's perfectly happy being Fredric Hammer. But Johnny is next on my list. Do you know where we can find him?'

Lex nodded. 'I dropped him off at his club, before I came here.'

'His club?' said Alice. 'What sort of club would accept Johnny Wilde as a member?'

'The kind that only accepts people like him,' said Lex.

'I didn't know there was anyone else like the Wild Card,' I said.

'You'd be surprised,' said Lex. 'Do you have a car?'

'Any minute now,' I said.

There were three luxury cars parked outside Ethel's house, all of them far too flashy and expensive for this kind of neighbourhood. I strolled over for a closer look, and Alice and Lex followed at a safe distance to see what I would do. It only took me a moment to establish that all three cars were empty.

'Jerry always did like to travel in style,' I said.

Alice frowned as she looked up and down the street. 'I don't see any of his people.'

'Maybe Ethel got rid of them when she got rid of Jerry,' said Lex.

The three of us moved closer together, like soldiers who'd just dodged a whole bunch of bullets.

'I'm sure Jerry would want us to take one of these, to make up for all the trouble he caused us,' I said.

'I'm pretty sure he wouldn't,' said Alice.

I turned to Lex and gestured at the most extravagant vehicle. 'Think you can open this one?'

As he drew back a fist to smash in the driver's window, the door swung open invitingly. We all stood very still and looked at it.

'It would appear Ethel is still keeping an eye on us,' I said.

'Get us out of here, Gideon,' said Alice. 'And I mean *really quickly*.'

I slipped in behind the steering wheel and wasn't at all surprised to find the key waiting in the ignition. Alice got in beside me as I started the engine, and Lex settled himself heavily in the back. I sent the car shooting off down the road the moment I heard the doors slam, and didn't look back once. There wasn't any other traffic around, which was probably just as well for the other traffic, because I wasn't thinking about anything except putting as much distance as possible between us and the woman who only thought she wasn't an angel. After a while, I shot Lex a look in the rear-view mirror.

'Where are we going, Lex?'

'Club Lethe, in Soho.'

'Name doesn't ring any bells,' I said. 'And I thought I knew every low dive and special interest club in this city.'

'Lethe doesn't advertise,' said Lex.

'Oh,' said Alice. 'One of those.'

'What is the Wild Card doing in a club like that?' I said.

'Looking for himself,' said Lex.

'I wouldn't, if I were him,' said Alice.

'Drive,' Lex said calmly. 'I'll give you directions after we've crossed into Soho.'

Alice turned around in her seat, so she could stare at Lex.

'How did you get here? I can't see you hailing a taxi.'

'They never stop for me,' said Lex. 'I don't know why; I'm a really good tipper. But in the end, someone gave me a lift.'

'Did they want to?' I said.

'Not really,' said Lex.

'I won't ask,' I said.

'Best not to,' said Lex.

His directions took us deep into darkest Soho. Where all the best and worst establishments prefer to remain hidden in the shadows, away from curious eyes. Evening was descending into night as I steered the car through increasingly narrow streets. There wasn't much traffic, but people crowded the pavements, avoiding each other's eyes and keeping themselves to themselves. It wasn't the kind of place you wanted to meet anyone you knew. The first neon signs were just stirring into life, like predators becoming aware of approaching prey.

'What kind of place is Club Lethe?' said Alice.

'Very private and very strange,' said Lex. 'I look in now and again, to keep an eye on Johnny. He hasn't been the same since he nearly died in Hammer's vault.'

'I would have thought that was a good thing,' said Alice.

I finally brought the car to a halt at the end of a street where half the lights weren't working because people preferred it that way. I parked the car on a double yellow line, got out and walked away. Alice soon caught up, but Lex strode past us to take the lead. I let him, because he knew where we were going. I didn't look back at the car. If it was still there when we got back, all well and good; if it wasn't, we'd find some other way to get home. I try not to worry about things like that.

The street was lined with boarded-up windows, firmly closed doors, and bars and clubs whose signs had letters missing. It was all just camouflage for the kind of businesses that preferred not to speak their names out loud. There are still parts of Soho you couldn't drive upmarket with a whip and a cattle prod. The streets and squares that don't appear on any map, where people go to enquire after things they know are bad for them, or somebody else.

Subterranean culture – where the cut and thrust of the night circus goes head to head with the darkest impulses of the human spirit, and the sinning is easy.

Most of the people we passed stuck to the shadows and minded their own business. Alice and I walked proudly in what light there was, trusting to our reputations to ward off unwanted attentions. Lex didn't have to make an effort: he was the Damned. People took one look at him and hid in doorways.

Lex suddenly disappeared down a set of stone steps you wouldn't even notice if you didn't know where to look. Alice and I followed him down past street level to a single door, pinned to which was the name of the club handwritten on a piece of cardboard.

'This is taking downmarket to a whole new level,' said Alice.

Lex waved me forward. I tried the door handle and wasn't in the least surprised to find it wouldn't turn. I could have knocked and waited, but I really wasn't in the mood, so I dug out my skeleton key and unlocked the door with a flourish. Lex kicked it open and we all barged into a narrow hallway, where we surprised an unusually large man sitting on a chair and leafing through a cooking magazine. He threw it to one side, rose to his feet and moved to block our way. He was wearing a monk's robe, gathered in at the waist by a length of rope, with the hood pulled far enough forward to hide most of his face.

'Members only,' he snarled, squaring his shoulders to make himself appear bigger and more imposing. 'And you don't look like members. You look like trouble.'

Lex's look suggested serious violence was on its way, so I quickly placed myself between the Damned and the monk before things could get unpleasant.

'Let's all try being civilized,' I said smoothly. 'We're quite happy to take out temporary memberships.'

I showed the monk a fifty-pound note, because you don't want to appear cheap at moments like this. He snatched the money out of my hand and made it disappear about his person.

'Not enough! We don't want your kind here. Disappear, tourists, before I decide to jump up and down on you with both feet.'

You can't help some people, because they won't let you. I nodded to Lex. He grabbed a handful of the monk's robe, lifted him off his feet and banged his cowled head against the ceiling. There was a dull thud, and the monk hung limply from Lex's grasp like so much washing. Lex dumped the unconscious man back on his chair and then leaned him against the wall so he wouldn't fall off. Lex can be surprisingly solicitous on occasion. I searched the monk and retrieved my money, and then searched him some more to see if he had any other money on him. I took that off him, too. For being unnecessarily uncivilized. We moved on down the hallway until it ended in another door. It saw Lex approaching and opened on its own. And just like that, we were inside Club Lethe.

Which turned out to be one dimly lit room with bare stone walls, a low ceiling and nothing that could even pass as ambience. A handful of people were sitting in a circle, on rickety wooden chairs, talking quietly. They didn't even glance round at us. Alice moved a little closer to me.

'This doesn't feel even a little bit friendly, Gideon. Maybe I should have brought Emma, after all.'

'You can't talk to people if they're unconscious,' I said firmly. 'But there's no need to be concerned. We have Lex.'

'You make me sound like a guard dog,' said the Damned.

'Be good and I'll take you for walkies later,' I said.

'Well, woof,' said Lex.

Alice allowed herself a small smile. 'Good thing he's big enough for both of us to hide behind.'

Johnny Wilde was sitting quietly with the other people in the circle. A stout, middle-aged man, in an old tweed suit with leather patches on the elbows, Johnny had a round face and kind eyes. He looked like a retired professor because that's what he was. He listened attentively as the others talked, and it occurred to me that they all had the same kind of face: tired and beaten down by life. And probably by other things, too.

'OK . . .' I said. 'Really not what I was expecting. The group seems harmless enough, and Johnny looks astonishingly calm and together.'

'Look closely,' said Lex. Because it would have killed him to say appearances can be deceptive. He always had to be the most taciturn man in the room.

Johnny wasn't exactly sitting on his chair. He tended to sink down through it when he wasn't concentrating. One of his neighbours would notice and lean in for a quick word, and then Johnny would bob back up again. I wasn't surprised; Johnny and the material world haven't been on speaking terms in ages.

A tall and seriously gaunt old man in a vintage Grateful Dead T-shirt, grubby jeans and open-toed sandals emerged from an adjoining kitchen and ambled over to join us. His face had so many wrinkles it looked as if it could use a good ironing, and his long, grey hair was pulled back in a ponytail. Basically, he looked like an old hippie who hadn't eaten regularly since the Woodstock food drops. He eased to a halt, swayed for a moment as though catching up with himself and then showed us all the same gentle smile.

'Hi, I'm Aldo, steward for Club Lethe. Please keep your voices down, so as not to disturb the club's members. They're disturbed enough as it us. Hello, Lex; back already?'

'I'm just here for Johnny,' said Lex. 'You know how he is.'

'Not really,' said Aldo.

'Hold hard there,' I said to Lex. 'If you're a regular visitor, why didn't the monk recognize you?'

'Gordon only started an hour ago,' said the steward. 'And it must be said, he's not the brightest button in the box.'

'Why was he dressed as a monk?' asked Alice.

'Because he doesn't want to be recognized,' said Aldo. 'He only took the job because I asked his mother if she could recommend someone, and she was fed up having him around the house. He'd really much prefer to be a doorman at one of those upmarket BDSM clubs.' Aldo paused, as a thought caught up with him, and he looked reproachfully at Lex. 'You've done something to him, haven't you?'

'He'll be fine,' said Lex. 'When he wakes up.'

The steward winced. 'You have no idea how difficult it is to get staff around here, and we have to have someone. Our members take their privacy very seriously. They have to; it's all some of them have left.'

'How is Johnny?' said Lex.

'As disturbing as ever.'

'Don't you mean disturbed?' I said.

'No,' said the steward. 'Please watch quietly, and don't interrupt until the members have finished speaking. Then we usually have cocoa and biscuits. A small contribution would be appreciated, to help us pay the rent on the room. You wouldn't think they'd have the nerve to charge for a dump like this, would you? But they do.'

'What is this place?' said Alice, lowering her voice in spite of herself, because the steward's gentle smile would have made her feel like a barbarian if she hadn't.

'Club Lethe is a self-help and support group,' said Aldo. 'For people who have damaged their minds and their souls experimenting with new drugs. This bunch didn't just expand their consciousness; they shoved a whole stick of dynamite up its arse and blew it to pieces. I like to think of them as explorers into the greatest unknown of all – the point where the mind and the universe meet.'

'Here there be tygers,' said Lex, just a bit unexpectedly.

'Exactly,' said the steward. 'And some of them burn very brightly, in the alchemical forests of the night.'

'How did you end up Steward of a Club like this?' said Alice.

Aldo's gentle smile warmed his faded blue eyes. 'Someone has to be here, to ground the members when they start to drift away.'

'Would I be right in thinking you have experience in that area?' I said politely.

His smile widened into a grin. 'Back in the day, when dragons and unicorns roamed the mass unconscious, I had an endless appetite for unusual chemicals. If you could smoke it, swallow it, inject it or stick it where the sun doesn't shine, you could always find me at the front of the queue, asking if there was a discount for bulk buying. It frankly amazes me I still have a few working synapses to bang together.'

'But you don't do that any more?' said Alice.

'It wasn't the same after the sixties,' said the steward. 'The magic went away. These days I'm just here to help fellow travellers find their way down the road, and warn them about hidden pot-holes and unexpected detours.'

'We need to talk to Johnny,' said Lex, entirely unmoved by this wander through the land of myth and metaphor.

'I think they're getting to the end of the session,' said Aldo. 'Pay attention; you might find this interesting. And maybe even enlightening.'

He took us a little closer to the circle, where Johnny was explaining to the others why he was there. He sounded unusually calm and collected.

'I'm Johnny Wilde. Known here and there as the Wild Card. I took a drug that allowed me to see the world as it really is and step behind the curtains of reality. Sometimes I go backstage and move things around. And sometimes I get lost, trying to sort out what's inside my head, and what isn't. I see so many things . . . and only some of them share the same world as the rest of you.

'I should have died in Fredric Hammer's secret vault. A guard shot me repeatedly, at point-blank range. The impact of the bullets threw me to the floor, and I lay there expecting to be dead . . . until I realized I wasn't, and I wondered why I was still lying there. I bounced back, because that's what I do; but ever since I've been wondering . . . if I only continue to exist because I believe I do.'

He looked expectantly around the circle. The others seemed a little overawed by his presence among them. The Wild Card's reputation ranged far and wide, as a very cautionary tale.

'All the members of Club Lethe have some experience of what's on the Other Side,' Aldo murmured. 'And none of them are even a little bit happy about what they found there.'

One of the other people in the circle leaned forward. He was a large, flabby sort, all but spilling out of his cheap suit, so leaning forward took a lot of effort. His red face perspired heavily.

'I'm Nathan Thorpe,' he said in a deep rumble of a voice. 'My drug allows me to slow down my metabolism, so seconds can pass as hours. I use this to study the world in great detail. Searching for patterns, and perhaps the maker's signature. I'd settle for a hidden message, or even a few Easter eggs. But more and more I get the feeling that no one is looking back . . . that we are all alone, trapped in an empty room.'

He stopped talking. No one seemed to have anything to say in response. The woman sitting next to him kept her gaze fixed on the floor as she talked, so she wouldn't have to look anywhere else. A painfully thin woman in her late thirties, with dark skin and close-cropped hair, she wore a smart blouse and skirt, and an air of quiet desperation.

'I'm Jean Lynne. I took a drug to let me see ghosts. It never crossed my mind that they would be able to see me. They're attracted to me, like moths to a light, because I'm the only one who can see them, and they're so alone . . . But there are more and more of them all the time, and I can't stop seeing them . . .'

She stopped talking, but her lips kept moving, saying the same thing over and over.

Go away. Please, go away . . .

A grey-haired, anonymous little man, the kind you'd walk straight past in the street and never notice, started speaking the moment Lynne stopped.

'My name is Thomas Norton. I took a drug that was supposed to make me young again. And I am, but only inside my head. I'm a young man trapped in an old man's body.'

After that, the conversation moved slowly round the circle, everyone speaking in quiet, defeated voices as they tried to help each other. The big man, Thorpe, asked Lynne if she'd considered an exorcism.

'I'm not possessed,' she said, still not looking up. 'I'm haunted. And anyway, I'm not religious.'

Thorpe frowned, taken aback. 'But if you can see the dead . . .'

'That's just it!' said Lynne. 'If there is a Heaven and a Hell, why are they all still here? Unless there's nowhere else for them to go . . .'

Eventually, they turned to Johnny. The man who'd been through so much more than all of them and hadn't let it break him.

'How do you cope?' said Thorpe.

'How do you stay focused?' said Norton.

'How do you stay sane?' Lynne lifted her head for the first time to look at Johnny.

'Some people will tell you I haven't,' said Johnny. 'These days I cope by helping other people, when I can't help myself. Let me take a look at these ghosts of yours.'

He stood up and looked around the empty room. And just like

that, we could all see the ghosts. Rank after rank of them, filling the whole cellar, packed together so tightly they overlapped each other. Just dim glowing forms, without faces or definition. As though they'd been dead for so long they'd forgotten who they used to be.

Alice clung tightly to my arm, and I did my best to stand firm, for her. Lex just looked interested. Aldo beamed happily, entranced. Johnny shook his head slowly and then cleared his throat loudly. And every single ghost in the room turned their head to look at him. Hundreds of blank and empty faces, with no eyes, but they could see him. I felt something move through the packed ranks of the ghosts, as they realized someone else knew they were there. They stared fixedly at Johnny, their indistinct bodies suddenly blazing with a hunger and a need that would not let them rest. Johnny smiled easily back at them.

My skin crawled, as I realized the ghosts were starting to become aware of the rest of us, too. Alice stood a little straighter and glared right back at them, refusing to be intimidated. Lex stirred uneasily, and his silver bracelets began to glow as they recognized a clear and imminent threat.

The steward stared entranced at the glowing forms, his face full of a simple wonder.

The ghosts started towards us, slowly gathering speed. The other club members rose quickly to their feet and backed away as far as they could get. Lynne shook her head, *No, no, no . . .* The other two moved to put themselves between her and the ghosts, although it was clear from their faces that they had no idea what they could do to stop the oncoming ghosts. They just knew they had to do something.

Johnny raised one hand and drew a line across the floor, separating us from the hungry ghosts. The glowing forms slammed up against the unseen barrier and stopped, held where they were by the power of the Wild Card's will. But still they kept pressing forward, as though they could force their way through by sheer pressure of numbers. And I wasn't sure they couldn't.

'Everyone get behind me,' Lex said quietly. 'I'm going to put on my armour.'

'You really think that can help against ghosts?' said Alice.

'I am armoured by Heaven and Hell,' Lex said steadily. 'And that covers pretty much all the ground there is.'

'Don't be so dramatic,' said Johnny, not taking his eyes off the ghosts. 'And a little hush, please. I'm working.'

He looked thoughtfully at the ghosts, as though they were just another problem that needed solving, and then raised one arm and pointed at the far wall. All the ghostly heads turned to look, and I did, too. There was a door in the wall that I was certain hadn't been there just a moment before. A simple, everyday door, with a large neon sign above it, saying *EXIT*. Johnny nodded at the door and it swung slowly open. A marvellous, brilliant light spilled out of it, pushing back the gloom of the cellar. Like the beam of a lighthouse, offering a safe way through the storm. A slow movement, of something that might have been recognition, moved through the massed ranks of the ghosts. They forgot all about the line on the floor and the living people crowded behind it, and concentrated only on the door.

They stared, fascinated, into that wonderous light, and so did I. It felt like home, like where I belonged, like where I came from before I was me. The home that was waiting for all of us, at the end. The light was full of peace and comfort, and everything I'd ever wanted. I took a step towards it, and then I stopped and looked at Alice. She was staring entranced into the light as well, but when I said her name, she turned her face away to look at me. I put out my hand, and she took hold of it, and we shared a smile.

I checked the others were still where they should be and then turned to Lex. And out of all of us, he was the only one not looking at the light. His face was turned away, as though it was too painful to look at.

'There's no need to be afraid of the light, Lex,' said Johnny.

'I'm not afraid,' said Lex. 'It's just . . . it hurts too much. Because that's not where I'm going. I don't belong there.'

'You say the dumbest things sometimes, Lex,' said Johnny.

He turned to address the ghosts, and all their empty heads snapped round to face him as he started talking.

'Go home,' he said. 'What are you hanging around here for? Playtime is over and your tea's waiting. Go into the light, where everyone you ever lost or cared for is waiting for you.'

And just like that, all the ghosts were gone. There was no sense of movement or transition, more like so many candles that had finally been blown out. The door slowly closed itself, and the wonderful light faded away and was gone. I felt like a drowning man who'd just had his lifeline snatched away. And then Alice squeezed my hand, and I squeezed hers, and as we smiled at each other, I was already forgetting what I'd seen.

The steward smiled quietly. He looked as if he'd just met an old friend that he hadn't seen in a long time. The club members were babbling excitedly together. Lex Talon stood stooped, with his head hanging down, looking horribly tired. But before I could say anything, his head came up and his shoulders squared, as though he had picked up his burden again and stood ready to carry it as far as he had to.

Lynne sobbed wildly, with relief and gratitude, and rushed over to wring Johnny's hand with both of hers. He let her do that for a while and then quietly eased his hand free.

'They won't bother you again. I've changed the drug so it won't affect you any more. The ghosts won't see you, because you can't see them.'

'There must be some way I can thank you,' said Lynne.

'Live a normal life,' said Johnny. 'For those of us who can't.' He turned to Thorpe. 'You – just stop looking. If God had meant to leave us a message, he wouldn't have hidden it.'

Thorpe started to say something, thought about it and didn't. Johnny looked at Norton.

'Your drug didn't work. Everyone feels like you do.'

He got up and walked away from the circle, leaving them to chatter excitedly behind him. He nodded to the steward, who saluted him as he passed, and came over to join me and my crew. He was frowning.

'What's wrong?' I said. 'I thought you did a good job.'

'I can help them,' said Johnny, 'But I can't help myself. I keep coming here, looking for someone who can do for me what I do for them, but there's no one. I'm stuck being the Wild Card.'

'You need something to keep you busy,' I said. 'I'm planning a new heist, and I could use the Wild Card. What do you say?'

Johnny beamed happily. 'Of course! I had so much fun being part of your crew.' He winked at Alice. 'Peek-a-boo! I see you, Annie Anybody!' And then he leaped on Lex like an eager puppy, hugging him tightly and wrapping his legs around the Damned's waist. 'Oh, it's good to be back!'

Lex stood there and let Johnny do it, until he let go and climbed down.

'Good to see you, too, you weird little man,' said Lex.

'Can you come with us right now, Johnny?' I said quickly.

'Yes,' he said, not even glancing back at the circle.

'So that's it,' said Alice. 'The crew is back together again!'

'We still need one more specialist,' I said.

'Who do you have in mind?' said Lex.

'Switch It Sally,' I said.

'But . . . You must know you can't trust her!' said Alice. 'Nobody can!'

'We can work around that,' I said.

SIX

It's All a Matter of Taste

To the crew's mutual astonishment, the expensive car was still parked where I'd left it. All four wheels still attached and not even a key mark on the paintwork. I allowed myself a slightly smug smile.

Alice gave Johnny a stern look. 'Have you been messing with reality again?'

'Not at all,' he said loftily. 'Sometimes the universe is just kinder than we expect.'

'That has not been my experience,' said Lex.

I got them all into the car with a minimum of squabbling over who got to ride shotgun. Alice won, by getting into the passenger seat while Lex and Johnny were still arguing. They seemed to regard that as cheating and grumbled loudly as they arranged themselves in the back. I set off through London again. Lex ended up sitting quietly, not looking at anything in particular, while Johnny bounced around, looking out of one window after another and taking a keen interest in everything. I wondered if he did that to ground himself in what was real, as opposed to what went on inside his head.

'Where are we going?' said Alice after a while.

'Somewhere more upmarket,' I said.

She sniffed. 'That shouldn't be difficult. But what would Sally be doing, mixing with the upper crust?'

'Conning someone,' I said cheerfully.

'Who is this Switch It Sally?' said Lex. 'I don't know the name, and I thought I'd at least heard of all the major players.'

'Sally is not major,' I said, cutting off an over-confident taxi cab with great satisfaction. 'She barely qualifies as minor. Basically, she's just a low-rent grifter, running one small con after another because she doesn't have the ambition to go after anything bigger.'

'What makes you think she'll want to be part of our crew?' said Alice, just a bit pointedly.

'Because no one has ever offered her a chance to play with the big boys,' I said.

'We're the big boys?' said Johnny. 'I am so proud . . . Oh, look, an ostrich!'

I didn't look. I was pretty sure there wasn't one, and if there was, I didn't want to think about how it got there.

'The reason no one ever wants Switch It Sally on their team is that she's betrayed everyone she ever worked with,' Alice said flatly. 'She's a selfish, scheming little minx who never wants to share with anyone. And those are her good qualities.'

'But her special gift makes her perfect for this heist,' I said. I caught Lex's eye in the rear-view mirror, because he was the one who needed to be convinced. 'Sally can exchange any object for another of similar size, from a distance, without anyone noticing. And that is exactly what we need to snatch the Masque of Ra from the Khuffu Casino. Harry is providing us with an exact duplicate.'

'You know this Sally well?' said Lex.

'We worked a few cons together, back in the day,' I said. 'Before I was Gideon Sable.'

'Before I came along to rescue you,' said Alice.

'Why did you stop working with her?' said Lex.

Alice snorted loudly. 'Because she sold him out and sprinted for the horizon, leaving him holding the bag. Just like we all told him she would.'

'Explain to me again why having this woman on our team is a good idea,' said Lex. 'Because if there was a good reason, I think I missed it.'

'She'll be fine,' I said firmly. 'As long as we keep her on a really short leash.'

'You could have a gun permanently attached to her head and I still wouldn't trust her further than I could throw a wet camel,' said Alice.

'I did that once,' said Johnny. Everyone ignored him. It seemed safest.

'I don't work with people I can't trust,' said Lex.

'You don't normally work with anyone,' I said. 'But you had a good time working with us.'

'I trust you,' said Lex.

Everyone took a moment to react to that. It was a big step for the Damned.

'Then trust me,' I said carefully, 'to stay on top of Sally.'

Alice produced a short snort of laughter. 'Paging Doctor Freud . . .'

'She just needs careful handling,' I said.

'You're giving me ammunition now,' said Alice.

And then she broke off, as she realized we were driving past shops with expensive brand names and really impressive storefronts. The kind of places where most people couldn't even afford to window-shop.

Alice scowled. 'What are we doing in an up-itself area like this?'

'We are going to a wine tasting,' I said. 'Where Sally is running her latest con.'

'Around here? They'll eat her alive.' Alice looked at me suspiciously. 'How do you know so much about where she is and what she's doing?'

'Well, first I consulted my special compass, and the needle almost bent itself in half pointing to her. Which is how I know she's essential to my plan. And then I asked Harry.'

'Him again!'

'I'm afraid so.'

'It'll all end in tears,' Alice said darkly.

We ended up in an extravagant little enclave, dedicated to selling the very best in cuisine to people who almost certainly didn't appreciate it. The kind of restaurants where if you want a reservation, your parents have to put your name down the moment you're born. We cruised unhurriedly past very select establishments offering specialized dining experiences – such as eating endangered species in complete darkness, the better to savour the flavour and hide your shame while you do it. Or a converted dungeon, where naked slaves will feed you delicate morsels with their bare hands. And, taking the concept of game bird to its logical conclusion, a restaurant that specialized in zombie fowl – apparently, your meal would actually walk across the table to drop on to your plate. And for all I knew, look at you reproachfully while you ate it.

I finally spotted an empty space at the side of the road and jammed the car into it before anyone else beat me to it. I was pretty sure I wasn't allowed to park there, but that just added to the pleasure of the moment. As we got out of the car, Alice was already shaking her head.

'Someone is bound to come along and clamp it, or haul it away.'

'Let them,' I said. 'Easy come, easy go.'

And then I stopped to peer down a shadowy alley at a parked van.

'What's the matter?' said Alice.

'I've seen this vehicle before,' I said.

'It's just a standard white van,' said Alice. 'Or at least it might be white if the owner ever gets around to cleaning it. There are hundreds just like it bombing up and down the streets of London, getting in everyone's way and not giving a damn.'

'But you wouldn't expect to see something as common as this parked here,' I said. 'Even the delivery men are encouraged to move on the moment they're finished unloading, to avoid lowering the tone. And I know I've seen this particular van before, because I recognize the heavy tyres – specially designed to facilitate fast getaways. Sally is here.'

'I thought you already knew that?' said Alice.

'It's nice to have it confirmed,' I said.

I led the crew to an anonymous front door in a very anonymous building. One of those places that doesn't need to advertise, because all the right people already know where it is. I felt like drawing a cock and balls on the door, just on principle. The only thing that stood out was the large muscular gentleman standing guard, in an exquisitely tailored suit. He watched us approach with a cold gaze that said very clearly *Move along. You don't belong here.* Alice leaned in beside me, to murmur in my ear.

'Tell me you've spotted the bulge under his jacket, from the gun in his concealed shoulder holster.'

'Of course,' I said. 'I'd be surprised if he wasn't packing, given the kind of rare and expensive vintages he's protecting. And all the rich and important personages, of course.'

'How do you know so much about this wine tasting?' said Alice.

'Harry,' I admitted.

Alice scowled. 'He is far too involved in what is supposed to be *our* heist. And I still say this sounds like far too grand a gathering for someone like Switch It Sally.'

'Trust the compass,' I said.

'How are we getting in?' said Alice. 'Even without the gun, that guard looks like he could break us in two just by coughing loudly.'

'Watch . . . and marvel,' I said.

I walked up to the guard, smiling easily. He didn't smile back, just fixed me with a steady gaze that dared me to try anything. I stopped before him and raised an eyebrow, in a way that suggested I was surprised he was still blocking my way.

'I'm going to need to see your invitation, sir,' said the guard, in a tone that made it very clear he didn't believe I had one.

'I've already shown it to you,' I said sharply.

Of all the answers he'd been expecting, that wasn't one of them. Suddenly caught on the back foot, he looked at me blankly.

'What?'

'I only left the wine tasting half an hour ago,' I said sternly. 'To collect my friends. And now we're back.'

'I don't remember you, sir,' said the guard.

I drew myself up and glared at him.

'You'll be saying next that you don't recognize the Damned, either.'

Lex made a low growling noise. The guard took one look at him and quickly decided he wasn't being paid enough to do anything that might upset the Damned. He opened the front door for us and stepped well back. I strode past him as though

I'd never expected any other outcome. Alice stuck her nose even more in the air. Lex didn't so much as glance at the guard, for which the guard seemed very grateful. Johnny just bounced along in the rear, smiling sweetly, and raised a bowler hat that he hadn't been wearing a moment before. The guard pretended he hadn't seen that and hurriedly closed the door behind us.

Alice waited till we were halfway down the extravagantly appointed hallway before she smiled at me appreciatively.

'Good to see you haven't lost your touch.'

'I don't just rely on my special toys,' I said.

'What would you have done if I hadn't been there to back you up?' said Lex.

'Gone to Plan B,' I said.

'There's a Plan B?' said Johnny. He picked up an expensive china vase from an antique table, threw away the flowers and started to eat it.

'There's always a Plan B,' I said. 'And a C, and a D. After that, I tend to fall back on a subtle blend of improvisation and blind panic.'

'I don't want to rain on your parade,' Alice said quietly, 'but we are getting very close to the guards at the next door. I've seen less scary things glowering down at me from cathedral roofs.'

'Time for Plan B?' said Lex.

'Watch, learn and applaud afterwards,' I said.

We came to a halt in front of the two Neanderthals in tuxedos, and the larger of them started speaking before I could say anything.

'We'll need to see your invitations before you can go any further. Sir.'

I glared at him. 'You're new, aren't you? Stand up straight when I'm speaking to you!'

Both guards snapped to attention, responding automatically to the authority in my voice.

'Sorry, sir,' said the guard. 'If you could please identify yourself . . .'

'I'm in charge of security for this whole damned tasting,' I said coldly. 'Weren't you briefed when you got here? What's your name? No, never mind; just go inside and tell the organizer I'm here.'

'Yes, sir,' the guard said quickly, happy to do anything that would get him out from under my glare. 'If you could just give me your name . . .'

I gave him my very best scowl, and he actually fell back a step. 'You don't even know my name? What kind of amateur-night set-up is this? It doesn't matter; the organizer will know me. Why are you still standing there?'

The guard bobbed his head quickly, opened the door and hurried inside. The other guard frowned hard, the beginnings of suspicion starting to form in his face. I turned to Lex.

'Take him down, but don't break him.'

Lex moved quickly forward, raised a closed fist and hit the guard on top of his head. The man collapsed, and Lex caught him before he hit the floor. I'd already spotted a storage space in the far wall, and gestured to Alice. She hurried over to open the closet, and Lex dumped the unconscious guard inside it. An elderly and very well-dressed couple passing by went so far as to raise an eyebrow. I smiled at them calmly.

'I'd avoid the claret, if I were you. That second growth always was malignant.'

The couple nodded and disappeared through the main door. Alice closed the closet and came back to join me.

'I didn't know you spoke wine.'

'I can fake it with the best of them,' I said. 'Now, I've bought us some time by baffling the guards with bullshit, but we need to get in there, find Sally and get out, before I have to resort to Plan C.'

'Is that the one which involves running around like a chicken that's just had its head cut off?' Alice said sweetly.

'Nothing so organized,' I said.

'I love to watch a professional at work,' said Lex.

'We have a professional?' said Johnny, looking around.

'You've been very restrained so far, Johnny,' I said carefully. 'And I do appreciate that you haven't held long conversations with people who aren't there, or tap-danced on the ceiling. If you could keep on not doing things like that for just a little while longer, it would be very helpful.'

'I can remember when you were fun,' Johnny said sadly. 'I'd better get to do something to express the real me before we have to leave.'

'I think I can pretty much guarantee something like that will become necessary at some point,' I said.

'I get to do bad things to people who deserve it?' said Johnny, his face lighting up like a child who'd just been promised a treat.

'Definitely,' I said.

'What about me?' said Lex, in a voice that made it clear he had no intention of being left out of any forthcoming mayhem.

'I'm sure there will be opportunities for you to kick some entitled backsides,' I said.

Lex sniffed. 'There had better be. I have my reputation to think of.'

Johnny grinned. 'I've missed you guys . . .'

I led the way through the main door. Alice slipped an arm through mine and leaned in close.

'It's like riding herd on a couple of kids.'

'Kids with thermonuclear capabilities,' I said. 'If I let myself think about what could happen if the Damned and the Wild Card really got out of hand, I'd have to go home and hide under the bed until it was a whole different year.'

'At least they're on our side,' said Alice. 'They like you.'

'They like you, too,' I said.

'Well, of course,' said Alice. 'Everyone likes me. Whoever I happen to be.'

The reception area turned out to be a great barn of a place, full of people decked out in magnificent finery. Personally tailored tuxedos and designer evening gowns clashed with the very latest in exotic fashions, all of them worn with the same assured arrogance. The kind that says *I look great. If you think otherwise, it's because you're too far down the pecking order to know better.* My crew and I received a number of surprised glances as we made our way through the throng – partly over our lack of finery, but mostly because it had been a long time since people this select had seen anyone they didn't recognize who wasn't a servant. I smiled easily in all directions, as though I felt perfectly at home in such a refined environment.

Alice quickly realized she couldn't compete with the levels of arrogance going on around her and settled for looking professional. Lex didn't give a damn what anybody thought, and walked straight at people until they jumped out of his way.

They didn't mean to, but something about Lex persuaded them to do it now and complain later. They might be a selfish and pampered elite, but there was nothing wrong with their self-preservation instincts.

Johnny just strolled along, smiling happily, taking a cheerful interest in everything. Including some things that weren't there. People smiled indulgently, in case he was someone's relative.

Row upon row of dusty wine bottles had been set out on display, with uniformed staff standing ready to uncork and decant as necessary. People in small groups were doing all the things expected at a wine tasting: savouring the bouquet with exaggerated facial expressions, swilling the wine around their mouths before spitting it into a handy bucket, then rhapsodizing loudly in a series of evocative non sequiturs. All performed and received with perfectly straight faces.

'I never did understand wine tastings,' said Lex. 'Even the low-key affairs I used to attend, back when I was just a minor historian. I once ordered red wine with fish, and the head of my department wouldn't speak to me for a week.'

'It's nothing to do with the wine,' I said. 'It's all about snobbery and one-upmanship. You could slip a standard house red into any of these bottles, and everyone here would still go into ecstasies over the taste.'

A supercilious uniformed waiter presented us with a silver platter of assorted small cheeses. Alice started to reach for one, but I stopped her with a quick gesture.

'Not a good idea. The ones that don't have industrial-strength bacteria have cheese mites on steroids. Not so much an acquired taste, more about proving the elite are ready to eat things no one else will touch.'

Johnny grabbed half a dozen different cheeses and crammed all of them into his mouth at the same time. The waiter departed, not even trying to hide his disgust. Lex looked sorrowfully at Johnny.

'Can't take you anywhere.'

Johnny just shrugged, chewing manfully.

'How do you know so much about wine tastings, Gideon?' said Alice.

I grinned. 'It's just another con game. And I know all there is to know about cons. Ah . . . I spy with my little eye that devious diva Switch It Sally.'

I nodded at a tall and apparently aristocratic young woman, in a sky-blue evening dress and elbow-length white silk gloves. She had very dark skin, sparkling eyes, a beaming smile and dyed blonde hair in a bowl cut. I had to smile as I heard her speak in a cut-glass finishing-school accent I knew for a fact she wasn't entitled to.

'She's changed her look,' said Alice.

'Hark who's talking,' I said.

'What's she doing?'

'Working.'

Sally was surrounded by a small crowd of very attentive young men. They hung on her every bon mot, laughed loudly when she delivered a bitchy comment, and competed to be the one who could impress her most with some flashy story from their business or social lives. But they weren't charming her; she was charming them. Just by paying attention, she was picking up all kinds of useful personal information that she could use later, to help her crack their passwords and plunder their bank accounts. She was robbing them blind, and they didn't even know it.

I left my crew keeping an eye out for security and advanced steadily on Sally. I barged artlessly through her crowd of admirers, planted myself right in front of her and smiled easily. Sally quickly worked out it would be more advantageous to acknowledge me than to freeze me out. She knew I'd only make a scene if she claimed not to know me. So she gasped in delight, threw her white-gloved arms in the air and hit me with her most dazzlingly smile.

'Gideon, darling! How wonderful to see you here!'

We leaned forward, embraced warmly, kissed the air somewhere near each other's cheeks and then stepped back and smiled fondly at each other. All the young men were glaring at me now, indignant at having their quality time with Sally interrupted, but I just ignored them. Knowing that would annoy them most.

'Sorry to break in, but you just have to come with me,' I said to Sally. 'They're about to open a particularly impressive little vintage that I just know will rain heaven on your taste buds; I wouldn't want you to miss it.'

I took a firm hold on her arm and steered her away with a certain amount of brute force. Sally waited till we'd gone far enough that we wouldn't be overheard by her admirers, and then pulled her arm free and glared at me.

'What the hell are you doing here, Gideon? I don't come to where you work and stop you stealing the pennies off a dead man's eyes. Honestly, darling, this is a bit much. What are you even doing at a gathering like this? It's really not your sort of thing . . .'

'I could say the same about you,' I said. 'Punching a bit above your social weight, aren't you?'

'Some of us have spent the last few years improving ourselves, darling,' Sally said airily. 'As opposed to walking around in a dead man's reputation. I mean, that is just a bit ghoulish, isn't it? Now, what do you want with me, Gideon? I am just the teensiest bit busy right now.'

'I have a place for you in my crew,' I said.

She looked at me coldly. 'Please, darling, I do have standards.'

'News to me,' I said. 'Let me see if I can work out what your current con is.'

I looked around, taking in all the conspicuously elegant people worshipping at the altar of aged bottles, and then I remembered what I'd said earlier about house reds. I grinned at Sally.

'You've been using your gift to surreptitiously switch out the expensive wines, one at a time, replacing them with cheap plonk from bottles stored in your van. I recognized it in a side alley, on the way in.'

Sally scowled, and her shoulders slumped just a little. 'Oh, poo! Can't a girl have a little fun, darling?'

'These are not good people to be messing with,' I said sternly. 'They are, in fact, really bad people.'

'I know that!' said Sally, her eyes flashing indignantly. 'Only the really bad people have things worth stealing. You taught me that.' And then she looked around quickly, to make sure she hadn't been overheard. Reassured, she went back to glaring at me. 'All right, now you know why I'm here, darling. So why don't you make like a tree and leaf, so I can get back to what I do best – squeezing these ripe little plums till the pips fly?'

'It won't be long before someone in security spots what you're doing,' I said. 'And then large men with guns, and a huge hole where their sense of humour should be, will come for you.' I stopped as a thought struck me. 'This isn't your usual cup of larceny, Sally . . . So I have to ask: who put you up to it?'

She smiled brightly and made firm eye contact, confirming that she was about to lie to me.

'I'm sure I don't know what you're talking about, darling. This is my very own brilliant scheme, and it was all going perfectly until you showed up to piss on my parade.'

'You were never this bright, Sally,' I said. 'And you've never had the contacts to get into somewhere like this before. So if you want my help and protection when it finally all hits the fan and clogs up the works . . .'

She pouted, sticking her lower lip right out and making a real production of it. 'Why do you always have to spoil my fun, darling?'

'Because you will keep walking into minefields and not noticing,' I said. 'I am saving your pretend aristocratic arse. Now, who put you up to this?'

Sally realized the pout wasn't working and abandoned it in favour of a shrug and a guileless smile.

'Oh, all right. If I must . . . One of the big London wine merchants got really upset over not receiving an invitation this year, so he put the word out he was looking for someone who could make some trouble at the tasting. Eventually, the word got round to me, and when I said I thought I could really ruin the occasion, he made all the arrangements.'

'And it never even occurred to you to wonder why everyone else turned it down?' I asked.

She shrugged prettily. 'I was lucky to get it, darling, and you don't look a gift horse in the enclosure.'

'You didn't take any safeguards with the wine merchant?'

'Of course, darling! I made him pay cash, in advance. He got me a proper invitation, RSVP and everything.'

I looked at her speechlessly. It honestly hadn't occurred to Sally that she'd been set up as the patsy in the deal. The merchant had probably already contacted the organizers to let them know about her, so they would be grateful enough to invite him back next year. While Sally . . . would never be seen again. People who organized events like this took their wine and their reputations very seriously.

'I'm planning a heist in Las Vegas,' I said. 'I could use your special gift . . . and I think it would be best for you if you couldn't be found for a while.'

Sally's eyes widened, and she squealed delightedly. 'Vegas! Oh, darling, why didn't you say? Of course I am in, sweetie! I take back everything I ever said about you, even if most of it was true. When do we start?'

'As soon as we can get out of here,' I said.

I looked around and then winced internally as I saw the guard I'd double-talked at the main door heading through the crowd towards us, with a look of grim retaliation on his face and several hard men following on behind. I grabbed Sally's arm.

'I think we should leave. Right now, if not sooner.'

'Whatever you say, darling.'

I plunged through the crowd, dragging Sally along with me. I glanced at the exit and saw more guards moving into position to block the way. I stopped and thought hard. Sally had seen the security men, too, and looked at me with huge eyes.

'That's probably not a good thing, is it, darling?'

'Not really, no.'

'They do look awfully serious. I've got nothing against strong, silent types, but you can have too much of a good thing. Tell me you have a suitably dramatic plan to get us out of here, darling.'

'You know me,' I said. 'I've always got a plan.'

I led her quickly over to my people. 'Sally, this is the crew. Crew, this is Switch It Sally. Everyone play nicely or I'll send you all to bed without even a hot water bottle to chew on.'

Sally smiled brightly at everyone, although the smile dimmed a little when she recognized Annie in Alice. Interestingly, it was obvious she had no idea at all who Lex or Johnny were. She extended an elegant hand to them, to be shaken or kissed. Lex just looked at her, and then Sally jumped a little as an invisible hand grabbed hold of hers and shook it firmly. Lex gave Johnny a hard look. Alice grabbed me by the arm and moved us a little away.

'How can she not recognize the Damned?'

'Sally is only ever interested in things that affect her personally,' I said. 'Now, in case you hadn't noticed, we are being approached by some professionally dangerous persons.'

'Of course I noticed,' said Alice. 'I had to stop Lex from launching a pre-emptive strike with the nearest furniture. He forgets that while he might be bulletproof in his armour, the rest of us aren't. So what's the plan, Gideon?'

I couldn't help thinking that, just once, it might be nice if somebody else came up with a plan, but of course I wouldn't have trusted it if they had. I escorted Alice back to the others and nodded to Johnny, who was absently tapping his foot to music only he could hear.

'See the muscle in the good suits, heading straight for us?' I said to him. 'I could use a distraction. Something that will hold everyone's attention . . . without actually endangering their lives.'

'I'm hurt you felt it necessary to add that last bit,' said Johnny.

'The guards really are getting very close,' I said.

'Well, I can't think what I'm going to do if you keep pressuring me!' Johnny looked back and forth, and then his eyes lit up. 'Oh, I know . . .'

He gestured grandly at all the people tasting wine, and there was suddenly mass spitting and cries of outrage. The air was full of loud remonstrations, accompanied by much waving of arms, followed by even more spitting.

'Johnny . . .' said Alice. 'What did you change the wine into?'

'Piledrivers,' said Johnny. 'A very popular drink back when I was a student. Vodka with prune juice.'

'You animal!' said Lex.

Johnny lowered his head. 'I am so ashamed . . .'

'No, you're not,' said Lex. 'You don't know the meaning of the word.'

'There are lots of things I'm not sure about any more,' Johnny said cheerfully.

The crowd was getting seriously out of hand, as accusations of fraud and sabotage flew in all directions. I took advantage of the chaos to steer my crew toward the door. The guards did their best to come after us, barging people out of the way with no regard for status and completely ignoring their outraged protestations. But the sheer press of the crowd worked in our favour, buying us some time.

And then I lurched to a halt, gesturing sharply for the others to stop with me, as even more guards spilled through the main door from the outer hallway, blocking our way out. I looked around quickly, calculating the odds and weighing the possibilities. We were trapped between two sets of guards and facing an angry crowd who were going to become a whole lot angrier once it became clear we were responsible for the really bad day they were having. They definitely didn't look as if they were in the mood to accept an apology.

Even so, much as I despised pretty much everyone in the room, I still didn't want to unleash the Damned and the Wild Card on them. Both men had all the subtlety of a flying half brick and nothing even remotely resembling restraint. I didn't want to be responsible for starting a bloodbath.

Of course, the guards heading in our direction from both ends of the room didn't know that, and probably wouldn't have cared if they had. They all had guns in their hands and looked as though they were more than ready to use them once they'd got through enough of the crowd to get a clear shot. Even as I thought that, one of the guards raised his gun and fired a shot over the heads of the people in front of him. The well-dressed men and women cried out, ducked down low and then scattered, scrabbling quickly away in all directions to get out of the line of fire. Suddenly, there was no one at all standing between me and my crew . . . and a whole lot of men with guns.

Lex put on his armour. The silver bracelets at his wrists glowed blindingly bright, and what had once been the halos of two murdered angels swept over Lex's body in a moment, covering him from head to toe and sealing him off from the world. Everyone in the room made some kind of noise and turned their heads away, unable to face a man armoured by Heaven and Hell. The guards and the guests, the organizers and the staff couldn't bring themselves to look directly at armour divided into light and dark. One half shone like the sun, with a fierce unforgiving light; the other half was made out of a darkness so deep it was like staring into the abyss.

The guards lowered their weapons. Some of them threw their guns away. The guard who'd fired the first shot, and shown himself to be the man in charge, forced himself to stare at the Damned and raised his voice to the other guards.

'Stand your ground! And pick up those guns! We're supposed to be professionals, so do your job!'

'But that's the Damned!' wailed one of the guards.

'Then today is the day we earn our pay,' said the senior guard.

'I want a raise,' said a voice at the back.

Johnny Wilde stepped forward to stand beside the Damned. There was a pause as everyone looked at the quietly smiling little man in the battered old jacket with leather patches on the elbows. And then Johnny stopped smiling, and everything changed. Just standing there, quiet and composed, he was the most dangerous thing in the room, and everyone knew it. The senior guard switched his gun from the Damned to Johnny. When he spoke, his voice was as steady as his arm.

'Who are you?'

'I'm the Wild Card,' said Johnny. 'I am the lightning out of clear blue sky and the heart attack you never saw coming. I am everything that ever scared you. I am bad luck on two legs, and I am looking right at you.'

'Oh, shit,' said a quiet voice at the back.

Everyone in the room was standing very still now, because no one wanted the Wild Card to look at them. The senior guard sighed quietly and lowered his gun.

'Some days, things wouldn't go right if you offered them a bonus.'

I stepped forward to stand on the Damned's other side, and everyone's eyes went to me. I gave them my best *We can work this out* smile, and put a staying hand on the Damned's armoured arm. And then I snatched my hand away again, because it felt like nudging God's arm to get his attention. I nodded easily to the senior guard.

'Why don't we all just try to be reasonable? We don't have to start a mass slaughter here if we don't want to.'

'That's good to hear,' the guard said cautiously.

'They started it,' said the Damned. His voice was cold and remorseless as it issued from behind the featureless mask of his face.

'And I really don't like people who think they can threaten me,' said the Wild Card. 'If these guards are so keen to show everyone what they're made of, perhaps I should just turn them inside out, so we can all get a good look.'

Several of the guards made high, whining noises.

'Don't scare them, Johnny,' I said quickly. 'Scared people

make really bad life choices – scared people with guns even more so. Remember: we're thieves, not killers.'

'Speak for yourself,' said the Damned.

'I thought you were trying to put that behind you?' I said.

The featureless mask turned slowly to face me. 'Who told you that?'

'But it's true, isn't it?' I said. 'You went to see the rogue angel because you were looking for a way out of being the Damned. That could start right here.'

'You don't have to be the Damned all the time, Lex,' said Johnny. 'Anyone can change.'

'Even you?' said the Damned.

'That's what I believe,' said Johnny, smiling.

The Damned stood very still. I had no idea at all what he was thinking. I turned carefully to the senior guard.

'Tell your people to lower their weapons, and we might all walk out of this room alive.'

'I do like the sound of that,' said the guard.

He gave the order, and his men competed to see how quickly they could carry it out. They'd signed on to defend a wine tasting against people like Sally, not the Damned and the Wild Card.

One of the organizers shouldered his way through the crowd to glare at the guards.

'What the hell do you think you're doing? We hired you to protect us! Pick up those guns and kill all these criminals! That's an order!'

The senior guard looked at him thoughtfully. 'There isn't a bottle here worth dying for. You want these people dead? Do it yourself.'

The organizer spluttered furiously and then stopped as the guard grabbed his hand and thrust his gun into it.

'Go ahead. Give it your best shot. And see how far that gets you.'

The organizer looked at the gun and then at the Damned and the Wild Card. He looked around for support, but no one wanted anything to do with him. He started to say something and then swallowed hard. He opened his hand and let the gun fall to the floor. It made a really loud clatter in the quiet.

I cleared my throat in a meaningful way, and everyone's gaze snapped back to me.

'I think it's time we were leaving.'

'Fine by me,' said the senior guard.

'Always best not to outstay your welcome,' said Johnny. 'Mind you, that's how I feel about life.'

He put a hand on the Damned's arm, turned him around and steered him towards the main exit. The feel of the armour didn't seem to bother him at all. I nodded to Alice and Sally, and we moved quickly in behind them. Everyone else stayed exactly where they were and watched us go, hoping the threat was finally over. Some of them looked as if they were only just starting to breathe again.

We had almost made it all the way to the main door when one of the guards there decided to be a hero. He grabbed Sally by the arm, pulled her in close as she squealed loudly and then stuck his gun in her face. And then he laughed at the Damned, too brave or too stupid to be properly scared of what he was doing.

'Lose the armour and surrender!' he said loudly. 'Or I'll blow her brains all over you!'

The Damned looked at him. Sally was keeping very still, her wide eyes pleading. And then the armour disappeared, back into the silver bracelets at Lex's wrists. He stood revealed again, meeting the guard's gaze steadily.

'Now let her go.'

The guard laughed again and shifted his aim to Lex's face. I saw his finger tighten on the trigger. And then Sally back-elbowed him viciously in the ribs. The guard bent in half, gasping for breath. His gun fired harmlessly into the open door. Sally grabbed a nearby bottle and hit him over the head with it. The bottle didn't smash; instead, there was a satisfyingly loud thud, and the guard fell unconscious to the floor. Sally tossed the bottle carelessly to one side and smiled dazzlingly at Lex.

'Thanks for the save, darling. Now, let's get out of here. These people don't appreciate a class act when they see one.'

Out in the hallway, I gathered my crew together and got them moving quickly towards the outer door. I led from the front, as befitted the man in charge. We pounded down the hallway, not looking back, even though I knew it wouldn't be long before the organizers promised enough extra money to get some of the guards to come after us. And while the Damned and the Wild Card might not have anything to fear from bullets, the rest of us did. The problem with armed guards is that they only have to get lucky once, and we have to be lucky all the time.

The outside guard was still standing by the door when we spilled out on to the street. Before he could say anything, I stuck my face right into his.

'It's all gone to hell in there!' I said loudly. 'The paramilitary wing of the Temperance Society has launched an attack! Get inside, barricade the inner door. And don't let anyone get past you!'

'Of course, sir,' said the guard and disappeared into the hall.

'That should buy us some time,' I said. I locked the door with my skeleton key. 'And I'd like to see them open that without a fire axe or a grenade launcher.'

Lex scowled at the closed door.

'I didn't get to do much this time.'

'For which we are all very grateful,' said Alice.

'There'll be time for you to indulge the violent and destructive side of your nature, once we're in Vegas,' I said. 'For now, let's concentrate on getting the hell out of here.'

'I'll get my van and catch up with you later, darling,' said Sally.

'No, you won't,' I said immediately. 'Because you'll just drive off and leave us, and we won't see you again until you've shifted all that stolen wine.'

'Honestly, darling . . .'

'Forget it, Sally,' said Alice. 'We know you. So behave yourself or I'll give you to Lex.'

Sally shot Lex a smouldering look. 'I like them big and dumb.'

He stared at her. 'Words fail me.'

'Exactly!' said Sally.

Johnny produced a big bunch of roses from out of nowhere and handed them to Sally. She beamed delightedly and then frowned.

'Darling, they smell of coffee!'

'I always fall down on the details,' said Johnny.

I started down the street towards where I'd parked the car,

only to stop again when I saw it wasn't there. Alice shook her head solemnly.

'Told you . . .'

'We need to be somewhere else in a hurry, before security catches up with us,' I said. 'We'll just have to use Sally's van.'

'Yay!' said Sally, punching the air with her hand full of flowers. Only to look a little surprised when she brought her hand down and the flowers weren't in it any more.

We hurried to the alley where her van was parked, and Sally raised her voice indignantly when I unlocked the front door with my skeleton key and climbed into the driving seat.

'I am the designated getaway driver, darling!'

'But you have a tendency to drive straight through things and people,' I said, slamming the skeleton key into the ignition. 'And I think we've attracted enough attention for the moment.'

Alice moved in beside me, and Lex moved in beside her, and that took up all the space in the front. Sally insisted on sitting on Lex's lap. Johnny jumped up on to the roof, in a single bound. I sent the van screeching out of the alley, just in time to scatter a whole bunch of armed guards. I drove off at speed, while the guards fired after us. Johnny performed a tap dance of triumph on the van's roof. Sally looked at me.

'You have the strangest friends, darling.'

'Then you should feel right at home,' I said. 'Does this piece of junk have satnav?'

'Be your age, darling,' said Sally, settling herself comfortably on Lex's lap while he tried not to notice. 'I couldn't even afford to have the brakes fixed. So . . . what's the job?'

'We are going to rob a casino in Las Vegas,' I said.

'Super cool!' said Sally. 'Who's behind this heist?'

'Judi Rifkin,' said Alice.

Sally opened the door and tried to jump out of the speeding van. Lex had to haul her back in and hold her while she struggled.

'That woman is crazy!' Sally said loudly.

'She's rich,' I said. 'She's allowed to be crazy. But not to worry, I have a plan.'

Sally slumped dejectedly. 'There'll be tears before bedtime, darling.'

SEVEN

At Home with the Crew

Some time later, I brought the van to a halt outside a pleasant little house in a quiet cul-de-sac, in a perfectly normal and respectable neighbourhood. I had to turn the engine off before my crew would accept that we weren't going any further. They took their time getting out of the van and then crowded together, staring at the house. Given that Lex used to spend most of his time in an abandoned Underground station, Johnny mostly hangs out in cemeteries listening to the graves, and Sally has to keep moving because there's always someone after her, I suppose the sheer normality of the setting came as something of a shock.

'How did you end up with a place this nice?' Lex said finally. 'No, don't tell me . . . You stole it, didn't you?'

'Something like that,' I said. 'Now, can you please all get inside before the neighbours see you.'

'You care what the neighbours think?' said Johnny. 'Oh, the horror, the horror . . .'

'Camouflage works best when you don't stand out,' I said. 'Aah . . . Excuse me for a moment.'

I went to join Alice, who had Sally bent forward over the van's bonnet in an armlock.

'I caught her sneaking into the driver's seat,' said Alice. 'So she could run out on us!'

'Let go of me, you big bully!' said Sally. 'Gideon, make her let go of me!'

'You'll notice she's not denying it,' said Alice.

I gestured for her to let Sally go. Alice did so, reluctantly, and Sally immediately straightened up and gave me the full-pout-and-demure-eyes bit.

'Honestly, darling . . .'

'You're not going anywhere,' I said firmly.

'Oh, but, sweetie . . . I have gallons of expensive wines cooling their heels in the back of this van. We are talking liquid gold!'

'You'll be lucky to get anything for them without the correct bottles and labels to provide a provenance,' I said. 'You really didn't think this one through, Sally.'

'No change there,' said Alice.

Sally's face dropped, but she still glared at me stubbornly. 'I can't just leave them sitting here!'

'Yes, you can,' said Alice. 'With what you stand to make in Vegas, this is just pocket change.'

Sally brightened immediately, and she smiled at Alice for the first time. 'Really, darling? Pinky promise and hope to die?'

'Get in the house, Sally,' I said. 'I'm not letting you out of my sight until this heist is safely under way.'

'Well, really, darling . . .' Sally shrugged prettily and fluttered her eyelashes at me. 'Anyone would think you didn't trust me.'

'Of course I don't,' I said. 'I know you.'

She dropped me a saucy wink. 'I haven't forgotten, darling.'

'Get in the house,' said Alice.

The moment we were inside, Alice went straight to her wardrobe rooms, so she could change into someone more comfortable. I led the others into the living room, and they looked around curiously. I think they were pleasantly surprised there weren't plastic covers on the furniture and a flight of plaster ducks on the wall.

'I suppose it's easier on the eye than the high-rise flat where we last met,' said Lex.

'And a hell of a lot nicer than that grubby bed-sitter we used to share, Gideon,' said Sally. 'Remember when we had to do a moonlight flit through the back window to avoid paying the landlord his rent?'

'I think that was somebody else,' I said.

Sally smiled knowingly at Lex. 'This was before he hooked up with Annie Anybody and got ideas above his station. Before he decided he could be Gideon Sable.'

Lex looked at me thoughtfully. 'Are you ever going to tell us your real name?'

'Gideon Sable is my real name now,' I said.

Sally stretched slowly, showing off her exquisite form to its best advantage. 'Of course, I would never dream of telling anyone who you used to be, darling. For the right price.'

I met her gaze steadily. 'Don't forget I know what you used to be, before you reinvented yourself as Switch It Sally.'

Her smiled disappeared in a moment. 'You'd never tell!'

'Wouldn't I?'

'Oh, poo,' said Sally. She threw herself into the most comfortable chair in the room, crossed her legs with a flourish and folded her arms tightly. 'I can remember when you used to be fun.'

While all this civilized conversation was going on, Johnny bounced happily around the room, examining everything with great interest.

'Please don't change any of the details, Johnny,' I said carefully. 'Annie and I like things just the way they are.'

'I used to live in a house like this,' Johnny said wistfully. 'At least, I think I did. It's so hard to be sure when your memory keeps playing multiple choice.'

'Can I just point out that your feet aren't reaching the floor?' I said tactfully.

He looked down and saw that he was floating a good three inches above the carpet. He smiled apologetically and then sat down in mid-air next to a perfectly good chair and crossed his legs comfortably.

'Sorry about that. I keep forgetting.'

'How long before we can make a start?' said Lex. 'I can't take too long away from putting the fear of God into people, or they'll start thinking they can get away with things.'

'You need a full briefing on the heist,' I said. 'And I'm still waiting to hear how we're going to get to Vegas without being noticed.'

Sally coughed discreetly. 'Can I just point out that I don't have my passport with me?'

I looked at her. 'You have a passport?'

She smiled winningly. 'Well, I've got somebody's passport.'

'Relax,' I said. 'You won't need it. We'll be using the hidden ways.'

Sally looked at me for a moment and then indicated to me with a quick jerk of her head that she had something she wanted to say privately. I nodded resignedly, and she rose out of her chair in a single lithe movement. We put some distance between us and the others, and lowered our voices. Lex pretended not to notice, and Johnny probably didn't.

'It has been a while, hasn't it?' said Sally.

'Probably for the best,' I said.

Sally glanced at the door Alice had disappeared through. 'Why her and not me? She let you down just as badly as I did.'

'But she felt bad about it,' I said.

Sally shrugged. 'You know I never look back, darling.'

'Of course not,' I said. 'You might see your sins catching up with you.'

Sally looked at me steadily. 'If you never let anyone get close, no one can ever hurt you.'

'That's no way to live.'

'You say that like I have a choice.' She smiled suddenly. 'We did have some good times together, didn't we, darling?'

'But I wanted more than just jumping from one small-time con to the next,' I said. 'I wanted to be somebody.'

'And now you are,' said Sally. 'Gideon Sable, master thief! Just tell me this. Are you happy . . . with her?'

'Yes,' I said. 'Are you happy, Sally?'

She flashed me her most devastating smile. 'I'm always happy, darling; you know that. Especially now we're heading to Las Vegas to plunder a casino! It was so good of you to bring me on board for this one. I'll have to think of a very special way to say thank you . . .'

'Annie would stab you to death with your own high heels,' I said sternly.

Sally just smiled. 'I notice that wasn't a no.'

'Just restrain your natural impulse to cheat and betray everyone, and we'll get along fine,' I said. 'In return, I won't even hint to the others that you originally trained to be an accountant.'

'That was a long time ago, darling,' Sally said coldly. 'A gentleman would have erased such a thing from his memory.'

And then we all looked round as Annie emerged from the back room. The business look was gone, replaced by an ordinary woman in a faded dressing gown. The long black wig and heavy glasses had been discarded, in favour of no makeup and hair cropped in a buzzcut. When she wasn't busy being somebody else, Annie could make so little impression on a room that she almost wasn't there.

'Annie, darling . . . you have let yourself go,' said Sally.

'I think it's time we got down to business,' I said quickly.

I led everyone over to the table in the middle of the room. Johnny had to lever himself up out of his non-existent chair to join us. I opened Judi Rifkin's mission file, and Sally turned up her nose.

'You could have splashed out on a laptop, darling,' she said. 'So we could link to whatever extra information we needed.'

'The key to any successful con is to never leave a trail,' I said. 'You can't hack paper.'

'Get on with it,' said Lex. 'What's the heist, who's the target and what's the plan?'

'We are going to steal the Masque of Ra,' I said. 'A supernatural object from ancient Egypt that's supposed to be a shortcut to immortality. It's currently in the hands of a Vegas casino owner, Saul Montressor. Some years ago, he killed two friends of mine. Which is why we're also going to destroy Saul's life while we're there.'

Lex shot me a hard look. 'Is this a heist or a vendetta?'

'If we get it right, both,' I said.

I spread out photos of the Montressors. 'This is Saul, and these are his children – Frank, Tony and Joyce. All of them Vegas mobsters, red in tooth and claw.'

'This is starting to sound more like my kind of business than yours,' said Lex. 'Is that why you went out of your way to bring me back?'

'No,' I said steadily. 'I don't need you to kill anyone, Lex. I brought you back in because we work well together. And because we're going to have to get past some seriously gifted security people.'

I took out the photographs of Double Down Dan, Soulful Sam and the Enchanted Enforcer, and provided a quick rundown on what they could do. Lex just sniffed.

'The cheaper the crooks, the gaudier the personas.'

'They must be good at what they do,' I said, 'or Saul wouldn't have hired them.'

'I think they look cute,' said Sally.

'You would,' said Annie.

'Judi Rifkin has hired us to get her the masque,' I said, putting us back on track. 'In return, she has promised to never bother us again – and provide a very generous payoff.'

'How generous?' Sally said immediately.

'Five million pounds, in cash.'

Sally squealed delightedly and clapped her hands. 'Oh, darlings! There is nothing I wouldn't do for that kind of money! Just point me at the casino and stand back!'

'I wouldn't start counting your share just yet,' I said. 'We can't trust Judi to make good on anything she's promised.'

'Of course not, darling,' said Sally. 'She's crazy.'

'But if we play this right,' I said, 'we should come out of this heist with armfuls of money and Judi Rifkin off our back for ever. And I will have had my revenge on Saul Montressor.'

'Because you've got a plan,' said Lex.

'Gideon always has a plan,' said Annie.

I showed them exterior views of the Khuffu Casino, a huge pyramid with flashing neon stylings and extravagant surroundings. The crew took it in their stride. This was Vegas, after all. Next, photos of the interior, with its ancient Egyptian trappings and hanging chandeliers, rows of slot machines and any number of gaming tables. The floor was crowded with gamblers, all of them eager to throw away everything they had on games of chance they didn't properly understand.

'The main floor is always going to be packed solid,' I said. 'From the moment the doors open till they boot everyone out in the early hours.'

'I like crowds,' said Sally. 'They can hide a multitude of sins.'

Annie looked at Lex and Johnny. 'Of course, some people stand out more than others . . .'

'But this is Vegas,' I said. 'Where loud and outrageous comes as standard. We can use that.'

I showed them a large publicity still of the Masque of Ra, on display in the casino lobby. And right beside it, standing upright in his open sarcophagus, the mummy of the Pharaoh Khuffu. Sally stirred restlessly.

'I've never liked mummies,' she said quietly. 'I used to watch those old movies on television when I was a kid, and they always scared the crap out of me.'

'If this one gives us any trouble, I'll tie its bandages in knots,' said Lex.

Sally smiled widely. 'I never thought I'd have the Damned as my very own bodyguard. You must stick close to me at all times, Lex. In case I need you.'

'The casino is guarded from top to bottom, with twenty-four-hour camera coverage,' I said. 'Along with motion trackers, hidden microphones with computers listening for target words and phrases, and pressure sensors in the floor of every backstage room and passageway. All backed up by the usual small army of security guards.'

'Will they have guns?' said Sally.

'This is America,' said Annie. 'Of course they'll have guns.'

'Don't worry, Sally,' said Johnny. 'You can always hide behind me.'

'You're not very wide,' said Sally. 'I'd rather stand behind Lex.'

She smiled dazzlingly at the Damned, and he looked blankly back at her. He seemed a little discomforted by her constant interest. I made a mental note to warn him that Sally always made a play for the biggest man in the crew, so she would have someone ready to take the fall when she inevitably did a runner.

'We're going to need computer fiends with serious skills, to get us past the security systems,' said Sally. 'Fortunately, darlings, I know a few who owe me favours. Geeks are so easy to charm.'

'No,' I said. 'That's what the casino will be expecting. We do this old school: lateral thinking and applied misdirection.'

'And when it comes to making technology do what we need it to do, I have some experience in that area,' said Annie.

Sally looked at her sharply. 'It's true, then? You really can make machines fall in love with you?'

'Yes,' said Annie.

Sally grinned. 'How are you with cash machines, darling?'

'Raise your sights, Sally,' I said. 'This is no time to be thinking small. We're going to take a Vegas casino to the cleaners.'

'I'm still waiting to hear the plan,' said Lex. 'How are we going to do this?'

'By convincing the Montressors that we're after the cash in their vault,' I said steadily. 'And while they put all their efforts into protecting that, we grab the Masque of Ra and get the hell out of Vegas.'

'How are we going to break into a casino vault?' said Sally. 'We are talking solid steel doors, electronic locking systems and the kind of protections that would stop a charging rhino in its tracks and send it home crying to its mother.'

'It's all about misdirection,' I said. 'Annie and I are going to set up meetings with Saul and his children. Ostensibly to discuss selling them a London casino.'

'Are you sure Saul will be interested after his failure last time?' said Annie.

'That must still rankle,' I said. 'But if we can get him interested, his children will be as well, because what affects Saul affects them.'

'What has that got to do with the masque and the vault?' said Lex.

'If Saul agrees to a meeting, he'll invite us in,' I said. 'Which means we'll be waved past all the usual security protections.'

Sally frowned. 'But why do you need to talk to the young Montressors?'

'Because the whole point of these meetings is to spread dissension inside the family,' said Annie. 'We'll be telling all of them different things, so that when the attack on the vault happens, they'll be too busy blaming each other to realize what's actually going on.'

'Divide and conquer,' I said. 'Lex and Johnny, you'll be talking with the casino's security people, offering to sell them upgraded protections and protocols.'

'Wait just a minute!' said Lex. 'I can't do that! I have no idea what you just said. Anyway, they'd be bound to check up on us, to make sure we are who we say we are. You can't just bluff people with an impressive business card these days.'

'You don't even have to give them the name of your company,' I said. 'Just smile mysteriously and say you're a new start-up, and this is their chance to get in on the ground floor. You want to be in business with the Montressors, so you can use their name to get you more business. They'll understand that. Then you just casually happen to mention that you've heard a rumour someone wants to break into their vault, and that's why they need your new protections.'

'What sort of rumour?' said Lex, with the air of someone doing his best to keep up.

'The vaguer the better,' I said patiently. 'That way, they'll provide the details, according to what they're most afraid of. Look, don't worry; I'll write all of this out, and you and Johnny can memorize it on the trip over.'

Lex shook his head. 'This really isn't me. I don't do talking to people. I just kill people who need killing. Why don't I just wipe out the Montressors while you grab the masque?'

'Because even your armour might not be able to cope with some of the protections the casino is supposed to have,' I said. 'Come on, Lex; it'll be fun. That is why you came back into the crew, isn't it?'

Lex didn't look convinced. Johnny threw a comforting arm over his shoulders, though he had to stand on tiptoe to do it.

'Don't worry, Lex. I'll be right there with you, to make sure nothing goes wrong.'

Lex looked at him. 'That really fills me with confidence.'

Johnny beamed at him. 'I knew it would!'

'Security will be so keen to prove they don't need your assistance that they'll be bound to take you down to the vault so you can see for yourself,' I said. 'All you have to do then is remember what they show you, and pass it on to me so I can plan the assault.'

Sally raised a hand, like a child at school. 'Excuse me for asking, but what am I supposed to be doing while all of this is going on?'

'Play tourist,' I said. 'Wander round the casino, see the sights and drop a little money at the tables. But no using your gift to cheat; security would pounce on that in a moment. Just get me the layout, including all the less obvious entrances and exits. Bat your eyelashes at some of the more impressionable members of staff, so they'll tell you all the backstage stuff no one else knows.'

Sally nodded. 'I can do that.'

I turned back to Lex and Johnny. 'Once Annie and I have reduced the Montressors to a fever pitch of paranoia, I'll give you the signal to attack the vault. You in your armour, Lex, and Johnny . . . well, just be yourself.'

'I can do that,' Johnny said cheerfully. 'Suddenly and strangely and all over the place.'

'The rest of us will be in the lobby,' I said, 'waiting for the alarms to go off. Then Sally makes the switch, and we walk away with the real masque, leaving the replica in its place. Judi gets what she wants, and I get to see Saul's reputation destroyed.'

Annie looked at me steadily. 'We need to make a decision

right now, Gideon. Which has priority? Stealing the masque or getting revenge on Saul?'

'If we do this right, we can have both,' I said.

'But if we can't?'

'Then we go for the masque,' I said steadily. 'We can always go after that bastard again, once Judi is off our backs.'

Annie didn't seem entirely convinced, but nodded to show she was ready to go along, for now.

'This is all a bit cold-blooded for you, isn't it, Gideon?' said Sally.

'Saul killed my friends,' I said. 'And, according to Harry, the younger Montressors have killed their share of other people's friends.'

'Then let me take care of them,' said Lex. 'Cold-blooded is what *I* do, not you.'

'I don't want them killed,' I said. 'I'm not feeling that merciful. I want them to suffer.'

'You have changed,' said Sally.

'I told you,' I said. 'I'm Gideon Sable now.'

My crew members looked at each other. I could tell they weren't happy. Lex cleared his throat, indicating he was about to change the subject.

'Is there anything in this vault worth having, apart from the cash? I think we deserve to walk away with something a bit special, particularly if we can't rely on our payout from Judi.'

'Let's not get greedy,' I said.

'Oh, please, let's!' said Sally.

I thought about it. 'I haven't heard of Saul storing anything out of the ordinary in his vault.'

Johnny grinned at me. 'You always said that the best way to get revenge on the bad guys was to hit them where it hurts. In the money bags.'

'I didn't know you were paying attention,' I said.

He bristled. 'I can be practical when I have to.'

'If we're going up against Las Vegas mobsters, let's make sure it's for something worthwhile, darlings,' said Sally.

'She may be loud,' said Annie, 'but she has a point.'

'Who's loud?' said Sally.

'Is there any way we could find out what Saul has in his vault?' said Lex.

'There might be,' said Annie, looking at me meaningfully.

I nodded. 'The eye . . .'

'What eye?' said Sally, immediately suspicious. 'Have you been holding out on us, Gideon?'

I reached into my pocket and brought out the crystal eyeball. I held it up, so the others could get a good look at it. They didn't seem particularly impressed.

'Where did you get that?' said Lex.

'From Madam Osiris,' I said. 'In return for my getting you to promise never to hurt her.'

'I wasn't planning to,' said Lex.

'I still need the promise,' I said.

He shrugged. 'Sure. Why not?'

I had a feeling that was going to come back to bite one of us on the arse, but I didn't say anything.

'I didn't know you went in for crystal ball gazing, darling,' Sally said archly. 'How are you on lottery numbers?'

'This one is special,' I said.

'That's what they all say,' said Sally.

I held the eyeball up before my right eye, and looked through it. Suddenly, I was looking down on the great pyramid of the Khuffu Casino. I soared around it and then dived at one of the windows like a bird of prey zeroing in on its victim. There were secrets locked inside that pyramid, and I hungered for them. Or the eye did . . . But my rapid descent slammed to an abrupt halt, as I was held back by an unseen force. I could feel the eye straining against it, struggling to get closer, but whatever guarded the casino was simply too powerful.

I lowered the crystal eye.

'What did you see, darling?' Sally said quickly.

'I couldn't get inside the casino, never mind the vault,' I said. 'There are some seriously powerful protections in place.'

'Saul wouldn't need that just for the masque,' said Annie.

'It was probably put in place long ago, to protect the casino,' I said. 'This is Las Vegas, after all. I'll take another look, once I'm inside the casino's protections. If there does turn out to be something . . . Lex, Johnny, once you're inside the vault, feel free to grab whatever looks interesting. Providing you can carry it out.'

Johnny grinned at Lex. 'I told you this would be fun.'

Sally clapped her hands loudly. 'Yay, team!'

'Let's not get sidetracked, people,' I said sternly. 'We're going after the masque first, and Saul second; anything else only if there's time.'

'Oh, of course, darling,' said Sally.

I looked at her suspiciously but decided to move on. I nodded to Lex and Johnny.

'After you've finished with the vault, fall back to the main floor. And make as much of a disruption there as you can, to hold everyone's attention. I want security focused on you, not the lobby.'

'I'll just change the odds so everyone is winning!' said Johnny. 'How much more confusion could you ask for?'

'You sound very focused and together, Johnny,' I said.

'I do, don't I?' said Johnny. 'You're such a good influence on me.'

I smiled confidently at my crew. 'It's the classic con. Fool the mark into concentrating on one thing, while we go after another. Anything else that anyone needs to discuss?'

'If there are forces in place to protect the casino, I'll need to get in really close to switch out the masque,' said Sally.

'How close?' I said.

'Arm's length.'

I nodded. 'We can work around that. Anything else?'

They all looked at each other, but no one said anything. They were all too busy thinking.

'One last thing,' I said. 'It's important to me that Saul understands why he's being punished.'

Annie stirred uneasily. 'It's never a good idea to mix business with pleasure.'

'Isn't that what we've always been about?' I said. 'Taking from the bad guys to make them feel the pain they've caused others?'

'But it isn't normally about us,' said Annie.

'This isn't a normal heist,' I said. I looked around the crew. 'Once we're in Vegas, we'll be a long way out of our comfort zones, so we have to depend on each other. Stick to the plan, and we can do this!'

'Yay team!' said Sally.

'Yay the plan,' I said.

EIGHT
On the Moonlight Express

After that, we all just sat around my living room, waiting for something to happen. Sally once again commandeered the most comfortable chair, but she couldn't settle, crossing and recrossing her long legs while constantly checking to see if anyone had noticed. And then looking upset when no one cared.

Lex sat very still, staring at nothing. I had no idea what was going through his mind, and I was pretty sure I didn't want to know. The Damned's thoughts often took him into dark places. One of the reasons I brought him back on to my crew was to keep him occupied, so he wouldn't get lost in his own darkness. I wanted to say something, but Lex had left simple human things like small talk far behind him.

Johnny had fallen asleep in an actual chair, with his legs stretched out and his mouth hanging open. He was snoring quietly, in stereo. Trying to get my head round how he was doing that disturbed the hell out of me, so I stopped trying. Johnny was only on nodding terms with reality at the best of times. I still hoped I could save Lex; I wasn't so sure about Johnny.

Annie rose suddenly to her feet. 'I think I'll just nip into the kitchen and make us all some tea.'

'Excellent idea,' I said quickly, getting to my feet. 'I'll give you a hand.'

Nobody said they actually wanted anything, but Annie and I were already hurrying to the kitchen. Anything had to be better than sitting in that room, listening to the clock tick. We shut the kitchen door firmly, so we could pretend we didn't hear if anyone called us back, and Annie busied herself finding five mugs. It took her a while. We don't get many visitors, and we like it that way. I filled the kettle and turned it on. Annie shot me a look.

'How much longer do you expect them to just sit around? The

atmosphere in that room is so thick you could spread it with a trowel.'

'Judi said she had a way to get us to Las Vegas unnoticed,' I said. 'Which is one more than I have. We have to wait until she gets in touch.'

Annie sniffed loudly. 'How long do you think it'll be before Sally says something that upsets the others so much they try to kill her? How long before Johnny starts having conversations with people who aren't there, and they start answering back? How long before Lex just walks out? These are not sociable people, and with good reason.'

She slammed the mugs down on the kitchen table. One of them said *World's Best Other Person*, another said *I'm Anybody's* and the other three showed elaborate images from Edwardian erotica. Because one of Annie's friends has very odd ideas as to what makes for a good house-warming present. If you poured hot water into the mugs, their clothes reappeared.

'We have to be patient,' I said.

'Something had better happen soon,' Annie said ominously. 'Before we're reduced to Trivial Pursuit.'

I shuddered at the thought. 'It's not like I have any way of contacting Judi.'

Annie looked at me sharply. 'But she knows how to find us?'

'She found us outside Old Harry's Place. And the only way she could do that was if she'd been watching us for some time.'

'Oh, hell,' said Annie. 'Are we going to have to move again?'

'Would you feel safe living here, knowing Judi's hard men could drop by at any hour of the day?'

'I can be out the front door and gone at the drop of a hint,' said Annie.

'What about all your disguises?' I said.

'They're not disguises, they're personas,' said Annie. 'But really it's just clothes. I can always get more clothes.' She smiled briefly. 'In our line of work, you can't afford to get attached to things, Gideon . . . Why are you frowning?'

'A thought just struck me. Harry knows where we are, as well.'

'Are you sure?'

'He didn't ask for an address when I asked him for a replica of the Masque of Ra. But then Harry knows everything.'

Annie nodded. 'It does feel that way.'

'He promised he'd get the replica to us before we had to leave for Vegas.'

'He'd better.'

A sudden blast of trumpets filled the kitchen, making both of us jump. Loud and triumphant, the music seemed to come out of everywhere at once, and then a cardboard box appeared in mid-air and dropped on to the kitchen table with a self-satisfied thud. The music cut off so abruptly it left echoes.

I glared at the box. 'Someone is showing off.'

'You told me this house had serious defences!' said Annie.

'It does,' I said. 'I spent ages setting up spiritual bear traps. And nearly lost the ghost of a finger doing it.'

There was the sound of rapidly approaching feet, and then Lex and Sally jammed themselves into the kitchen doorway. Johnny appeared behind them, jumping up and down so he could peer over their shoulders.

'We heard trumpets!' said Sally.

'Sounded like a whole brass section,' said Lex.

'We have just received a special delivery,' I said. 'It would appear Judi knows I have assembled a crew.'

'How could she know that?' said Sally. 'Is she watching us?'

'I don't think she's actually peering in through the windows,' said Annie. 'She probably has people to do that kind of thing for her.'

'There are always people watching me,' Johnny said confidentially. 'Some of them aren't even people.'

'Open the box,' said Lex. 'Or do you want me to put on my armour and do it for you?'

I did consider that, just long enough to make everyone nervous, and then I very carefully took the lid off the cardboard box. Inside was a perfect replica of the Masque of Ra . . . and a mobile phone.

'OK . . .' I said. 'This is actually just a bit disturbing. Because while I have been waiting for both of these items, I really didn't expect them to turn up together. The copy of the masque comes to us courtesy of Old Harry's Place, but the phone is from Judi Rifkin. And they are not supposed to be working together.'

'I said Harry's fingerprints were all over this heist,' said Annie. 'But why would he want to get involved with someone like Judi?'

'Maybe it's all about putting pressure on you and me,' I said, 'so we'll agree to do what he wants us to.'

'What does Harry want you to do?' said Sally, immediately suspicious.

'Help him break his lease,' I said.

I picked up the replica masque and looked it over carefully. It had the stylized human features found on the lid of every ancient Egyptian sarcophagus, cast in solid gold, but wafer thin. The expression seemed to be saying *I know things you wouldn't want to know.* I put the masque down and nodded to the others.

'A perfect copy, except that this weighs only a fraction of the original. Harry does good work.'

'Are you sure it's perfect?' said Lex. 'It has to fool some very suspicious people.'

'I was hired to steal the masque once before,' I said. 'I put a lot of time into researching everything about it.'

'If I didn't know better, I'd swear that was the real deal,' said Annie.

We didn't look at each other. It was Annie's betrayal over the theft of the original masque that split us up for so many years. I had forgiven her, but I wasn't sure she had forgiven herself. I turned away and picked up the phone. It faded in and out in my grasp, like a handful of cold air that came and went.

'What makes you so sure the phone is from Judi?' said Sally.

'Because that is a phantom phone,' said Annie. 'Those things cost an arm and a leg. Often someone else's. Besides, it's such a flashy and ostentatious way of making contact that it could only have come from Judi Rifkin.'

'What's a phantom phone?' said Sally. 'Something for talking to spirits?'

'It's not part of any regular network,' I said. 'It makes contact through the shadow lines. One use only, and then it goes back to where it was summoned from.'

'Guaranteed secure,' said Annie. 'From the living and the dead and everything in between.'

The phone rang: just a quiet chirp, like the ghost of a caged bird. I answered, and Judi's voice came through immediately, harsh and authoritative.

'Be in Hyde Park at midnight. The Moonlight Express will be

passing through. How you get the train to stop is your problem. And no, I'm not paying for the tickets.'

She stopped speaking, and the phone faded away in my hand and was gone. I checked my watch.

'We have just under two hours to get to Hyde Park and be in the right place at the right time to intercept the Moonlight Express.'

'Judi is paying for us to ride the Moonlight?' said Annie.

'No,' I said. 'She isn't.'

Annie frowned as she thought about that. Lex frowned, because that was what he did. Sally frowned, too, so as not to be left out. Johnny already looked as if he was thinking about something else.

'What, exactly, is the Moonlight Express?' said Sally, sounding more than a little annoyed at constantly having to play catchup.

'Transportation to anywhere in the world, faster than should be humanly possible,' I said. 'Very exclusive and completely undetectable. It travels on moonbeams, across the roof of the world.'

Sally looked at me. 'Really?'

I shrugged. 'So they say. But given how expensive a ticket is, I never expected to find out myself.'

Annie scowled. 'But if Judi isn't paying, how are we going to . . .'

'Don't look at me, darlings,' Sally said quickly. 'Money and I have only ever held the most fleeting of acquaintances.'

'I don't use money,' said Lex. 'Everyone is always very keen to give me whatever I need, as long as I promise to go away and leave them alone.'

Annie looked at Johnny. 'Couldn't you just conjure some up for us?'

'I don't believe in money,' Johnny said sadly. 'But then I don't believe in lots of things these days.'

Annie turned her attention back to me. 'Given that this heist is Judi's idea, why isn't she paying?'

'It's a test,' I said. 'If we're not good enough to con our way on board the Moonlight Express, then we're not good enough to con our way into the Khuffu Casino and acquire the Masque of Ra. As if this heist wasn't complicated enough . . . Right then, everyone grab their necessities, and let's get moving.'

'I can't go anywhere looking like this!' said Annie, indicating her whole look rather than just the faded dressing gown.

'Same here!' said Sally.

Annie shot her a look. 'I must have something that will fit you. But if you stretch anything, I will bury you somewhere they'll never find you. Certainly not before the air runs out.'

'Girlfriends together!' Sally said cheerfully.

'As quickly as possible, please,' I said, resisting the urge to make encouraging gestures at them. 'The clock is not on our side, ladies.'

Annie and Sally left the kitchen, already discussing new outfits and looks. Lex shook his head.

'In my experience, women don't hurry just because you ask them to. Particularly when it involves clothes.'

'Annie and Sally are professionals,' I said, doing my best to sound confident. 'They won't take long.'

'It's heart-warming you think that,' said Lex. 'I am going back to the living room, to make myself comfortable. Are you still going to make some tea?'

'A few biscuits would be nice,' Johnny said wistfully. 'I do love to dunk a Hobnob.'

'We won't have time,' I said firmly.

Thirty minutes later, Annie came back into the living room wearing a tan leather jacket over a ruffled purple blouse, designer jeans and flat shoes. Her new spectacles were so big they seemed to balance on her cheekbones, and the look was topped off with a curly blonde wig and almost tasteful makeup. She smiled easily round the room.

'I am Miriam. Professional poker player and reader of tells. Just point me at the tables, and I'll win us our fare home.'

Sally couldn't wait any longer for her moment in the spotlight. She shouldered past Miriam and struck an elegant pose, to show off her smart black suit, crisp white blouse, black string tie and a monocle screwed firmly into one eye.

'I am still Sally, and I have stuffed my pockets with all kinds of useful objects, for switching out other things.'

'Why the monocle?' I said.

'To distract people! Always give the mark something interesting to look at while you rob them blind, darling.'

'Are we ready to go?' said Miriam.

I carefully didn't mention the last thirty minutes. 'Hyde Park, here we come.'

'What have you done with the fake masque?' said Sally.

'Concealed it about my person,' I said. 'You could search me all day and never find it.'

Miriam smiled. 'Maybe later.'

We raced across London in Sally's old van and finally abandoned it on the outskirts of Hyde Park. I left the key in the ignition, because I didn't expect to be seeing the van again, and led the way into the park.

It was getting uncomfortably close to the midnight hour, so I stepped it out. Away from the brightly lit paths, the park's shadows were deep and dark, and the night was eerily quiet. I couldn't see anyone else, which was unusual enough to make me nervous. All kinds of people have all kinds of reasons for being in Hyde Park at night, but it seemed everyone else had decided this was not a good night to be out and about. I kept the crew moving, hurrying them between the tall dark trees and across spaces where moonlight shimmered like an expanse of open water.

Sally stayed quiet for longer than I expected, before finally moving up alongside me.

'Are you sure you know where you're going, darling? Only we have been walking for quite some time now, and if I'd known we were going on a hike, I wouldn't have chosen these shoes.'

'It's never easy to track down the Moonlight Express,' I said patiently. 'The real ghost train, the ride from nowhere. We have to be in exactly the right place to meet it, where the worlds of if and maybe come together, just for a moment.'

'I hate metaphors,' said Sally.

I finally led everyone into a small clearing surrounded by tall, leafless trees that stood like dark guardian figures outlined against the night sky. We were a long way from the brightly lit paths, and the cold night air was very still. I took a good look around, checked my watch and nodded quickly.

'This is it. We made it, with minutes to spare.'

My crew inspected the open space and then glanced at each other to see who would be the first to say something. As always, Sally got in first.

'I have to say, it doesn't look all that promising, darling. Are you positive the train will show up soon? Only I'm really not dressed for standing around in the cold.'

'I once stole a ticket for the Moonlight Express, for a man who didn't officially exist,' I said. 'In return, he told me where to be, if I ever needed to flag down the train from beyond.'

'Beyond what?' said Sally.

'Everything,' I said.

'What happened to this man who didn't exist?' said Miriam.

'I'm guessing he caught the train,' I said. 'Because I never saw him again. At least, given how many really appalling people were after him, I'm hoping that's what happened.'

'Nice story to set the mood, darling,' said Sally. She glowered around her. 'I'm not seeing anything but a whole lot of trees and grass and nature-y things, and I'm not terribly keen on any of them. I am not an outdoors person, darlings. I am at my best in smoky bars, and clubs with really bad reputations. I do not do the healthy outdoors thing.'

'I've never known anyone who could complain as much as you,' I said.

She flashed me a smile. 'It's a gift, darling.'

'This is where we need to be,' I said, 'to catch the train that can cross the world on the back of the moonbow.'

'How are we supposed to stop something like that?' said Lex.

'I have a plan,' I said.

'Of course you do,' said Miriam.

'Am I going to like this plan?' said Lex.

'Almost certainly not,' I said. 'But just do what I tell you, and everything will be fine.'

'Oh, we're doomed,' said Johnny, cheerfully enough.

I checked my watch. Only a few minutes left. I could feel a tension growing in the clearing, a sense of something waiting to happen. And then we all looked round sharply as a train's whistle came to us from out of the oceans of the night, high and piercing, like a demon wailing for its human lover.

And then, right on the stroke of the midnight hour, a great beam of moonlight flashed across the night sky, bent suddenly down and hit the earth, and then blazed a shimmering path across the open clearing, a foot or so above the grass.

An old-fashioned steam train came roaring along the

moonlight trail, a great black beast of an engine with silver and copper stylings, pulling half a dozen old-fashioned carriages in an elegant brown-and-cream livery. It took a long time to reach us, as though it was covering all kinds of space to get to where we were.

'How the hell are we supposed to stop something like that?' said Sally. 'Take off our underwear and wave it, like in *The Railway Children*?'

'That would be the first thing you'd think of,' said Miriam.

I turned to Lex. 'Put on your armour, step up on to the moonlight path and stand in front of that train.'

He looked at the massive steam engine and then at me. 'Really?'

'Yes! Right now!'

Lex shrugged, and Heaven and Hell's protection swept over him in a moment. When he stepped up on to the moonlit path, I was sure it dropped just a little under the weight of his armour. The Damned stood facing the oncoming train, staring it down with his featureless face. The engine grew larger and larger as it steamed out of the night, impossibly huge and intimidating, but the Damned stood his ground. There was a screech of brakes and a howl of venting steam, and the Moonlight Express ground to a halt just a few yards short of the Damned.

'You know,' I said, in the sudden hush, 'I wasn't entirely certain that would work.'

'Now you tell me,' said the Damned.

He dropped his armour but didn't take his gaze off the train. I stepped up on to the shimmering path beside him, and it felt as firm and solid as the ground I'd left behind. Miriam climbed up to stand on Lex's other side, and Sally and Johnny moved into position with us. And then we all stood there and waited to see what would happen.

'I love steam engines!' Johnny said brightly. 'They're so wonderfully functional. Look at the pistons on that!'

The front door on the leading carriage slammed open, and a man jumped down on to the moonlit path. He walked steadily toward us – a tall, distinguished figure in an old-fashioned uniform, complete with brightly polished brass buttons and a gleaming top hat. He stopped a nicely calculated distance away, produced a gold watch on a chain from his waistcoat pocket, flipped open the lid and checked the time. He then closed the lid with a snap, put the watch away and stared thoughtfully at Lex. When he spoke, his voice was cold but composed, a man with all the authority in the world.

'This is not an assigned stop.'

'I am the Damned,' said Lex.

'Of course you are. I am the Conductor. Your vocation buys you a few moments of my time and interest, but don't push your luck. Not even the Damned can interrupt the schedule of the Moonlight Express with impunity.'

'I am willing to bet,' said Lex, 'that if I put my armour back on, I could pick up your engine and throw it the length of this park.'

The Conductor smiled briefly. 'That is why we stopped. But I think it only fair to warn you that there are various personages and powers on this train that even the Damned in his armour might have trouble facing down.'

'Really?' said Lex. 'I'd like to meet them.'

'No, you wouldn't,' said the Conductor. 'Trust me on this.'

While they were politely facing off against each other, I turned to Sally and murmured in her ear.

'I need you to pick the pockets of five passengers on this train and switch out their tickets.'

Sally looked at me sharply. 'You could have given me some warning, darling! This train has serious protections!'

'But you are Switch It Sally,' I said.

She scowled, bit her lip and concentrated. For a long moment nothing seemed to be happening. Beads of sweat formed on her forehead and ran slowly down her face. And then she relaxed, reached into her jacket pocket and handed me five tickets. I checked them carefully. Heavy cardboard and stamped with the name of the train, they already had holes punched in them by the Conductor. I grinned at Sally.

'I knew I could rely on you.'

'No, you didn't,' said Sally. 'But thanks anyway, darling.'

I stepped forward and showed the tickets to the Conductor, holding them carefully so the punch holes weren't visible. He sighed quietly.

'Your destination?'

'Las Vegas,' I said.

The Conductor just nodded and led the way to the open carriage door. He pulled down a set of folding steps, stepped back and gestured courteously for us to climb on board. I went first, radiating confidence, and Miriam followed right behind, smiling graciously. Lex came next, with Sally hanging off his arm as though she belonged there, and Johnny brought up the rear, studying everything with great interest.

'Please don't do that,' said the Conductor.

'Do what?' said Johnny.

'Anything,' said the Conductor.

The first thing to catch my eye as I entered the carriage was the view outside the windows. Instead of Hyde Park at night, there was only an endless dark, with a vast array of stars. All of them different colours, like precious stones scattered across the night. Some expanded and fell back again, while others blinked on and off. A comet streaked past, leaving a sparkling trail behind it. Miriam tapped me surreptitiously on the arm, to remind me I was holding everyone else up. I moved on down the aisle.

The carriage rocked gently from side to side, just like any other train. Apparently, we were underway again, although I hadn't felt any lurch as we started. The carriage's interior was as defiantly old-fashioned as the engine pulling it, and very comfortable. The seats were widely spaced, to allow everyone plenty of leg room, and heavily padded under gleaming black leather. Ornate gas lamps shed a gentle golden glow over everything, and the carriage extended back quite a way, as though it was a lot longer than it appeared from the outside.

A well-stocked bar occupied most of the far end, where a number of people (and a handful of individuals quite definitely not people) were sitting on bar stools. Sally went *Oooh!* very loudly, grabbed Lex by the arm and dragged him down the aisle to the bar. He didn't seem to mind. Johnny watched them go, but made no move to join them. He just dropped into a seat and pushed it back into full recline mode. Judging by the look on the Conductor's face, I gathered the carriage's chairs weren't supposed to do that. Miriam tapped my arm again, but this time I stood my ground so I could study the other passengers.

A Nosferatu in a long grey coat, all pointed ears and rat teeth, lay stretched out full length in the luggage rack. Underneath him sat a pair of tall and spindly Grey aliens, wearing morning suits that made them look like undertakers, and conversing animatedly. Whatever they were discussing involved much waving of the arms, which left trails of glowing blue ectoplasm hanging on the air behind them. A dozen or so commuters, dressed in suits and fashions from half a dozen different eras, were smoking big cigars and reading newspapers in languages I didn't even recognize. Half a dozen Reptiloids, human lizards in long flowing robes with their tails sticking out the back, had turned their chairs around so they could play cards together. And then there was the handful of ghosts sitting at the bar, faded figures who were only technically present. Talking quietly, they occasionally reached out to comfort or console each other, but their hands always passed through the person sitting next to them. What I could see of their faces seemed horribly tired and sad.

The Conductor cleared his throat, and I realized he was still with us. I gestured at the semi-transparent figures.

'Do they get a special rate, for being deceased?'

'Oh, they're not dead,' said the Conductor, with not even a hint of a *sir* in his voice. 'Just people who've travelled so much they've come unstuck in Time and Space. Sundered spirits, if you like. They're hoping the Moonlight Express will take them somewhere they can become real and solid again.'

'Is that likely?' I said.

The Conductor shrugged. 'The Company just sells tickets. Everything else is down to the traveller.'

'But if they're unsubstantial,' Miriam said thoughtfully, 'how were they able to pay for their tickets?'

'With information,' said the Conductor. 'About where they come from and all the places they've visited. The Company is always keen to add new stops to the line. Your destination will be our next stop. Everyone else has much further to go. Now, if you'll excuse me, I see someone who definitely shouldn't be in first class.'

He glanced back down the carriage. 'I really don't like surprises during the run, so I'll be checking everyone's tickets again when I get back.'

He strode off down the aisle to confront what might have been a ragged-looking sasquatch, or just possibly a walking hearth rug. Big and burly and covered in greasy knotted hair, it kept banging its head against the ceiling as it peered around in a confused sort of way. Until it saw the Conductor coming, and then it backed quickly away, squeezing its large body through the narrow end door. The Conductor went out after it, and the door closed behind them. I started to say something to Miriam and then stopped as I spotted a tall, imposing figure in a blindingly white suit, sitting on his own. He was staring out of the window at the starry deep, apparently lost in thought.

'Gideon, if you'd gone any paler, I would be checking to see if you still had a pulse,' Miriam said quietly. 'What's the problem? Do you know that man?'

'Not personally,' I said, just as quietly. 'For which I am very grateful. That is Reynard du Bois, the Sinister Saint. Good, mad and dangerous to know. A man so religious he declared himself a living saint and immediately began performing miracles. But given some of the things he's done with his powers, there isn't a Church anywhere that would embrace him. Reynard is an unwavering defender of what he sees as the Good – and to Hell with anyone who disagrees with him.'

'Like the Damned?' said Miriam.

'Only more so,' I said.

'Is he as dangerous as Lex?'

'Only if you belong to some kind of minority.'

'Oh . . . One of those,' said Miriam. 'How does he feel about criminals?'

'Let's just hope he doesn't notice us, so we won't have to find out.'

'Could we please sit down?' said Miriam. 'It's been a very long day, my feet aren't talking to me, and people are starting to stare at us.'

Even as she said that, one of the commuters suddenly jumped to his feet and raised his voice, as his hands moved fruitlessly from one pocket to another.

'Someone has stolen my ticket! Everyone, check your pockets! Where's the Conductor? The thieves must still be on the train!'

Everyone searched for their tickets, and four more commuters stood up and loudly declared that they had been robbed, too. The first commuter stabbed an accusing finger at Miriam and me.

'I want those people arrested! They were the last ones to board, and everything was fine until they showed up!'

Lex and Sally came hurrying back from the bar to join us. Sally finished the last of her drink and tossed the empty shot glass over her shoulder. It bounced off a Grey's elongated head, but the alien merely looked a little puzzled. Lex and Sally moved quickly into position beside Miriam and me, and Lex gave the accusing commuter his coldest glare.

'I am the Damned, and these people are under my protection.'

Everyone went very quiet, including the aggrieved commuter. They'd heard of the Damned. But either the two Grey aliens hadn't or they just didn't care, because they rose up out of their seats and headed purposefully down the aisle toward us. They swayed from side to side as they advanced, swimming more than walking, as though breasting some invisible tide, and streaming blue ectoplasm behind them. The Grey faces held no expression I could understand, but their huge black eyes were like patches of night.

Lex stepped forward to block their way, but before he could put on his armour, the Greys whipped their arms forward, and great loops of ectoplasm shot out and wrapped around Lex. They pinned his arms to his sides and then tightened with such force they crushed all the air out of his lungs. Anyone else would have collapsed, but Lex just snarled at the Greys and put his armour on. All the passengers cried out as a new presence filled the carriage, beating on the air. The Damned thrust out his arms, and the blue coils shattered and fell away from him. The Grey aliens cried out as though they'd been wounded, and staggered back down the aisle. They dropped back into their seats and huddled together, shaking.

They passed the Reptiloids, coming in the other direction. All six of them had energy guns in their scaled hands, aimed unwaveringly at the Damned. They showed him disturbing grins, packed full of jagged teeth. The Damned raised his armoured fists, and the Reptiloids opened fire, but not one of their guns worked. The Reptiloids stopped and looked at their energy weapons. They shook them tentatively and then tried again, but still nothing happened. I caught the smile on Sally's face.

'All right,' I said quietly. 'What did you do?'

She smiled dazzlingly and opened one hand to reveal a small

metallic shape. 'I switched the energy packs out of their guns, darling.'

'How did you know they had any?'

She looked at me condescendingly. 'I watch *Star Trek*.'

'OK,' I said. 'What did you replace them with?'

'Matchboxes, darling,' said Sally. 'I collect them. They come in handy for all kinds of things.'

The Reptiloids put away their weapons and produced gleaming bone knives from inside their robes.

'That's really not going to help you,' said the Damned.

Johnny moved into position beside him and we all jumped a little, because none of us had seen him leave his seat.

'It's all right, Johnny,' the Damned said quickly. 'They can't hurt me.'

The Wild Card showed the Reptiloids his own disturbing smile. 'You've been hogging all the fun, Lex. Don't I get to play?'

'You play too roughly, Johnny. I can handle this.'

'But they threatened you,' said the Wild Card. 'And I can't have that.'

He stepped forward, and the Reptiloids raised their bone knives. Johnny shook his head sadly.

'I don't believe in lizard people.'

Slowly and relentlessly, the Reptiloids faded away and were gone, screaming silently to the last. A chill ran through me as I took in the Wild Card's smile. The Damned put off his armour and shook his head.

'That wasn't necessary.'

'They wanted to kill you,' said Johnny.

'You really think they could have hurt me?'

Johnny shrugged. 'It's the principle of the thing. And I don't have many principles left.'

Five of the commuters had gathered together in the aisle. They glared at us, outraged at losing their tickets, and suddenly the men in suits had been replaced by lean muscular wolves. They still stood on two feet, but a fierce hunger burned in their eyes, and they snarled viciously. One of them reached out and casually tore chunks of stuffing out of a nearby seat with one sweep of his clawed hand. They started down the aisle towards us, every movement charged with menace and malice.

Because they didn't understand what had just happened. They didn't know about the Wild Card. I moved quickly in beside Johnny and put a staying hand on his shoulder.

'Let me handle this,' I said. 'It's my turn.'

He nodded, and I stepped forward to face the advancing wolves. I shook my head slowly.

'More bloody werewolves . . .'

They stopped and looked at me, just a bit confused.

'There doesn't have to be any trouble,' I said.

They laughed at me, in a harsh, barking way, showing their teeth and flashing their claws. Their eyes sparkled viciously, craving blood and death. I took out my skeleton key and pointed it at them. They paused to see what it would do. I turned the key slowly in mid-air, unlocking the human shapes stored within them, just as I had at the Gallery of Ghosts. Only, this time, nothing happened. The wolves growled at me – a slow, chilling sound full of all the hate and hunger in the world. I lowered the key, and Miriam was quickly there at my side.

'What's wrong?' she said quietly.

'I don't know,' I said. 'Maybe where they're from, the change mechanism follows different rules.'

'There must be something you can do!'

I thought hard. The wolves had started forward again, taking their time so they could savour the killing to come. And I stabbed my skeleton key at the nearest carriage door. It swung back with a crash, opening on to the darkness and the stars. Air went whistling down the aisle, pulled out through the door, and the carriage rocked heavily from side to side. Everyone grabbed at their seats to steady themselves. But the werewolves dug their clawed feet into the thickly carpeted floor and just kept coming.

I went forward to meet them, because I'd had enough of being threatened. The nearest wolf reared up and snarled at me mockingly. And while it was busy doing that, I hit the button on my pen. Time crashed to a halt. I moved in behind the wolf, took a firm hold on its tail and restarted Time. Before the wolf realized what was happening, I dragged it over to the open doorway, spun it around and booted it out into space. The wolf didn't even have time to howl before it was swept away and left behind by the train.

I told myself I didn't feel guilty. Werewolves are just plague rats with delusions of grandeur. But even so, there was a limit to how much of a hard arse I was prepared to be. I turned back to the remaining wolves, held where they were by shock and horror.

'Change back,' I said, 'and we'll pretend none of this happened.'

The wolves looked at each other, and suddenly the commuters were back, as though they'd never been away. They returned to their seats and sat down, carefully not looking at me. I used my skeleton key to close the door, and the air settled down and the train stopped rocking. I thought the trouble was over, until Reynard du Bois got up out of his seat and came strolling down the aisle. His white suit seemed to glow with concentrated holiness. Lex quietly walked past me to face him. Reynard came to a halt and nodded pleasantly to Lex.

'The legendary Damned . . . I wasn't sure at first whether I should embrace you as a brother in arms or see you as a competitor.' He laughed softly, but there was no humour in the sound. 'Either way, this train isn't big enough for both of us. I should find it touching that you honestly believe you can save yourself from the Pit with a few good deeds; but I am the law and the lore, and your very existence offends me.'

He gestured with one elegant hand, and all the carriage doors sprang open. This time the air went howling out of the openings, and everyone clung desperately to their seats as the carriage lurched dangerously. Lex just stood his ground. Reynard smiled at him.

'Pick a door; you're leaving.'

'I don't serve the Good to save myself,' said Lex. 'I do it to save others. And to piss off Hell, one last time.'

Renard shook his head. 'You're a disgrace. Get out, before I throw you out.'

'I don't think so,' said Lex. 'I am the real thing, armoured by Heaven and Hell. You're just a wannabe in a nice suit. You lack . . . commitment.'

The Sinister Saint glared at him. 'I am God's Angry Man! Here to put things right and make sure everyone knows their place!'

'With you and your kind at the top of the pile, and everyone else at the bottom,' said Lex. 'I punish the guilty to protect the innocent; you do it because you're afraid of anyone who doesn't look like you. God is bigger than that.'

'How dare you speak to me like that!' screamed Reynard. 'I am a saint!'

'Self-appointed,' said Lex.

He put on his armour, and the light and the dark crashed into place around him. Reynard had to turn his eyes away, unable to face the blinding light and the terrible dark, as Heaven and Hell manifested in the carriage. He finally made himself look and thrust out a hand. Lightning stabbed down out of nowhere, raging energies that flared and crackled around the Damned's armour, but he just stood there, unmoved, and the lightning disappeared.

'Is that all you've got?' said the Damned.

The Sinister Saint howled wordlessly and threw himself forward. His hands locked around the Damned's throat, but he couldn't get past the armour. Reynard released his hold and struck at the Damned again and again, almost sobbing with frustrated rage. Finally, he ran out of strength and stumbled backwards. His suit wasn't glowing any more. Reynard glared at the Damned, snarling viciously like a cornered rat.

'I'll find a way to get to you! And then I'll kill you and all your friends!'

Johnny Wilde appeared out of nowhere, to stand beside the Damned.

'That's no way to talk,' he said calmly.

'I saw what you did to the lizards,' said Reynard. 'Don't think you can threaten me. I have God at my side!'

Johnny looked at him carefully. 'No . . . I don't see him. I think it's time you were leaving.'

He looked past Reynard, at the sundered spirits standing together at the bar. Semi-transparent and only just there, they were still fascinated by what was happening. Johnny smiled at them, and just like that all of them were solid and real again. They cried out in shock and joy and embraced each other, before turning their smiles on Johnny.

'Yes,' he said. 'I did that. If you'd like to show your appreciation, throw this arsehole off the train.'

The returned spirits strode down the aisle. Reynard threw his lightning at them, but they were so divorced from reality the energies couldn't touch them. They marched right up to the Sinister Saint, laid their newly solid hands on him and hauled him away. He fought them, shouting and protesting, right up to the moment they threw him out of the nearest door. He was gone in a moment, lost in the dark, and everyone else in the carriage applauded loudly. One by one the doors closed, and the air and the carriage grew still again. Johnny smiled easily.

'He could have helped them, but he didn't.' He nodded to the returned spirits. 'Enjoy your new life.'

The spirits clapped each other on the shoulder and went back to the bar, where they ordered a great many drinks. I got the feeling they'd been looking forward to that for a really long time.

The end door opened, and the Conductor came back into the carriage. One of the commuters stood up, shot me a defiant look and addressed the Conductor in a loud and carrying voice.

'Those people stole our tickets!'

The other aggrieved commuters quickly joined in, backing him up. But their voices quickly fell away, silenced by the complete lack of sympathy in the Conductor's face.

'All passengers without valid tickets must get off the train,' he said. 'That's Company policy.'

He didn't gesture or even look around, but once again a carriage door swung open. Only this time there was no disturbance in the air or any change in the motion of the carriage. The commuters stared in horror at the darkness and the stars outside the door. The one on his feet put on an ingratiating smile and tried an appeal to reason.

'We all paid for our tickets! It's not our fault they were stolen. You have a duty to take us where you promised!'

'You have a duty to look after your tickets,' said the Conductor. 'Company policy clearly states that every passenger needs a valid ticket to travel on the Moonlight Express. No excuses.'

And just like that, all the commuters were dragged into the aisle by some unseen force. They screamed and protested and looked beseechingly at the other passengers, but they were all keeping their heads down and hoping not to be noticed. The commuters stared at the open doors, and the sheer horror of what lay beyond stole the words from their mouths.

'Oh, hell,' I said.

'What?' said Miriam.

'I'm going to have to do something.'

'They turned into wolves and tried to kill us,' Miriam said reasonably. 'So if it's us or them, I vote them. They are not nice people, and we really need to get to Vegas.'

'There's a limit to how much damage I'm prepared to do to people's lives,' I said. 'Or we'll end up as bad as the people we go after.' I turned to Lex. 'I'm about to do something really dumb, because it's the right thing. Back me up?'

'Any time,' said Lex.

'Sounds like fun to me,' said Johnny.

Sally smiled brilliantly. 'Anything for an interesting life, darling.'

I looked at Miriam, and she nodded resignedly.

'Go ahead. Snatch defeat from the jaws of victory.'

I raised my voice and addressed the Conductor. 'Leave those people alone! Or else.'

The Conductor turned to face me, and the commuters slammed to a halt, just short of the open door. They looked desperately at me, not quite daring to hope. I walked steadily down the aisle to confront the Conductor, and he waited patiently for me to join him.

'Or else?' he said calmly, as though he was just requesting information.

'You'd better believe it,' I said cheerfully.

'I'm not sure what it is you're objecting to,' said the Conductor. 'After what you did to the wolf.'

'That was self-defence,' I said. 'This isn't necessary.'

'They have no tickets,' said the Conductor.

'I know,' I said. 'My friends and I stole them.'

'Now, that is also against Company policy,' said the Conductor. 'I'm afraid you'll have to leave the train.'

He didn't look at the open door. He didn't have to.

'We'll get off the train when we get to Vegas,' I said. 'Not before.'

'I could make you leave,' said the Conductor.

'I am Gideon Sable, master thief,' I said flatly. 'This my crew: the Damned and the Wild Card, Annie Anybody and Switch It Sally. You really think you can make us do one thing we don't want to?'

The Conductor considered the matter.

'And you are the one who let us on the train, with stolen tickets,' I said.

The Conductor nodded. 'Sit down and behave yourselves. I'll tell you when we've reached Las Vegas.'

The door closed quietly, and the commuters quietly returned to their seats. The Conductor gave me a final hard look and something that might have been a very brief smile, and then he turned and left the carriage through the end door. I went back to my crew, doing my best to look as though I wasn't still shaking inside.

'Could he really have thrown us off?' said Miriam.

'Some say the Conductor has the strength of the whole train,' I said. 'That he is in fact the human manifestation of the Moonlight Express.'

Lex looked at me. 'Really?'

I smiled. 'People say a lot of things.'

Not long after, there was a great squealing of brakes and a venting of steam as the Moonlight Express came to a halt. The darkness and the stars disappeared from outside the windows, replaced by blazing neon, rushing traffic and packed city streets. I didn't see the Conductor come back in, but suddenly his voice was filling the carriage.

'Las Vegas! Everyone who is travelling to Las Vegas, off the train!'

A single door opened. I gestured for my crew to go first, while I kept an eye on the Conductor. When I was the only one left, I took the five tickets out of my pocket, and he came forward to take them.

'See they get back to their owners,' I said.

'Thank you for using the Moonlight Express,' he said calmly. 'I hope to see you again someday.'

I jumped down from the open door, and it slammed behind me. When I looked back, the Moonlight Express was gone. I grinned at my crew.

'Welcome to Las Vegas!'

NINE
Hungry Fish in Murky Waters

Las Vegas didn't seem at all interested in our arrival. Heavy traffic roared up and down a street lined with dozens of casinos, all of them magnificently garish, with enough flashing neon to be seen from the moon. Because understatement gets you nowhere in Vegas.

The pavement was packed with people, all of them in a hurry to be somewhere else. No one was just strolling along, enjoying the sights, for fear of being taken for a tourist. They all wanted people to think they were someone important, on their way to do something that mattered. Las Vegas is the city where no one ever sleeps for fear they might be missing out on something, or because someone else might be sneaking up on them.

My crew stared openly about them, acclimatizing themselves to their new setting, and I saw no reason to hurry them. We received a lot of angry glances from passers-by just for being in the way, but nobody said anything. The Damned's presence might have had something to do with that. The irritated crowd might not know who he was, but they could still sense the danger. Because Vegas knows all there is to know about predators.

Miriam was the first to tear her gaze away from the gaudy facades. 'How are we supposed to find the Khuffu Casino in the midst of all this?'

Sally smiled brightly and wiggled her long fingers. 'I could always relieve someone of their phone, darlings, and look for a map.'

'Control those itchy fingers, Sally,' I said. 'We are right where we're supposed to be.'

I pointed directly across the street to the massive pyramid of the Khuffu Casino, which stood proudly behind an impressive display of dancing fountains and brilliant spotlights.

'How on earth did we miss that?' said Johnny. 'If it was any more colourful, it would stain your eyeballs.'

'More importantly, how did the Conductor know to drop us here?' said Lex. 'We didn't tell him where in Vegas we were going.'

'All part of the service on the Moonlight Express,' I said.

Sally scowled at the traffic, which showed no sign of ever slowing down, never mind stopping.

'How are we supposed to get to the Khuffu, darlings? Call a taxi to take us to the other side of the street?'

Miriam turned to Lex, a smile tugging at her lips. 'If you could stop the Moonlight Express . . .'

Lex marched straight out into the middle of the road. Cars blared their horns as they shot past him without slowing, but Lex just turned unhurriedly and glared at the oncoming traffic. And all the cars came crashing to a halt in a mass squealing of brakes. I'm not sure any of the drivers could have said why. Lex wasn't wearing his armour, and I doubted anyone in Vegas had even heard of the Damned. But something in his expression hit them right where their self-preservation instincts lived.

Lex turned around to face the traffic coming in the other direction, and once again every driver found a compelling reason to stop. It was suddenly a whole lot quieter. I gathered up my crew and led them across the road to the Khuffu Casino. I kept my head well down, just in case anyone was filming the stopped traffic on their phones, but a quick glance around showed they were all too stunned.

'I really must try that on Oxford Street when we get back,' said Lex.

'Concentrate on what matters,' I said sternly, nodding at the casino's main doors. 'Remember, there's surveillance everywhere, and the guards in these places are actually encouraged to play rough.'

'Let them start something,' said Lex. 'I could use a little light exercise.'

'Even you couldn't fight a whole casino, darling,' said Sally.

'Want to bet?' said Lex.

'We are not here to draw attention to ourselves,' I said. 'Our only hope of getting away with this is to grab the masque when no one is looking, and then disappear. So the Montressors never know how it was done or who did it. We work best in the shadows, and the glare of all this neon is making me very nervous.'

'I could turn off all the lights, if you like,' Johnny said diffidently. 'Or strike everyone blind. Temporarily, of course.'

The Wild Card was never more worrying than when he was trying to be helpful. I gave him my best diplomatic smile.

'Not right now, thank you.'

I hurried my crew through the casino entrance, under the thoughtful gaze of the security guards, who weren't quite sure what to make of us. I just acted as though they weren't there, while Miriam smiled confidently at my side. Lex looked as if he was ready to walk right over anyone who got in his way, but then he always did. Sally hung on to his arm with both hands, tossing her hair and laughing happily, as though this was just another night out for her. And Johnny ambled along in the rear, nodding pleasantly to everyone, including several who weren't actually present.

The lobby had been designed to appear impressive, without being intimidating; no expense had been spared to make the entrance to the lion's den appear luxurious and inviting. The Masque of Ra had been given pride of place, set halfway up a stone pillar so it was the first thing everyone saw as they entered. We came to a halt in front of the masque and studied it carefully.

It looked exactly like the replica I had tucked away about my person, but face to face with the real thing, I had to admit the actual masque was much more impressive. Partly because of the staging, under carefully arranged lights, but mostly because this masque had a presence, and a depth, all its own. If I hadn't known better, I would have sworn it was staring back at me.

The sarcophagus of the Pharaoh Khuffu stood on its end beside the pillar, with the mummy propped up inside it. There were fewer lights trained on the mummy, perhaps to add a sense of drama, but more likely so the shadows would help to disguise bandages browned with age and ragged and rotting in places. The mummy had no discernible face, just a rough shape under layers of bandages, but two silver dollars had been set in place where the eyes should have been. I was pretty sure that wasn't an ancient Egyptian tradition.

Now I'd seen the state of the mummy, Judi's story about Khuffu getting out of his sarcophagus in the early hours to guard the masque seemed distinctly unlikely. One less thing to worry about.

A large sign described the history of the pharaoh and the masque. A few tourists stopped to take selfies of themselves with the mummy, but barely even glanced at the masque. To make it clear they were far too sophisticated to believe in such things. For them, it was all just part of the casino's general theme. But out of the corner of my eye, I couldn't help noticing that the guards were keeping a watchful eye on everyone who got too close to the masque.

I was about to gather up my crew and head for the main floor when a loud voice called my name. I looked round to discover the casino's resident stand-up comic bustling towards us, flashing his best professional smile.

Big Bill Buxton nodded easily to the security guards, in an *It's all right, they're with me* sort of way, and the guards relaxed a little. If Bill vouched for us, then we must be someone, even if they weren't sure who. Bill was wearing the same Hawaiian shirt and flappy shorts I'd seen in Old Harry's mirror, but in person he seemed even larger. A great butterball of a man, he carried himself with practised grace. His round red face was perspiring heavily, just from the exertion of his walk, but his eyes were sharp and focused. He crashed to a halt before me and thrust out a huge meaty hand.

'Hi, hello and how are you! Welcome to the Khuffu, Gideon Sable; I've been expecting you! Hell, I've been hanging around here for so long my shoes have put down roots!'

'Really?' I murmured, matching his hearty handshake with one of my own. 'We weren't expecting such a welcome, Mr Buxton.'

'Bill! Please, just call me Bill. Everyone does.' He chuckled loudly as he released my hand, but I got the feeling that was just something he did to put people at their ease. He met my gaze knowingly. 'A mutual friend told me you were on your way.'

'Of course,' I said. 'I should have known.'

I introduced Bill to the crew, and Bill insisted on shaking hands with all of them. Sally gave him her best sultry gaze.

'I am absolutely loving Las Vegas, Bill darling. It really is just like in all the movies!'

'We stand ready to offer you the full interactive experience,' said Bill. 'All the flash and glamour you can handle, in return for all the money you have on you. I have to say, I love your accent . . .'

'I should hope so, darling,' said Sally. 'I put enough work into it.'

'And the monocle is really cool.'

Sally shot me a triumphant look. Bill switched his relentless smile back to me and gestured grandly at the casino's main floor. 'Come inside; let me show you around. I will be your native guide and point out all the players and pitfalls.'

He dropped a companionable if somewhat weighty arm across my shoulders and urged me forward into the ever-ravenous maw of the beast.

The whole area was packed with people hitting the laws of chance head on and daring them to blink first. Crazed optimism and wild-eyed fervour slammed up against the brutal mechanics of probability, and money disappeared in the greatest conjuring trick of all: where the casino fools you into thinking you ever had a chance. It was like one big adventure playground, with all the fun of the fair and endless traps for the unwary. Gambler beware . . . The roar of the crowd was almost a match for the traffic outside, and the stench of mass sweat and desperation was almost overwhelming. Bill smiled out across the great sprawl of greed and avarice, as though it all belonged to him.

Rows of slot machines stretched away before us, manned by devoted souls sitting determinedly on uncomfortable plastic stools, holding a paper cup of coins in one hand while they endlessly hauled down handles with the other. They never took their eyes off the spinning images before them, and their arms never seemed to get tired, though I felt worn out just watching them. It was as if they were hypnotized by the machines in some strange ritual of worship and sacrifice. Occasionally, a bell would ring to draw attention to a winner, but the prize never seemed big enough to justify the excitement. Bill grinned as he caught my expression.

'Got to keep dropping some chum into the water, to keep the fish hungry. Of course, these are just the small fish. The sharks stick to the gaming tables, and the whales prefer to play big-stakes poker in the back rooms.'

'Whales?' I said politely, just to show I was hanging on to the metaphor.

'The really big spenders,' said Bill. 'The ones with so much to give . . . Think of all this as the ocean, and the casino goes fishing every day.' He chuckled loudly at his own cleverness. 'Oh, and, Gideon, there's no need to keep glancing at the security guards. You're with me, so that makes you distinguished guests – ready to be taken for everything you've got.'

'You do like your metaphors, don't you?'

'That's Vegas for you,' Bill said comfortably. 'Layers and layers of surface, with nothing underneath.'

'Why are you so keen to give us the grand tour?' Miriam said bluntly. 'We know all about casinos.'

'But this is Vegas,' said Bill. 'And we know all there is to know about shearing the sheep.' Bill waved his free arm expansively at the main floor, and I took the opportunity to duck out from under the one lying heavily on my shoulders. Bill just carried on talking. 'Think of this as one big battleground, where the casino is at war with the gamblers for every penny they have on them. They might arrive in Vegas in a nice car, with all kinds of hopes and dreams, but we'll send them home on a Greyhound bus, with a much better understanding of how the world works. Because all's fair in love and war. Not that there's much difference in Vegas.'

I put up a hand to stop him.

'Why the ancient Egyptian theme? Why all the fake hieroglyphics on the walls, and the far-from-accurate costumes? Most of it looks like out-takes from Elizabeth Taylor's *Cleopatra*.'

Bill shrugged. 'This used to be the old Howling Timber Wolf Casino, before Saul got hold of it. He's never said, but I've always assumed the new look is something to do with the masque. I know Saul was really proud when he brought that thing home. Don't ask me how he got his hands on it; he won't say. And this is a man who lives to boast.

'The old casino had definitely become a bit shabby – the kind of place where the glamour comes off on your hands, and it takes forever to get the ambience out of your clothes. The Khuffu looks more like what a modern casino is supposed to be: the ultimate honey trap. But what most people don't know is that this is Saul's last roll of the dice. He's invested a lifetime's savings into rebranding this casino, and he needs it to pay off big. Of course, no one can be allowed to know that because sharks can smell blood in the water, so he just carries on living it large, like he doesn't have a care in the world.'

'What about Saul's children?' I said. 'Do they know?'

'They're not supposed to,' said Bill. 'But of course they do. The kids are working really hard to squeeze all the profit they can out of the Khuffu, because it's their only inheritance. But there's a limit to how much influence they can have. Saul always has to be the man in charge, and he has very fixed ideas on how to run things.'

He paused and shot me a sidelong glance. 'Do you know Saul?'

'I know of him,' I said carefully. 'I've never actually met the man.'

'Saul and I go way back,' Bill said easily. 'Started out together, back when we both had nothing. Except I could make people laugh, and he could make money. We've come a long way . . .'

He finally stopped talking as he looked out over the floor, his eyes lost in nostalgia. I took the opportunity to immerse myself in the Khuffu experience. The topless waitresses all had black wigs and heavy black eye makeup, and short leather skirts. They seemed to be taking it in their stride, and I couldn't see a tan line anywhere. The male staff were also bare-chested, though they'd oiled to show off their muscles, and their minimalist outfits made them look as if they'd just stepped out of a posing competition. Everyone else, from the card dealers to the bar staff to the pit bosses, were arrayed in elaborate costumes that owed more to old mummy movies than anything from actual Egyptian history.

There was no sense of playfulness or fun in any of their faces; as far as the staff was concerned, it was just work clothes.

I turned to Lex and discovered he was standing dangerously still: like a predator that had just spotted a new quarry. A chill ran through me as I realized the Damned had recognized someone, and not in a good way. Sally was looking anxiously at Lex and squeezing his arm hard, trying to get him to look at her.

'What is it, darling? What's wrong?'

Lex ignored her. His face was inhumanly cold, and there was death in his eyes. I gestured sharply for Sally to stand back, and moved in close beside Lex. He started speaking without even looking at me, his voice cold but casual, like a hunter who'd just decided on his next kill.

'See the tall man, in the grey suit and flowery waistcoat, with a long scar on his face?'

It didn't take me long to pick the man out. Standing alone by the chemin-de-fer table, but taking only a polite interest in the proceedings, he didn't so much have a scar as a reminder of when someone had made a determined effort to rip half his face off.

'I gave him that scar,' said Lex. 'One of the few real scumbags to get away from me. Creighton Price . . . He steals identities. Quite literally. He kills people, takes on their appearance, then moves into their lives . . . replacing them so completely that no one can tell the difference. He steals everything worth taking, destroying friends and family in the process, and then just disappears, so he can move on to the next victim. I kill people who need killing, and no one qualifies more than him.'

'That's not what we're here for,' I said firmly. 'He can wait until after we've got the masque. You wanted to be part of this crew, and that means you have a responsibility not to screw things up for the rest of us.'

I couldn't tell if anything I said was reaching him. But finally he nodded slowly, never taking his eyes off Price.

'Later . . .'

I breathed a quiet sigh of relief and shot a meaningful look at Sally. She grabbed hold of Lex's arm with both hands again and chattered cheerfully to him until he started to look less like the Damned. I turned back to Bill, who was looking at me sharply.

'What just happened there? The big guy looked like he was ready to bite chunks out of someone.'

'He thought he saw someone he knew.' I looked at Bill thoughtfully. 'Didn't Judi brief you on who we are?'

'All she gave me were names and descriptions,' said Bill. 'She did say you were all considered heavy hitters, back in London. But you're in Vegas now. The big league.'

I just nodded and let that one go. Bill frowned at Lex, who had calmed down enough to smile indulgently at Sally.

'Is the big guy going to be trouble? He looks like he could do a lot of damage if he put his mind to it. Can you guarantee you can keep a tight leash on him, or do I need to call in some muscle?'

'Lex will do what he will do,' I said. 'But I can usually point him in the right direction.'

Bill nodded reluctantly. 'So, Gideon . . . what do you need to get started?'

'A personal meeting with Saul,' I said. 'And then with all three of his children. To discuss selling them a London casino.'

Bill grinned delightedly. 'You couldn't have chosen better bait. Saul is still mad as hell over missing out on acquiring a casino in London, some years back. One of the few times he got his ass handed to him. And he could use a bolthole to run to, if the Khuffu should crash and burn. Yeah . . . I can see Saul going for that in a big way. And the kids will want to know all about it, if only to protect themselves. They don't want to be left with nothing but a tarted-up money pit as their only inheritance.'

'Any chance they might try to sabotage the deal?' I said.

'Oh, they'll definitely be interested in taking it over for themselves,' said Bill. 'A chance to stab Daddy in the back and get their hands on a casino of their own? They'll dry-hump that one to death.'

Miriam fixed him with a chilly look. 'You're being very helpful, Bill, but I have to ask: why have you turned on your old friend?'

Bill stopped smiling for the first time and met her gaze steadily. 'Because he's going to be young and strong again, and live more lifetimes, and I'm not. We're old friends, so I always assumed we'd grow old together. But now he's going to get a second chance, while I'm to be left here to rot? I could forgive him anything but that.'

'You really believe the Masque of Ra can do all of that?' said Miriam.

Bill shrugged. 'Saul believes it, and he's not an easy man to fool. So you do whatever it takes to bring him down. And then Saul and I will be right back where we used to be. Two old friends sharing the twilight of their lives. That's all I want.'

'How long will it take you to set up these meetings?' I said.

Bill's cheerful grin returned. 'Saul will insist on seeing you first thing tomorrow morning, once I tell him what you have to offer. But you're going to have to be really convincing, Gideon . . .'

'Relax,' I said. 'This is what I do.'

He seemed to find something reassuring in my face and relaxed a little. 'Once the kids hear what's happening, and I'll make sure they do without being too obvious about it, they'll find time to see you in the afternoon.'

'Three separate meetings,' I said.

'Of course,' said Bill. 'The kids will insist on it. They weren't raised to trust each other.'

'So there's no chance of their presenting a united front against their father?' I said. 'Even if it's in their best interests?'

'Baby piranhas do not cooperate,' said Bill. 'Especially when there's blood in the water. When Dana, their mother, was still alive, she could sometimes get them to see reason, but now she's dead . . .'

'I heard a car accident,' I said.

'Yeah,' said Bill. 'That's what I heard, too.'

And for a moment we both looked at each other, without having to say anything.

'Well,' Miriam said brightly, 'since we've got some free time before the meetings, I think I'll wander off and find a card game to board and plunder.'

I steered her a cautious distance away from Bill and lowered my voice. 'Can you really play cards?'

She looked at me sternly. 'Miriam can. Don't fuss, Gideon; I can look after myself.'

'Of course you can,' I said.

She kissed a fingertip, pressed it against my forehead and then set off for the card tables like a wolf that had just scented a flock of sheep. When I looked back, Sally was already dragging Lex off to the gaming tables. He didn't seem to mind.

'I feel like I should have warned them more about what they're getting into,' said Bill.

'Miriam knows cards,' I said. 'And Sally knows all there is to know about having a good time. And Lex . . . isn't easily fooled.'

I turned to Johnny, but he'd disappeared. I looked quickly around, but there were none of the usual signs that went with Johnny taking too much of an interest in his surroundings – things appearing and disappearing, the laws of common sense having a nervous breakdown, people screaming . . . So I just shrugged and turned back to Bill.

'I understand Saul has security personnel with supernatural gifts,' I said. 'I need to take a look at them.'

Bill nodded quickly. 'Nothing easier. Saul insists that they show themselves off. Some casinos have clowns and acrobats; Saul has supernatural attack dogs. They make regular patrols of the main floor and pose for selfies with the tourists. Who assume they're fakes, because everything else is.'

'But they're not,' I said.

'If they were, Saul wouldn't have hired them,' said Bill.

He led me through the packed crowd. A lot of people recognized Bill, and he had a quick smile and a joke for all of them. A few people glanced at me and then looked quickly away again, not wanting to waste their time on someone who wasn't anybody. Bill finally pointed out Double Down Dan, who was busy keeping a watchful eye on a big winner at the roulette wheel. The lucky man was jumping up and down and whooping loudly, as the croupier pushed a big pile of chips towards him. Everyone around him smiled and laughed and clapped him on the shoulder, in case his luck might rub off.

Double Down Dan was the same rat-faced, sharp-suited type I'd seen in the talking mirror. In person, he looked like a vulture waiting for someone to die, ready to help the matter along, if need be.

Bill tapped me on the arm to get my attention and then pointed at the far side of the floor. There was Dan again, standing by the elevators. I looked back and forth between the two men, and Double Down Dan was quite definitely in two different places at the same time. Bill waited till I was sure of that, and then pointed out a third Dan downing a drink at the bar.

'Is that all of him?' I said.

'Isn't that enough?' said Bill. 'How many of him do you want?'

An elderly couple burst out of the crowd and beamed happily at Bill. They were both wearing the same T-shirts, saying *We're Throwing Away Our Children's Inheritance And Loving Every Minute Of It!* Bill hit them with his best professional smile, and they nodded fondly back at him.

'We always make a point of coming to see you, every time we're in Vegas,' the husband said proudly.

'We've been enjoying your act for years!' said the wife.

'And it never changes!' said the husband.

'Of course not,' said Bill, grinning. 'That's how good it is!'

They all laughed, and Bill posed for a photo with them before waving them on their way.

While all that was going on, I took a surreptitious peek through my crystal eye at the Double Down Dan by the roulette wheel. He was immediately replaced by a vision of all three Dans drinking together in a hotel room. From the look of them, they'd been doing that for some time. They toasted each other with whisky in chunky glasses.

'To the Tripani Brothers!' said one Dan.

'God bless triplets!' said the second.

'Easiest money we ever made!' said the third.

They knocked back their drinks and then laughed raucously at the trick they were pulling – on the casino and the world.

I slipped the crystal eye back into my pocket. A simple explanation after all; Dan could be in three places at the same time because there were three of him. Bill came back to join me, his professional smile undimmed by constant use.

'Got to keep the old fans happy. The ones who stay loyal, even though they've heard all the jokes before. Perhaps because it's good to have some things in life you can depend on. Are you finished with Dan?'

'Oh, yes,' I said. 'We're done.'

'OK!' said Bill. 'Next up – Soulful Sam!'

'Can he really see the guilt in anyone?' I said. 'And use it to punish them?'

'That's him,' said Bill. 'Scary son of a bitch, even for Vegas. This way.'

We headed for the roulette table. The big winner was screaming his head off, because he'd lost everything on one turn of the wheel. His winning streak had crashed and burned, and now he was howling abuse at everyone and claiming the wheel was rigged. I looked at Bill.

'Is it?'

'No need,' said Bill. 'The game is already heavily stacked in our favour. If people really understood the odds on that wheel, they'd just throw all their money on the table and walk away.'

The people who'd been happy enough to cheer the man on

while he was winning were now drifting away, because losing might be contagious. Everyone else at the wheel stayed put, because Double Down Dan had sent for Soulful Sam.

A hugely overweight figure in a plain white suit, with a pale face and colourless hair, Sam drifted through the crowd like a ghostly dirigible, and everyone fell back to give him plenty of room. He planted himself in front of the aggrieved man and looked him in the eye, and suddenly the disappointed gambler was standing very still and saying nothing. The two men seemed to be standing in their own little pool of quiet, untroubled by the noise and bustle of the casino.

'You knew she was pregnant when you pushed her down the stairs,' said Sam. 'Because you were afraid it wasn't yours. But it was.'

The gambler started crying and couldn't stop. Sam turned and walked away, his job done. The other gamblers watched the crying man hungrily, savouring the moment, until Dan gestured to the nearest security guards, and they came and took the sobbing man away.

'That one got off lightly,' said Bill. 'I once saw a man rip his own throat out because of what Sam said to him. I wasn't close enough to hear the actual words . . . and I've always been a bit grateful for that.'

'Any idea how he does it?' I said.

Bill shrugged. 'I've heard stories. There are always stories, in Vegas. Some say he was thrown out of his Church after stealing an ancient reliquary. Others say that it stole him. Either way, he can use whatever it is to look into your soul, and see the one thing you never told anyone. Sam once told me, after an evening's hard drinking, that he'd give the reliquary back in a moment if he could. But he can't, because it's still hungry.'

'Hold it,' I said. 'You drink with Soulful Sam?'

Bill's grin returned. 'I drink with everyone. That's how I know so much. I've been a hard-drinking man for so long I can keep my head when everyone else is running off at the mouth – and remember it all the next day. A very useful skill in a town like Vegas. Where do you want to go now?'

'Are any of the young Montressors on the main floor tonight?' I said.

'Wouldn't have thought so,' said Bill. He took a quick look

around and then shook his head. 'The boys don't normally work this late, and when they have to, they stick to their offices on the next floor. They only show their faces when there's a real problem, or when Saul makes them. They see coming down here as beneath their dignity. Not Saul, though; he takes regular strolls through the tables every day, so he can see where his money is coming from.'

I made a mental note to get the details on that; it might be something I could use.

'There is one other person you should see,' said Bill. 'Come with me, and I'll introduce you to the casino's resident songbird, the lovely Adelaide.'

'I've heard a lot about her,' I said.

Bill led me off the main floor and down a narrow corridor to a side room, where an unobtrusive sign said simply *The Lovely Adelaide*. Inside, tables and chairs had been set out before a small stage. Perhaps twenty or thirty people were sitting and drinking, while Adelaide sang.

She stood alone on the stage, in a spotlight that did its best to follow her around. A tall, statuesque blonde in a gown of silver sequins, Adelaide was glamorous in a professional kind of way, and doing her best to enchant her audience with a torch song that dated back to when Sinatra was King of Vegas. Bill and I stood at the back and listened to her sing, while I remembered the other vision I'd seen of her, at Old Harry's Place. The woman in the white silk mask.

'Not a bad voice,' said Bill. 'But there's lots like her in Vegas. Good, but never quite good enough.' He dropped me a sly wink. 'You know why Saul keeps her around?'

'Because she's also the Enchanted Enforcer,' I said. 'Does she really have the Evil Eye?'

Bill rolled his eyes. 'Act your age. That's just Vegas flimflam.'

'So how does she kill her victims?'

Bill looked back at the stage, rather than meet my gaze. 'No one knows. There are never any witnesses or clues, and the people Saul sends her after are never seen again. But there's an awful lot of desert outside Vegas, just made for burying bodies.'

The show ended abruptly. The background music cut off,

Adelaide stopped singing, and she left the stage without a bow or a goodbye, to desultory applause. Bill took me backstage to Adelaide's dressing room. There was no star on the door. Bill knocked briefly and barged right in. The room wasn't much bigger than a converted closet, with minimum furnishings and a few dresses on hangers. Adelaide was sitting before a brightly lit mirror, staring at herself. She barely managed a smile as Bill greeted her cheerfully, and didn't get up, but she did suffer him to kiss her on the cheek. She offered me a hand, which I shook politely.

'This is Gideon,' said Bill. 'He's a high flyer from London, here to do business with Saul.'

'Watch your back,' said Adelaide. 'It's never a good deal for Saul unless someone else ends up bleeding.'

And then the door behind us slammed open, and Joyce Montressor came charging in. A short, plump woman in a smart suit that still managed to look shabby, she had a determined, square face and flat dark hair cut in bangs. But Adelaide's face lit up the moment she saw her. She jumped up and hugged Joyce tightly, and the two of them clung together like orphans lost in the storm. Bill quietly indicated it was time for us to leave.

Outside in the corridor, I gave Bill a hard look. 'That was Saul's daughter. How can they keep that kind of relationship secret from him?'

'What makes you think he doesn't know?' said Bill.

'I was told he wouldn't approve.'

'He doesn't. Saul can be very old-fashioned in some ways. But as long as he doesn't know officially, he doesn't have to do anything about it. One of these days Joyce is going to get angry or desperate enough to confront Saul and rub his nose in it, in public. And then it will hit the fan so hard the fan will break.'

'If Saul did turn on Joyce,' I said thoughtfully, 'would he send the Enchanted Enforcer to dispose of her?'

'That's a nasty thought,' said Bill. He scowled as he considered the possibilities. 'Nasty enough that Saul might just do it. He'd find it fitting, and the perfect way to test Adelaide's loyalty. Would she do it? I don't know . . . But this is Vegas. People will do anything for money in Vegas. You just hope Saul doesn't ever feel the need to send the Enchanted Enforcer after you.'

'I've faced worse,' I said.

Something in my voice made Bill look at me sharply. 'Maybe you have.'

He escorted me back through the casino, in something of a hurry now our business was over. I didn't see any sign of my crew. Once we were out in the plaza, Bill thrust a key card into my hand.

'Judi told me to arrange hotel rooms for all of you, so I've booked you into separate rooms in the Delite Deluxe, just down the street. Very nice, very discreet; you won't like it, but don't worry because you won't be staying there long. I'll make sure the rest of your people get their keys.

'I'll contact you in the morning, after I've arranged your meeting with Saul. Welcome to Vegas, Gideon Sable. And always remember, when you're going fishing, make sure you've got a really big club to finish off the catch when you land it.'

He flashed me one last smile, slapped me companionably on the shoulder and strolled back into the casino as if he was coming home.

TEN

Lies, Damned Lies and Misleading Questions

The Delite Deluxe turned out to be a motel, and a grubby, downmarket, last-chance-for-a-roof-over-your-head motel at that. But admittedly not the kind of place anyone would expect to find me. So maybe Bill knew what he was doing after all. I looked the layout over carefully, because in my line of work it's always wise to know where the nearest exit is. The Delite Deluxe was basically just a collection of small rectangular rooms packed together on different levels, as though the architect had spent too much time as a child playing with Lego bricks. The rooms surrounded an open square with only one way in, which meant at least I'd have a decent chance of spotting anyone who did come looking for me.

I'd stayed in worse.

I had to climb two flights of metal stairs to find my room, stepping carefully around and over things I preferred not to look at too closely. All the while ignoring the peeling paint and the weather-beaten facades, and televisions that competed to blast soap operas and game shows through the paper-thin walls. I finally found the right room number and let myself in. I was so tired after my very long day that I just glanced around the room, winced briefly and then crashed fully clothed on the bed and escaped into sleep.

I was awakened by the relentless alarm of a ringing telephone. I sat up slowly, feeling like death warmed up and allowed to congeal, and checked the time on the bedside clock. It was six a.m. I spent some time explaining to the world how I felt about being disturbed at such an ungodly hour, and then rolled off the bed and went looking for the phone. I finally tracked it down in the bathroom, where some thoughtful soul had left it lying beside the toilet bowl. I used a handkerchief to pick it up and answered it with something that probably sounded like a growl.

'This is Bill,' said a far too cheerful voice for such an early hour. 'Saul will meet you at eight a.m. Yes, I know . . . but he's an early riser and thinks everyone else should be, too. I've primed the pump on your behalf, and he is very keen to hear what you have to say.'

'Good,' I said.

'You're not an early-morning person, are you?' said Bill.

'No,' I said.

'Take my advice, and be half an hour early,' said Bill. 'If you're even a little bit late, he won't see you. I'll meet you in the lobby and escort you up to his office.'

'Good of you,' I said.

'How are you enjoying the Delite Deluxe? Is it everything you thought it would be?'

'Lean closer,' I said. 'So I can reach down this phone and throttle you.'

Bill laughed. 'Welcome to Vegas.'

I went back into the main room, dropped the phone on the bed and made a few optimistic attempts at pulling my rumpled clothing back into shape. I studied myself in the streaky mirror and shrugged. Looking a little down on my luck might be just what I needed to convince Saul I really needed to sell my casino. I was just wondering whether I could manage another hour's sleep before I had to go out when there was a knock at my door. I looked at it thoughtfully. Only Bill and my crew were supposed to know I was here. But if it wasn't them, then I really needed to find out who it was. There was no spyhole, so I just unlocked the door and hauled it open.

Miriam strode straight past me and looked around my room. Then she looked me over and shook her head sadly.

'Don't start,' I said, closing the door. 'I slept in these clothes to protect myself from the bed. And I'm not the one whose outfit stinks of stale booze and cigar smoke. Have you been at the casino all night?'

'Pretty much,' Miriam said cheerfully. 'Who needs sleep when you've got adrenalin?' She showed me the new designer bag on her arm, opened it up and spilled great wads of cash on the bed. 'I told you I could play cards!'

'But did you learn anything useful?' I said, deliberately unimpressed.

'Of course,' said Miriam.

She pulled up a chair, gave the seat a good rub with her sleeve and sat down. I dropped on to the edge of the bed, facing her. One of my hands started to reach out to the money, but I pulled it back.

'You can count it later,' Miriam said sweetly. 'And then use it to upgrade us to a better class of hotel. Somewhere without hot and cold running cockroaches.'

'What did you learn?' I said.

'That the security guards only pay real attention to the games when serious money is changing hands,' she said briskly. 'That the casino staff treat paper money like it isn't real, and don't even bother to pick up any that falls on the floor. And, most importantly, that all the surveillance cameras covering the main floor think I'm wonderful and can't wait to do something nice for me.'

She leaned forward to fix me with a steady gaze. 'I also watched Saul Montressor make one of his regular visits to the main floor. Not so much an amble through his territory – more like a regal procession. He was surrounded by security guards and followed by a long train of businesspeople desperate to attract his attention. I got the impression he deliberately kept them waiting, to remind them who was in charge. It also seemed to me that he probably only makes these regular appearances so everyone can see him being rich and important.'

I nodded to show I was paying attention. Bill said Saul was having financial difficulties. The best way to keep sharks from circling is to make them think you're a bigger shark.

'All the staff on the main floor are scared shitless of Saul,' said Miriam. 'They kept their heads well down until he was safely past. After he was gone, I charmed the dealer at my table into telling a few tales out of school. He said Saul likes to fire people at random on these little appearances, just to put the fear of God into everyone and keep them on their toes.'

'Told you he was a bastard,' I said.

Miriam looked at me. 'He killed your friends. I hadn't forgotten. I don't think I ever knew them, did I?'

'Robert and Doug,' I said. 'They were before your time.'

'Did they really mean so much to you?' said Miriam. 'Only you never mentioned them to me before.'

'I don't talk about them, because they mattered so much,' I said. 'They were the brothers I never had. And Saul killed them just because he could.'

There was another knock on my door. I got up to answer it, while Miriam moved quickly to block its view of the money on the bed. I opened the door, and Lex and Sally breezed straight in, beaming all over their faces. I checked to make sure they hadn't been followed, closed the door and then stared at them. Sally was wearing a bridal veil and clinging proudly to Lex's arm. They were both covered in confetti.

'Guess what, darlings?' said Sally. 'We got married!'

Just when you think you're on top of everything, life whips the rug out from under your feet. I looked from Sally to Lex, and his entirely out-of-character smile actually widened a little.

'Best decision I ever made.'

I was prepared to bet all the money on my bed that it had been Sally's decision, not his, but when I glared at her, she just smiled defiantly back.

'Isn't this a bit sudden?' said Miriam.

'I've been alone for too long,' said Lex. 'And you have no idea how rare it is to find a woman who isn't afraid of me.'

I cleared my throat meaningfully. 'Have you told her about . . .'

'Yes,' said Lex. 'We have no secrets between us.'

I was ready to bet all the money in Saul's vault that wasn't true, but Sally was busy sparkling again.

'He really did tell me the whole story, darlings!' she said brightly. 'Honestly, I was so flattered he felt he could be that open with me! I'm not used to people trusting me!'

'There's a reason for that,' I said.

'You can get married anywhere in Vegas!' said Sally. 'We were married by Elvis! Well, I mean, it probably wasn't him, but . . . who knows? This is Vegas!'

I grabbed hold of Sally and hauled her off to one side, while Miriam distracted Lex by beating the confetti off his shoulders.

'Are you crazy, Sally?' I said, lowering my voice. 'You married the Damned?'

She glared right back at me. 'He's really very sweet, once you get to know him.'

'I know you always go for the biggest man in the crew,' I said. 'Because it makes you feel safer, knowing someone has your back when you're finally ready to make your play and shaft the rest of us. But I never thought you'd go this far.'

'This is different,' said Sally.

'That's what you always say.'

'Why can't you just be happy for us, darling?' said Sally, giving me the full pout.

'Because I know you,' I said. 'And I know Lex.'

'No,' said Sally. 'You only ever want him to be the Damned, but there's more to Lex than that. He needs me. No one has ever needed me before. He doesn't care about my past, because his is so much worse.'

'And the whole damned-to-Hell bit doesn't worry you at all?'

Sally shrugged. 'I never was religious. Look, Lex is mine now, darling. So you'd better get used to it.'

She went back to Lex, to find Miriam had given up on the confetti and backed him up against a wall, so she could tell him to his face that he was batshit crazy. Fortunately, he seemed to find that amusing. Sally squeezed in between them, draped herself over Lex and thrust out a hand to show off the heavy gold ring on her finger.

'Very nice,' I said. 'Is anyone looking for it?'

Sally sniffed. 'You always think the worst of me.'

'With good reason,' I said.

'I bought it for her,' said Lex.

'Where did you get the money?' said Miriam.

Lex reached inside his jacket and produced a great wad of cash. 'Turns out I have a gift for roulette.'

'I think he intimidated the wheel,' Sally said wisely. 'The croupier couldn't believe it. He changed the ball twice.'

She finally spotted all the cash on my bed and raised an eyebrow.

'Turns out I have a gift for cards,' said Miriam.

Sally smiled dazzlingly. 'We should have come to Vegas long ago, darlings. We are going to pick this town up by the heels and shake it till it rains money!'

I gave my full attention to Lex. 'Have you seen the Wild Card anywhere?'

Lex scowled and put his money away.

'No. What happened to Johnny?'

'He disappeared,' I said. 'Right after you went off with Sally.'

'Oh, hell,' said Lex.

Sally looked at him sharply. 'What's wrong, sweetie?'

'I'm his only real friend,' said Lex. 'But ever since I came back into this crew, I've been so taken up with you that I had no time for him. It's dangerous to leave Johnny on his own; he gets whimsical and strange. If he's gone wandering off around Vegas, there's no telling what he might do to keep himself occupied. Or amused.'

'I watched the early-morning news in my room before I came here,' said Miriam. 'There were no reports of anything particularly weird or unnatural.'

'But this is Vegas,' I said. 'It could take a while before anybody noticed.'

'I don't understand, darlings,' said Sally. 'He's just this funny little man who can do conjuring tricks. We can still do the heist without him, can't we?'

'Johnny is the Wild Card,' I said. 'The joker in the pack, the poison in the cup, and a one-man *Tales of the Unexpected.* He hasn't been on speaking terms with reality for years, because he can make it do anything.'

'He could make the whole of Vegas disappear, just because he's in a bad mood,' said Miriam.

'Really?' said Sally. 'That's kind of cool, actually . . .'

'Sally,' said Miriam, 'we're in Vegas.'

'Oh . . .' said Sally. 'Yes . . .' She turned quickly to Lex. 'He's your friend, darling. You can handle him, can't you?'

'If we can find him,' said Lex. 'Johnny can part the curtains of reality and walk backstage of the world, move things around to suit himself. He could be anywhere.'

There was another knock at the door. We all turned slowly to look at it. If Johnny had really lost the plot, there could be anything at all on the other side. I grabbed on to my courage with both hands, walked over to the door and opened it. Johnny Wilde greeted me with a perfectly calm and sane smile.

'Good morning! Isn't it an absolutely wonderful day? And don't you just love this place? It's so full of character.'

I gestured quickly for him to come in, and he strolled past me, looking perfectly normal. I took a good look around outside to see if Johnny had brought anything unusual home with him, and then checked the parking space for police cars, ambulances or fire engines. It all seemed peaceful enough, so I closed the door. Johnny smiled happily round the room, looking not at all like an unexploded bomb that might start ticking at any moment.

'Hello, crew! What's been happening while I've been absent without leave? Is the heist progressing? Are the bad guys shaking in their boots?'

And then he looked at Lex and Sally, took in the bridal veil and confetti, and smiled broadly.

'You got married! Good for you!'

A shower of rose petals fell out of nowhere on to the happy couple.

'You should have been my best man,' said Lex.

'Oh, it's been a long time since I was the best anything,' said Johnny. 'I sort of lost the knack.'

'You don't mind that we're married?' said Sally. 'You're not upset, are you, darling?'

'Of course not!' said Johnny. 'I always said being alone was bad for you, Lex. It makes you think dark thoughts. And I can't always be there to shine a light. I have so much to do – places to fix, things to be. That sun doesn't just keep coming up on its own, you know. I hope you'll both be very happy together! I know I was, with my wife.' He stopped to think about that. 'Or at least, I think I was. She disappeared. It is entirely possible that she never really existed, and I just made up the memory to comfort myself.'

'What have you been doing, Johnny?' said Miriam, breaking into a flow of conversation that showed no signs of stopping on its own.

He smiled happily. 'Just seeing Vegas, and walking up and down in it. This city is so weird it makes me feel normal.'

'But what have you been doing?' I said, a little more sharply than I intended.

'I've been good,' said Johnny. 'Mostly. Nothing anyone will notice – at least, not till after we've gone. I look on them as improvements.'

I didn't ask. I was pretty sure I didn't want to know. Johnny realized the rose petals were still falling on the happy couple and stopped them with a gesture.

'All right,' I said, in my best drawing-everyone's-attention voice. 'Now we're all here, it's time to set the plan in motion. Miriam and I have a meeting booked with Saul Montressor for eight a.m. Bill will be there, to introduce us.'

'He is being very helpful, isn't he?' said Miriam. 'You don't find that just a bit suspicious?'

'He has good reason to be on our side,' I said. 'But I don't trust him, of course. This is Vegas. As long as we can use him while he thinks he's using us . . .'

'What if his agenda gets in the way of our heist?' said Miriam.

'If he makes any trouble, I will throw him through a wall,' Lex said calmly.

'But he seems such a nice man, darling!' said Sally.

'You don't get to be Saul Montressor's best friend by being nice,' I said. I looked at Miriam. 'Are you ready for the meeting?'

'You hit him with the financials, and I will belabour him with charm,' said Miriam. 'He won't know what hit him. Have you decided on a name for the casino we're selling him?'

I looked at her. 'What?'

'He's bound to ask,' said Miriam.

'The Magnificat,' I said.

Miriam looked at me. 'Really? That's what you're going with?'

'This is Vegas,' I said. 'He'll probably think it's classy. Remember, the meeting is just a chance for us to spread rumours and disinformation. Especially about what his children are getting up to behind his back.'

'It's sad when you can't trust your own family,' said Sally, just a touch unexpectedly.

'What do we say when we meet the other Montressors?' said Miriam. 'Frank and Tony and Joyce?'

'We point out that if Saul is planning to use the Masque of Ra to make himself immortal,' I said patiently, 'they'll never get to inherit anything. It shouldn't be too difficult to set them at each other's throats. And then they'll be so busy fighting each other that they won't realize what we're really up to until it's too late.'

'Saul murdered your friends,' Miriam said carefully. 'Are you sure you can keep this on a business level, once you're face to face with the man?'

'Please,' I said. 'I am a professional.' I turned to Lex and Johnny. 'I'll have Bill set up a meeting for you with Double Down Dan and Soulful Sam about new protections for the Khuffu vault, so you can get a good look at it. Tony is head of security, but we need him concentrating on family matters.'

'I really don't think I'm the one who should be doing this,' said Lex. 'I don't have your experience when it comes to lying to people. I'm just muscle. Point me in the right direction and let me lay waste to the enemy.'

'I have complete faith in you, darling,' said Sally, kissing him resoundingly. 'So you should, too.'

'Exactly!' said Johnny. 'Which is why you and Lex should take this meeting and leave me out of it. I'm never good with people, because I keep thinking they might be something else. No . . . Keep me in reserve for emergencies. You know it makes sense.'

I nodded reluctantly. 'OK, Sally, you're up. But you're going to have to keep your head down, Johnny, and not do anything that might get you noticed. You know you don't find that easy.'

'I'll just stay in my room and watch television,' he said calmly.

'Are you feeling all right, Johnny?' said Miriam. 'Only this isn't like you. It's an improvement, but it isn't like you.'

'I've been much more grounded since I came back from the dead,' said Johnny.

Sally did a double-take and, interestingly, looked to me for confirmation rather than Lex. I nodded solemnly, and Sally moved to put Lex between her and Johnny. I wasn't entirely convinced by Johnny's new rational facade, but went along with it for the moment. I checked the clock by my bed.

'Time to get moving. Let's get this heist on the road.'

Sally put her hand in the air. 'Aren't you forgetting something, darling? This whole heist relies on my switching out the Masque of Ra for Harry's replica. And I haven't seen that since we were at your place. Where is it?'

I reached up my sleeve and pulled out a long golden cylinder that had been wrapped around my arm. I tapped it smartly and it sprang into shape as the Masque of Ra.

'It's wafer thin,' I said, 'but with the memory of the masque built in, so it will always return to its original shape. Harry designed it to be easily concealed.'

'How is it you know so much about the replica?' said Sally.

'Because he designed it for me, the first time I tried to steal the masque,' I said.

I slipped the replica back up my sleeve.

'You're taking it with you to the meeting?' Miriam said steadily. 'Is that wise?'

'Wiser than leaving it in a dump like this,' I said.

'We could always drop it off in a safe-deposit box,' said Sally.

'And draw attention to it?' I said. 'No, the replica will be perfectly safe with me.'

Miriam frowned. 'I still don't like how much Harry is involved with this heist. And not knowing why he's working with Judi.'

'No doubt all will become clear in time,' I said. 'For now, we concentrate on what's in front of us.'

'But what if Harry has sabotaged the replica?' said Miriam.

'Why would he want to?' I said.

'Why would he want to partner up with the infamous and very crazy Judi Rifkin?'

'Concentrate on the heist,' I said firmly. 'We'll deal with everything else when we come to it. Judi may be very rich, and Harry may be very weird, but neither of them understands the art of the con like we do.'

Miriam subsided reluctantly. I looked around at the crew.

'We have a plan. Everyone stick to their assigned roles and do their job, and we'll all get what we want out of this.'

'And if the plan goes wrong?' said Lex.

'Improvise,' I said. 'Miriam, pick up your money. And, Sally, lose the veil.'

Miriam and I returned to the Khuffu Casino, where once again Big Bill Buxton was waiting in the lobby to greet us, wearing an even more garish Hawaiian shirt that made him look even larger. He seemed fresh and at ease, as though he'd just had a good night's sleep somewhere comfortable. We all had to shake hands again.

'I need you to set up another meeting,' I said as soon as I got the chance. 'Between Double Down Dan and Soulful Sam, and Lex and Sally. They'll be here soon. You do remember them?'

'Your friends make a hell of an impression,' Bill said dryly. 'When do you need this meeting?'

'As soon as possible,' I said.

'Shouldn't be a problem,' said Bill. 'What's it all about? I have to tell Dan and Sam something.'

'Lex and Sally will be security consultants, here to discuss adding new safety measures to the Khuffu's vault,' I said. 'And you'd better tell Dan and Sam that Saul has approved this meeting, so they'll take it seriously.'

Bill shrugged. 'You know what you're doing . . . You do know what you're doing, don't you?'

'I have a plan,' I said.

'He always has a plan,' said Miriam.

'Really?' said Bill. 'Me, too!'

He led us across the main floor to the private elevators at the back of the room. But as we made our way through the rows of slot machines, Miriam became increasingly fascinated by the faces of the people working them. That terrible mixture of devotion and desperation. She stopped suddenly, and Bill and I had to stop with her.

'Please don't do anything that would attract attention,' I said quietly.

'They'll never know it was me,' said Miriam.

She seemed to stand a little taller as she raised her gift, and just like that, all the slot machines fell in love with her and hit the jackpot simultaneously. Bells rang out, celebrating the wins, and all the players screamed and howled with delight as jangling coins burst out of the slot machines in endless streams. Casino staff came running from all directions, followed by gamblers from all over the floor, keen to see what was happening. Bill stared wildly about him.

'This never happens!'

'Maybe it's a good omen,' I said.

Bill didn't seem convinced. He grabbed Miriam and me by the arms and hustled us through the excited crowd to the private elevators. He hit the button for the top floor and all but forced us inside. The doors closed slowly on the chaos filling the main floor. Bill shook his head and fixed me with a steady stare.

'I've got Saul all fired up to talk to you. Though, of course, he won't show it. Just remember, he is very keen to buy what you have to sell.'

I smiled and nodded and stood patiently as we travelled swiftly up to the top of the pyramid. I always feel most alive when I'm about to launch a new con – tap-dancing on the edge, following a plan but ready to wing it on the details. Trusting to my skills and expertise to get me through any difficulties. And, most of all, sticking it to the bad guys, one more time. Miriam caught the look on my face and sighed quietly.

The long elevator ride was followed by a long walk down an empty corridor. It was eerily quiet, with no names or titles on any of the closed doors. I couldn't see any surveillance cameras, but I made a point of strolling along as though I didn't have a care in the world. Miriam concentrated on looking businesslike. I kept a careful eye on Bill, but he seemed entirely relaxed about betraying his oldest friend.

Two large and surprisingly well-dressed security men were standing guard outside Saul's office. I didn't look for bulges under their jackets; I just assumed they were armed. Bill spoke to me out of the corner of his mouth as we drew nearer.

'Please don't try to be funny. These guys are famous for their complete lack of humour. So whatever they want, just go along.'

'Of course,' I said.

Bill nodded easily to the guards as we came to a halt in front of them, and they nodded back. One of them fixed me with a calm stare.

'We have to search you before we can let you in to see Mr Montressor. Standing orders.'

'What if we say no?' said Miriam.

'Then you don't get to see Mr Montressor,' said the other guard.

'It's all right, Miriam,' I said. 'We don't have anything to hide.'

'Then that makes you unique in Vegas,' said the first guard.

I looked at Bill. 'I thought you said they have no sense of humour?'

'He's new,' said Bill.

I was careful to hold both arms up high, so the guards wouldn't notice the gold cylinder up my sleeve. They patted me and Miriam down, thoroughly and professionally, and then the first guard opened the door and waved us through. Bill quickly pushed past us to take the lead.

The office was bigger than most hotel rooms I've stayed in, and it was filled with every comfort and luxury money could buy. Including a whole bunch of paintings that all but crowded each other off the walls. Given the clashing styles, I guessed they'd been chosen for their value.

Sitting behind a massive wooden desk, like an ogre in his cave, Saul looked exactly as I'd seen him in Harry's mirror. A large man in his late seventies, wearing an expensive suit in a careless way, he had a harsh face, a bald head, cold eyes and a mouth that looked as if it didn't believe in smiling. A man who'd spent his whole life learning how to be dangerous. He barely acknowledged Miriam and me, but nodded easily to Bill.

'Thanks for the tip,' he said. 'There'll be a little something extra in your pay packet at the end of the week. Buy yourself something nice.'

'No problem,' said Bill. He smiled easily at everyone and left without waiting to be dismissed.

'The only man in this place I can depend on,' said Saul. 'So when he says I should listen to you, I do.'

He looked at Miriam and me for a long moment and then gestured brusquely for us to sit down. I dropped on to the expensive chair as though I was completely at home with luxury, while Miriam still went with businesslike.

'So,' said Saul. 'You're from London. I had a bad experience the last time I was there.'

'So I've heard,' I said. 'But that was then and this is now. I am here to offer you what you couldn't buy last time.'

'Why do you want to sell your casino?' Saul said bluntly.

'I believe the term is "cash poor",' I said smoothly. 'And I owe rather a lot of money to some very unpleasant people. I am therefore ready to make a down-and-dirty deal, in return for a quick sale.'

'Who's she?' said Saul, not even glancing at Miriam.

'My business partner. She's good with the facts and figures.'

'What's your casino called?' said Saul.

'The Magnificat,' I said grandly.

'Have to change that,' said Saul. 'Why not sell to one of the other casino owners in London?'

'Because they want my place to fail,' I said. 'Less competition for them.'

Saul nodded slowly. 'If I do buy your place, am I going to have problems with the other casino operators?'

'Wouldn't surprise me,' I said. 'But you look like someone who can handle problems.'

Saul smiled for the first time, like a wolf baring its teeth at the prospect of a kill.

'I like handling problems.'

I remembered my dead friends but didn't let it touch my face. I was a professional.

'I want your casino,' said Saul. 'Let's talk details.'

I looked at him thoughtfully. 'Don't you need to run this past your children first?'

He stared at me. 'Why would I want to do that?'

'We were given to understand,' said Miriam, 'that you couldn't make any big financial decision without their approval.'

'And that they are currently investigating the possibility of taking legal responsibility for control of your finances,' I said. 'Because of your age.'

'They wouldn't dare . . .' said Saul. 'Who told you that?'

I shrugged. 'People are talking. You know how it is.'

'People are saying things,' said Miriam. 'We came to you first as a courtesy.'

'What are people saying?' Saul's voice was dangerously cold, and he leaned forward over his desk as though he was ready to shake the answers out of us.

'We did our research before we came to Vegas,' I said. 'And the word in the money markets is that your two sons are not at all happy with recent decisions you've made.'

'They are, understandably, concerned about their inheritance,' said Miriam.

'The last straw was your buying the Masque of Ra,' I said. 'If you make yourself immortal, they'll be left with nothing. Which is why they're working to seize control of your assets. They have also expressed an interest in buying my casino for themselves. In case their current plans don't work out.'

Saul sat back in his chair. I could see his mind racing.

'The Masque of Ra does have a reputation,' said Miriam.

'Many people are wondering why you haven't already used it,' I said.

'Unless some of the old stories are true,' said Miriam. 'That if you don't get the activating ritual exactly right, the masque will kill you. Horribly.'

'I have full control over all my financial dealings,' said Saul. 'And the masque is my business.'

'Of course,' I said. 'Why is why my partner and I are here, talking to you. We would much prefer to make a deal with a known quantity such as yourself, rather than take a risk on your sons. Though they do seem very keen to acquire my casino.'

Saul shot me a sudden look. 'Where would my boys get that kind of money?'

'They said that wouldn't be a problem,' said Miriam.

'Because the Khuffu's vault is always full of cash,' I said.

Saul brought one fist slamming down on his desk. The sound echoed through the room, filling it with the threat of barely repressed violence.

'Get out,' said Saul. 'I'll contact you when I'm ready to make an offer. Keep yourselves handy. And keep your mouths shut about all of this or I will have them closed permanently. Ask anyone in Vegas and they'll tell you Saul Montressor is a very bad man to cross.'

'So I've heard,' I said.

Outside in the corridor, Bill was leaning against the wall with his arms crossed. The moment we emerged, he hurried us off down the corridor until we were well out of the hearing of the guards.

'Well? How did it go?'

Miriam and I solemnly high-fived each other.

'Saul is thinking about it,' I said to Bill.

'He seemed very interested in what we had to say,' said Miriam.

Bill waited, but we just kept on walking, not looking at him.

'I'm taking you to meet Saul's oldest boy, Frank,' Bill said finally. 'He's very keen to see you.'

'I thought we couldn't see any of the family until this afternoon?' I said.

'Things move fast in Vegas,' said Bill.

We had to descend a couple of floors and walk down another long corridor to reach Frank Montressor. Again, there were guards at the door and a search to be endured before we were allowed to enter. Frank's office was smaller, but once again a lot of money had been spent on the fixtures and fittings. I got the feeling this was more because Frank felt the need to follow his father's example than because he had any style of his own.

Frank was in his mid-forties, large but soft, with a flushed face under flat black hair. Good clothes, but worn sloppily. He met us with a sour gaze and gestured sharply for Bill to leave. He did so without saying anything. Frank gave Miriam and me a hard look, to impress on us how important he was, but he didn't have his father's gift for menace. He waved impatiently for us to sit down.

'What have you been talking to Daddy about?'

'Not the Masque of Ra,' I said. 'Though that's what everyone else is talking about.'

'Because it really can do everything they say it can,' said Miriam.

Frank seemed genuinely taken aback. 'That old thing? I thought . . .'

'All your father has to do is locate the right ritual,' I said, 'and he will become young and strong again, and live for ever.'

'But that's not fair!' said Frank.

'Even after all your hard work,' said Miriam, 'the Khuffu will never be yours.'

'It's only a matter of time before your father decides he doesn't need you any more,' I said.

'Bill told me you're here to sell Daddy a casino in London,' said Frank, dragging us back to more familiar ground.

'Your father is looking for somewhere to go if the Khuffu keeps losing money,' I said. 'He's ready to disappear from Vegas and start a new life in London, and leave you and your brother and sister holding the can. Which is probably why Tony and Joyce reached out to us to buy our casino – so they'll have something for themselves.'

'Apparently, they don't trust you,' said Miriam. 'On a business or a personal level. They think you'll either screw up the deal or panic and go running to your father.'

'I'm the one who keeps this casino going!' said Frank. 'With no help from Tony or Joyce!'

'We are ready to make a deal with anyone,' I said. 'If you can get the money together, you could have your very own casino, without the Khuffu's debts. And be free of your father for ever.'

'What debts?' said Frank.

'People are talking,' said Miriam.

'About the things your father isn't telling you,' I said.

'Your brother and sister want to push you out of the way,' said Miriam.

'They do?' said Frank, struggling to keep up with all the rapid changes in direction.

'If I were you, I'd do some digging into what's really going on,' I said.

'You must know you can't trust anyone here,' said Miriam.

'If you do decide you want to make a deal with us, and get away from your family,' I said, 'just talk to Bill. He'll set it up.'

Frank looked at me. 'He's your inside man? But he's Daddy's oldest friend!'

'This is business,' I said.

'And it's amazing what a man will do,' said Miriam, 'for the right percentage.'

'I never thought he was funny,' said Frank. He scowled, thinking hard. 'You don't make a deal with anyone until I've got to the bottom of what's going on. You even try, and I'll have you dealt with. Now, get out of my office.'

'Don't leave it too long,' I said, as I got to my feet.

'Things are happening,' said Miriam, getting to hers.

The moment the door closed behind us, Bill was waiting to lead us away from the guards. This time he didn't say anything until we'd walked all the way back to the elevator.

'Frank has twice as much hidden surveillance as his father,' said Bill. 'So? How did it go?'

'Things are moving,' I said.

'But are you getting anywhere?'

'By the time we're through here, no one will trust anyone,' said Miriam.

Bill grinned. 'No change there. You're just forcing things to the surface.'

'They're all going to come to you at some point,' I said. 'Looking for answers. Remember: you don't know anything.'

Bill shot me a sideways smile. 'Kid, I was doing this dance before you were born. I know all the moves. OK, Tony is waiting to see you now. Be careful with him; he's smarter than Frank. And a lot tougher.'

We went down several floors and then along a somewhat shorter corridor to another set of guards and another search. I was starting to think I should have put something interesting in my pockets, just to entertain them. Bill didn't even try to come in with us.

Tony's office had the look of a place where work got done. He was in his late thirties, tall and fashionably slender, well dressed in a casual sort of way, dark-haired and dark-eyed. He sat behind his desk as though he was using it as a barrier against the world. He hardly gave Miriam and me time to sit down before he went on the attack.

'I'm in charge of security at the Khuffu. You don't make any kind of deal with my father unless you go through me first.'

'Are you interested in buying our casino?' I said politely. 'Like your father, and your brother and sister?'

Tony scowled. 'Frank and Joyce are interested?'

'They're putting their own deal together,' said Miriam. 'But we'll go with whoever makes the best offer.'

'Why would I want to buy a casino in London?' said Tony. 'I'm only working here for something to do.'

'If you owned a casino, you'd never have to worry about job security again,' I said.

'And if your brother and sister make the deal, and push your father and you to one side,' said Miriam, 'where would that leave you?'

'In such a situation, making your own deal could be seen as self-defence,' I said.

'And you know what your father is capable of,' said Miriam.

Tony looked at her sharply. 'What do you know about my mother?'

'People are saying things,' I said carefully.

'About how she died?' said Tony.

'There are questions,' said Miriam.

'What has that got to do with everyone being interested in your casino?' said Tony.

'Don't you think you should be asking your family that?' I said. 'What do they know that you don't?'

'That you ought to know,' said Miriam.

'What are they keeping from you?' I said.

'That's enough!' Tony thought hard for a moment and then glared at us. 'I don't give a damn about your casino, but I do want to know what's going on. In the meantime, you keep your mouths shut, or I'll have you dragged out into the desert and left there with your legs broken. Now, get out of my sight.'

This time, Bill made sure we were in the elevator and moving before he said anything.

'Tony is the clever one,' he said. 'Because he at least tried to make a life outside Vegas.'

'What about Joyce?' I said.

'She's the weak link in the family,' said Bill. 'But she's still a Montressor, so don't drop your guard.'

*   *   *

We had to go down quite a few flights and then follow Bill through a crowded corridor to reach a door with no guards. Bill stayed well back as we knocked and went in. Joyce's office wasn't much bigger than Adelaide's dressing room. Just a desk and a few chairs, and a big poster of Adelaide on one wall. All the time we were talking, Joyce would glance at her whenever she felt the need for emotional support.

She scowled at me. 'I remember you from the dressing room. People think I don't notice things, but I do. Bill says you can get me away from my family, so Adelaide and I can be together.'

'We have a casino to sell,' I said. 'But do you have the wherewithal to make an offer?'

'Your brothers seem sure you haven't,' said Miriam. 'That's why they're putting their own deal together and leaving you out of it. And outbidding your father, of course.'

'They think he won't be able to touch them, once they're in London,' I said.

'They'd go off and leave me here?' said Joyce. 'What else did they say?'

'They seemed to think there was something out of the ordinary about how your mother died,' I said.

Joyce looked at me. 'She died in a car accident.'

'That's not what everyone else is saying,' said Miriam.

'What are they saying?' said Joyce.

'I think you should find that out for yourself,' I said. 'Don't you?'

Joyce wasn't looking at us any more. Her gaze had turned inwards. 'He killed her. I've always known that. She was the best of us, and Daddy had her killed because she embarrassed him. And if he'd kill her, he'd kill me. Because of Adelaide.'

She sat still for a long moment. Thinking her own thoughts. I decided she needed a push.

'And then there's the Masque of Ra.'

She looked at me sharply. 'Could it really make Daddy live for ever?'

'A lot of people seem to think so,' I said.

'People who know about these things,' said Miriam.

'And if your father does become immortal,' I said, 'where would that leave you?'

'I have to get away,' said Joyce. 'But I don't have access to the kind of money it would take to buy a casino.'

'Neither do your brothers,' I said. 'But they did mention that there's always a lot of cash in the Khuffu's vault. Just waiting to be picked up.'

'They'd steal from the vault?' said Joyce. 'From Daddy?'

'You think they wouldn't dare?' said Miriam.

Joyce's eyes darted back and forth around the office before returning to the poster of Adelaide on the wall. That seemed to give her enough strength to glare at me and Miriam.

'You keep your mouths shut about all of this until I've talked to Adelaide. You do anything to threaten us and I'll send the Enchanted Enforcer after you! And you'll never be seen again!'

'We just want to make a deal,' I said. 'We don't care who with.'

But Joyce wasn't listening to us any more, so Miriam and I let ourselves out.

Bill raised an eyebrow as we left Joyce's office.

'That was quick.'

'Four meetings,' I said. 'And four death threats.'

'That's the Montressors for you,' Bill said cheerfully. 'Old-school Vegas.'

'Thanks for your help,' I said as we headed back to the elevator.

'Happy to do it,' said Bill. 'I've arranged a meeting between Dan and Sam and your people.'

'You'll find Lex and Sally on the main floor,' I said.

Bill looked at me thoughtfully. 'The big man made a lot of money at roulette last night.'

'So we heard,' said Miriam.

'The pit boss is still trying to figure out how he did it,' said Bill. 'They've taken that wheel apart twice, looking for answers. Is he naturally lucky?'

'I wouldn't have said so,' I said. 'Now, I could use a drink. How about you, Miriam?'

'I could use several drinks,' she said.

Bill escorted us all the way down to the main floor and led us through the crowd to the bar. He nodded familiarly to the bartender, who nodded back.

'Saul says drinks on the house for these two and their friends,' said Bill. He smiled easily at us. 'I'd better go find Lex and Sally, before they win even more of our money.'

And off he went. The bartender looked at us expressionlessly.

'Since the drinks are free,' I said, 'what have you got that's really expensive?'

'Might I suggest the Napoleon brandy?' said the bartender. 'It's from Mr Montressor's private stock.'

'I'm sure he won't mind,' I said.

'So give us a bottle and two glasses,' said Miriam.

'And when you've done that, go stand at the other end of the bar,' I said.

He just nodded, as though he was used to getting such instructions. He produced the brandy and the glasses, opened the bottle with a flourish and then moved unhurriedly away to give us some privacy. Miriam and I toasted each other. It was very good brandy.

'I thought the meetings went as well as could be expected,' I said finally.

'They did most of the work themselves,' said Miriam. 'All we had to do was nudge them in the right directions.'

'It's always easiest to make people believe what they want to believe,' I said.

Miriam shook her head. 'There's a real barrel of worms at the bottom of that family. Do you believe Saul had his wife killed?'

'His children seem to think so,' I said. 'But they didn't do anything about it. Not while there was still money to be made out of being a Montressor. And they were all ready to order us killed, just to keep us from talking. I told you they were bad guys.'

'I wonder what they're doing right now?' said Miriam in a meaningful sort of way.

I took the crystal eye out of my pocket, but no matter which Montressor I tried, the eye didn't show me anything.

'The family must have serious protections in place,' I said finally.

'Isn't there anyone you can see?' said Miriam.

I thought about it. 'Lex is usually resistant to security measures, because the halos protect him from outside influences. I wonder . . .'

* * *

The eye showed me a vision of Lex and Sally meeting with one of the Double Down Dans and Soulful Sam in a gloomy little back office. The kind of place where security would take troublemakers to throw a scare into them. Dan sat behind the desk, with Sam standing beside him. Lex and Sally stood facing them, with Lex appearing more than usually tall and impressive, while Sally concentrated on looking cute and decorous. Bill stuck around just long enough to make the introductions and remind Dan and Sam that Saul had approved this meeting, and then he left.

Lex and Sam glared at each other. Sam looked away first. Dan seemed shocked by that, though he did his best to hide it. Sally decided she'd better get the ball rolling.

'We're here to discuss new security updates for the Khuffu's vault,' she said brightly. 'And we have so much to offer you.'

'We don't need any updates,' said Dan. 'Our security is state of the art.'

'Then why is there a rumour going round that someone is planning an attack on your vault in the near future?' said Lex.

Dan sat up straight and exchanged a startled look with Sam.

'We haven't heard anything,' said Sam.

'We have,' said Sally. 'That's why we're here. And why you need what we have to offer.'

'Our vault is impregnable,' said Dan.

'That's what everyone thinks,' said Sally. 'Until someone comes along and suddenly proves it isn't.'

'What rumours are we talking about?' said Sam. 'Who is supposed to be planning this attack?'

'It's just gossip,' Sally said airily. 'You know how it is in the security game. People talk about all kinds of things.'

Dan rose to his feet. 'Come with us and take a look at the vault. See for yourselves how well protected it is.'

Sam looked at him sharply. 'You really think that's a good idea?'

'Mr Montressor must have heard the gossip,' said Dan, just as sharply. 'That's why he wanted us to have this meeting. We show these two what we've got, so they can tell everyone else how strong our defences are.' He smiled coldly at Lex and Sally. 'The best protection is a good reputation.'

* * *

I lowered the crystal eye and filled Miriam in on what had happened.

'Everything seems to be going according to plan,' she said.

'Lex missed a lot of cues,' I said. 'But Sally jumped right in. Good thing we didn't send Johnny.'

Miriam nodded slowly. 'This new reasonable attitude certainly isn't like him.'

'Dying and coming back changed him,' I said. 'And then, on top of that, Lex marries Sally! I really didn't see that one coming.'

'I think it's very sweet,' Miriam said firmly. 'Lex needs someone in his life.'

'Not a predator like Sally,' I said, just as firmly. 'She's up to something. I know her of old.'

Miriam looked at me for a long moment. 'You don't talk much about that part of your life.'

'Because I'm trying to forget most of it,' I said.

'Why did you team up with someone like Sally in the first place?'

'Her gift,' I said. 'I thought I could use it. But all the time she was using me. Just like she'll use Lex.'

'To do what?' said Miriam, frowning.

'To screw us over,' I said. 'It's what she does. She's planning something, and she thinks she's going to need Lex to protect her afterwards. I thought I could keep a lid on her, but I should have known better . . .'

'Lex needs a human relationship,' said Miriam. 'To bring him back to humanity. Johnny can't help with that, and we can't be there for Lex all the time.'

'He doesn't need someone like Sally,' I said. I raised the crystal eye again. 'They should have had time to get down to the vault by now.'

This time Lex and Sally were standing in a gleaming steel tunnel, facing the door to the Khuffu's vault. It was a large steel circle, which looked solid enough to shake off a direct hit by a pocket nuke. Dan and Sam were showing it off, while Lex and Sally did their best to appear unimpressed.

'That door weighs over four tons,' Dan said proudly. 'It has physical and electronic locks, and the tunnel you just walked through is lined with every form of surveillance you can think of – motion trackers, pressure sensors in the floor – and really nasty concealed weapons systems. There is no way an intruder could get this far, but even if they did, that door is impregnable.'

'But still,' said Lex. 'There are rumours . . .'

'What upgrades could you possibly provide?' said Dan.

'The next generation of smart-tech security,' Sally said smoothly. 'We are right at the forefront of what's happening, and you could be, too.'

Sam was studying Lex suspiciously, as though he was trying to remember something.

'We can provide you with all the latest tricks of the trade,' Sally said quickly. 'At a very reasonable discount, in return for being allowed to say that the Khuffu is using them. I think such a relationship could prove very beneficial to both sides.'

'We'll have to talk to Mr Montressor,' said Dan.

'You do that,' said Sally. She grabbed Lex by the arm, turned him around and hurried him back down the steel tunnel. She glanced back over her shoulder. 'We'll be back.'

Not long afterwards, Lex and Sally came striding out of the crowd to join us at the bar. Sally dropped on to a bar stool with an exaggerated sigh of relief, while Lex stood protectively behind her. I told them what I'd seen in my vision, and they seemed relieved at not having to make a detailed report after all.

'Ask the bartender for anything,' I said. 'Drinks are on the house.'

Sally squealed delightedly and clapped her hands together. 'Then let's have lots, darlings!'

The bartender returned from his exile at the other end of the bar without having to be summoned. Sally fixed him with a smouldering gaze, but Lex cut in first.

'If you're about to order one of those cute cocktails with amusingly pornographic names, this marriage is over.'

'But have you ever tried one, darling?' said Sally. 'You'd probably like them if they had big, butch, masculine names, like Top Gear or World Cup Fever.'

Lex considered the point and then nodded to the bartender. 'Set out one of everything, from A to Z, and we'll work our way through. Don't tell me what they are.'

The bartender set about mixing drinks. I shook my head.

'Please remember, we still have work to do.'

'Killjoy,' said Sally. 'I can remember when you used to be fun, darling.'

'I knew the bride when she used to rock and roll,' said Lex, just a bit unexpectedly. He looked at me steadily. 'What comes next in your great and complicated plan?'

'We give everyone time to think and brood,' I said. 'And make themselves even more paranoid. And then you make your attack on the vault.' I stopped and looked at Sally. 'I'm going to need you on hand to switch out the masque, and since Johnny's not involved any more, you're going to have to hit the vault on your own, Lex.'

'I am perfectly fine with that,' Sally said quickly. 'I'd hate to break a nail on that door, darlings.'

'I can open it,' said Lex. 'They only think it's protected because they've never seen my armour. Have you been able to see inside the vault yet?'

'No,' I said. 'I was only able to see the exterior because you were there. But don't get distracted, Lex. The masque is what it's all about.'

'Aren't you curious about what Saul might have squirrelled away?' said Sally.

'He's had a long time to think about protecting his treasures,' I said. 'There are bound to be surprises.'

'I can handle anything he's got,' said Lex.

'Of course you can, darling,' said Sally. She sipped the first of the cocktails, made happy sounds and knocked it back. Lex picked up the next glass, tried it and put it down again.

'I'd be happier if Johnny was doing this with you,' I said. 'He can cope with the unexpected, because that's his territory.'

'I don't think he's in any shape to be useful,' said Lex.

'We're going to have to do something about him,' said Miriam.

'After the heist,' said Lex.

'And after the honeymoon, darling,' Sally said reproachfully.

One of the Double Down Dans came striding out of the crowd towards us. He looked as if he'd uncovered something we'd been hiding, and couldn't wait to confront us with it. He crashed to a halt and smiled nastily, but I got in first.

'So,' I said lightly. 'Which of the three Tripani brothers are you?'

Dan stood very still, whatever he planned to say blown out of the water.

'I know your secret,' I said. 'Identical triplets, with no weird situational magic involved. I wonder what Saul would say if he found out he'd been paying top dollar for a simple con? But . . . no one else needs to know.'

'How did you find out?' said Dan.

'Someone always talks,' I said.

'What do you want?' said Dan.

'Lex will be the one breaking into your vault, late tomorrow afternoon,' I said. 'All you have to do is make sure security's attention is diverted somewhere else. In return, your secret is safe.'

He didn't argue. 'Deal.'

He turned and walked away, quickly disappearing back into the crowd.

'He was lying,' said Lex.

'Of course he was,' I said. 'He was just buying himself time to think. But it doesn't matter, because you'll be hitting the vault in the morning.'

'Quick thinking,' said Miriam.

'I thought so,' I said.

Some time later, the four of us walked out of the casino. Miriam and I had had enough brandy, and Lex and Sally had got bored with cocktails. Apparently, after the first dozen they all started to taste the same. We made it as far as the lobby before a loud voice called for us to stop. We turned and looked back to see Soulful Sam coming after us. There was enough anger burning in him to put actual touches of colour in his face, and his eyes blazed as he fixed his gaze on Lex. The huge figure finally slammed to a halt facing us, and he took a moment to get his breath before glaring into Lex's face.

'You might have shut Dan down, but I'm made of harder stuff,' he said. 'I finally remembered a report I saw on you, back when I was still with the Church. You're Lex Talon, the Damned!'

The guards in the lobby just stared at him blankly. Lex looked thoughtfully at Sam.

'I only kill people who need killing. The worst of the worst. You haven't made the list yet. Don't push your luck.'

'I can feel the guilt in you,' said Sam. 'So much guilt!'

'But it's mine,' said Lex. 'And you can't have it.'

Sam looked at the guards. 'Get out of here.'

None of them argued. They all but ran out of the lobby and into the main room. Because they didn't want to be anywhere near Soulful Sam when he raised his power. Lex nodded to Sam.

'Let's see what you've got.'

Sam's power suddenly filled the lobby. We could all feel its presence, beating like the wings of some giant bird. And I could tell the power wasn't coming from Sam. It was something using Sam. Sally fell back, leaving Lex to stand alone. Miriam moved in close beside me.

The halos at Lex's wrists suddenly blazed with light and darkness, meeting Sam's power with a greater force. The Damned was armoured by Heaven and Hell, and in the face of that, Sam's power rebounded and hit him with his own guilt. He started to say something, and his hands leaped up and tore out his throat. He stared at us with agonized eyes as blood spurted on the air, and then his legs gave out and he was dead before he hit the ground.

The halos shut themselves down, and Lex looked at the dead man.

'I wonder what he wanted to say?'

I thought about searching Sam, to see if he had the reliquary on him, but the body suddenly and silently vanished away. I looked quickly at the others, but they seemed just as startled as me.

Lex frowned. 'Johnny? Is that you?'

There was no answer.

'What are we going to do now?' said Miriam. 'He identified Lex as the Damned, in front of all those guards!'

'The name didn't mean anything to them,' I said. 'And by the time the Montressors have dug out the details, it will be too late.' I looked at Lex. 'Get yourself ready; you're going straight to the vault. The heist is on.'

ELEVEN

Everyone Gets What They Deserve

'Change of plan, people,' I said. 'Given the sheer amount of hidden technology and weapons systems guarding the way to the vault . . . Miriam, you'd better go with Lex. Charm everything and shut it all down.'

'That makes sense,' said Miriam. 'What are you going to be doing?'

'I have to be in the lobby with Sally while she switches out the masque.'

'Give me the replica, darling, and I can do it on my own,' said Sally.

'You can,' I said, 'but you're not going to.'

'You don't trust me!' said Sally.

'Of course not,' I said. 'I know you.' I turned to Lex. 'The original plan was just to get yourself noticed, as a distraction while we lift the masque, but given how well the vault is guarded, I think we need to know what Saul has hidden away in there. Are you sure you can break in?'

'I am armoured by Heaven and Hell,' he said calmly. 'There is nothing in this world that can stand against me.'

'Don't take too long inside the vault,' I said. 'We're here for the masque; anything else is just a bonus.'

Lex smiled. 'You'd be surprised at how much I can carry when I'm properly motivated.'

Sally hit him with her most dazzling smile. 'Bring me back something special, darling. And by special, I mean really expensive.'

I gave Lex my best hard look. 'Whatever happens, protect Miriam.'

'Always,' said Lex.

I led my crew back on to the main floor of the casino, where the usual crowds of people were throwing themselves into temptation's way, desperate to lose their money as quickly as possible. There were particularly long queues to try the slot machines. News of the big wins must have got around. I looked at Miriam.

'Are the surveillance systems still eager to please you?'

She grinned. 'They love me!'

'That's just weird,' said Sally.

'Some of us are more loveable than others,' said Miriam.

'Are the slot machines still charmed?' I said.

Miriam's smile broadened. 'When I charm something, they stay charmed.'

'How does that even work?' said Sally.

'Basically, it's a love charm that went wrong,' said Miriam.

Sally sniffed. 'I've never needed a spell to make anyone fall in love with me.'

'No,' I said, 'just a natural talent for double-dealing and back-stabbing.'

Lex moved in behind me and dropped a heavy hand on my shoulder. 'Let's agree to disagree on this, shall we?'

'Works for me,' I said.

He took his hand off my shoulder, and I stood up a little straighter. I nodded to Miriam.

'Set off all the slots again, and then shut down the cameras covering the main floor. That way, all the security guards will have to come here in person to find out what's going on.'

'Got it,' said Miriam. 'Let there be fireworks.'

And once again all the slot machines lost their collective minds. There was bedlam in the ranks as every machine paid off big time. Men and women jumped up and down, screaming and shouting, as waterfalls of coins emptied out of the machines. Bells rang out all across the main floor in what should have been a celebration but now sounded more like an alarm, and security men came running from all directions.

One of them shouted for all the slot machines to be shut down and overhauled. Another shouted for all the winners to be stopped from leaving until they'd been searched for electronic helpers. The gamblers clutched their prize money to their chests and defied the guards to take away their rightful winnings. Some of the guards looked ready to try. More and more people deserted the gambling tables to see what was happening and cheer on the lucky winners. It wasn't often they got to see the casino take a beating.

In all the excitement, no one noticed as I led Lex, Miriam and Sally through the crowd to the private elevator at the back of the room. Miriam quickly charmed its controls and persuaded the elevator to take her and Lex down to the vault area. I tapped my watch meaningfully as the doors closed, and Miriam gave me her best *I know what I'm doing* look.

'Back to the lobby?' said Sally.

'Not just yet,' I said.

I took her over to the bar, and we settled ourselves on the old-fashioned bar stools again.

'We can't make our move until Lex and Miriam have got to the vault and attracted security's attention,' I said quietly. 'Then we can switch out the Masque of Ra entirely unobserved and leave the replica in its place – and no one will know anything has happened. It's not just about stealing the masque; it's about getting away with it.'

'Spare me the lecture, darling' Sally said coldly. 'I have done this sort of thing before.'

The bartender came over and looked at us impassively. Sally opened her mouth, but I got in first.

'Two sparkling waters,' I said firmly. 'We need to keep our heads clear.'

'Oh, poo,' said Sally.

The bartender set two tall glasses of sparkling water in front of us and then drifted off to the other end of the bar without having to be told.

'What excellent service,' I said. 'If he keeps this up, I might have to consider leaving him a tip.'

Sally gave me a hard look. 'I am really not happy about Lex taking on the vault without me.'

'He has his armour,' I said. 'And Miriam's gift. Which means they're probably safer than we are. But I will keep an eye on them.'

I took the crystal eye out of my pocket and it showed me a vision.

Lex was striding along a gleaming steel corridor, while Miriam hurried along behind him, charming and shutting down one set of surveillance systems after another. Distorted reflections in the steel walls moved along with them like silent ghosts.

'Cameras, microphones, motion trackers, pressure sensors in the floor,' she muttered. 'Now the weapon systems . . . Lex. Hold it.'

He stopped immediately. 'What's wrong?'

'There's enough heavy-duty weaponry hidden behind these walls to stop an invading army,' said Miriam. 'Whatever Saul has locked away in this vault, he's gone to a great deal of trouble to make sure no one could get to it.'

'Should I put on my armour?' Lex said quietly.

'That might be a good idea,' said Miriam. 'Some of these systems are being very stubborn.'

The light and dark armour embraced Lex in a moment, and the steel floor creaked in protest as it suddenly had to support something so heavy that its presence alone was enough to change the course of the world. After a while, Miriam nodded slowly.

'I think that's everything. But we'd better get a move on. I'm not sure how long some of these systems will stay charmed.'

The Damned strode off down the corridor, and the steel floor rang loudly with every step. Miriam followed on behind, keeping her distance. She didn't like to look at the armour directly. They finally rounded the last corner, and there was the door to the vault. Standing in front of it were all three Double Down Dans with guns in their hands, all of them aimed at the Damned. He came to a halt, and Miriam ducked in behind him. The Dans winced at their first sight of the armour, but, interestingly, they didn't look away. Perhaps they shared the burden between the three of them.

'I saw what you did to Sam,' said the first Dan. 'And I heard that you were coming down here.'

'So we got here first,' said the middle Dan. 'If we stop you, that proves our loyalty to Saul Montressor, and then he won't care about our little deception.'

'And we need to avenge Sam,' said the third Dan. 'We didn't like him much – nobody did, including him – but he was our colleague. And when someone kills your colleague, you're supposed to do something about it.'

'Do you really think you can stop me, in my armour?' said

the Damned. The voice from behind his blank armoured face was disturbingly cold.

The Dans flinched at the sound of it but still held their ground, denying him access to the vault.

'We might not be able to keep you out,' said the first Dan. 'But we brought someone with us who can.'

And from out of a shadow that no one had noticed before stepped the tall and elegant figure of the Enchanted Enforcer. She was wearing her tuxedo and the white silk mask that covered her entire face. It had no eyeholes, just a pair of painted eyes in deepest black. The Damned turned his armoured face to her, and she didn't flinch at all.

'I am the Damned.'

'I know,' said the Enchanted Enforcer.

'And you think you can stop me?'

'It might be fun to try, some time,' said the Enchanted Enforcer. 'But that's not why I'm here.'

She turned to look at the three Double Down Dans, and one by one they blinked out of existence. None of them had time to say anything, and they didn't even leave a ripple on the air to mark their passing. Miriam moved in close behind the Damned, so she could peer over his shoulder.

'No wonder no one ever found a body,' she said. 'But the Evil Eye isn't supposed to work like that, is it?'

'It works for me,' said the Enchanted Enforcer.

And then she took off her white silk mask, crumpled it up and stuffed it into a pocket. Adelaide nodded easily to Miriam and the Damned.

'Joyce and I have been talking. We're going to need serious money if we're to get away from Saul, and it seems only fitting that he should provide it. Can you really open this door?'

'Couldn't you just make it disappear, like you did the Dans?' said Miriam.

'The Evil Eye only works on people,' said Adelaide.

The Damned looked at Miriam. 'Are there any defences left?'

Miriam studied the massive steel door. 'I've persuaded the electronic systems to open, but I can't do anything about the mechanical locks. They're too simple to qualify as machines. They can't hear me.'

'Then stand back and let me work,' said the Damned.

He strode forward and plunged his armoured hands deep into the solid steel of the door, forcing them in up to the wrist. The metal made deep groaning sounds, as though it was wounded. The Damned took a firm hold on the steel, braced himself and pulled hard. There was a terrible squealing of rending metal as lock mechanisms broke and shattered, and then the door swung slowly open. The Damned wrenched his hands out of the steel and pushed the door back against the tunnel wall. Automatic lights flickered on, illuminating the vault interior. Lex put off his armour and walked in, followed quickly by Miriam and Adelaide.

I had to lower the crystal eye at that point, because Saul Montressor was saying my name, and not in a good way. I slipped the eye back into my pocket and got up to face him. Sally scrambled down off her bar stool to stand beside me. Saul ignored her, his cold gaze fixed on me.

'Gideon Sable, master thief. I thought you'd be older.'

'I used to be,' I said.

'Did you really think I wouldn't have you checked out?' said Saul.

'I was hoping Bill's recommendation would be enough,' I said.

Saul looked at me contemptuously. 'There's a limit to how much I trust anyone. I have access to data bases on all you weird types who operate in the shadows. How do you think I found my supernatural people?

'I also keep a very close eye on everyone who wants to do me harm, including Judi Rifkin. She never was very tightly wrapped, even when she was married to Hammer, and she's been trying to stab me in the back for ages. If you were here, I knew she had to be involved . . . So I made a few enquiries, offered a little financial inducement . . . and one of Judi's own people told me she'd hired you to steal the Masque of Ra.'

'Shouldn't you have brought some security guards with you?' I said.

He showed me his cold smile. 'I don't need any help to deal with cheap punks like you.'

'You should never make it personal,' I said. 'It's important to be professional about these things. Soulful Sam let it get personal, and the Damned killed him.'

Saul frowned suddenly. 'Sam is dead? Wait . . . Where is the Damned?'

'Lex is keeping busy,' I said calmly. 'But, Saul . . . I know you came here to threaten me and Sally, but I feel I should point out that you have your own problems. Standing right behind you.'

He must have seen something in my face because he turned immediately to look. And there were Frank, Tony and Joyce, standing together and glaring at him. He glared right back.

'What are you doing here? Get back to work!'

'We thought the masque was just another toy for you to collect and show off,' said Frank. 'But it's the real thing, isn't it?'

'And if it can make you immortal,' said Joyce, 'what happens to us?'

'We made the Khuffu turn a profit in spite of you and all your old-fashioned ideas,' said Tony.

'I made the books balance,' said Frank.

'I made the casino secure,' said Tony.

'And I did everything you wanted me to,' said Joyce. 'I even kept my love secret, so as not to embarrass you.'

'And now you're planning to rob us of our inheritance?' said Tony.

Saul raked them all with his cold gaze, and they stopped talking.

'The casino is mine,' said Saul. 'And it'll stay mine.'

'Can I just ask something?' I said politely, and all their eyes turned sharply to me. 'You've had the masque all this time, Saul; why haven't you used it? Is it because you tried every ritual you could find, and none of them worked? That, in fact . . . you haven't found any way to make it do what it's supposed to do?'

Frank frowned and looked at Tony. 'Is he saying that the masque can't make Daddy immortal?'

Tony laughed at his father. 'All that money for a worthless piece of junk!'

'So our inheritance is safe, after all?' said Joyce.

'You'll get what I choose to give you,' said Saul. 'And only then if you've proved yourself worthy.'

'I knew you'd find some excuse to cheat us,' said Joyce. 'You don't care about any of us. You didn't even care about Mother!'

'I cared for her,' said Saul.

'You killed her!' said Joyce. She glared at her brothers. 'We should have done something.'

'There was no evidence,' said Tony.

'But we knew,' said Frank. 'And we all went on working for him anyway. Because we had nowhere else to go.'

'Speak for yourself,' said Tony. 'I could go anywhere.'

'But you didn't,' said Joyce.

Frank stared at Saul. 'I did everything you wanted. Tony ran away from home, while I stayed and worked my ass off for you. But when he screwed up his life and came crawling back, you gave him the best job in the casino and left me to do the shit work. Nothing I ever did was good enough for you! Now you're saying that even without the masque, you're still not going to leave me anything?'

'Stop whining, Frank,' said Saul. 'You never did have any backbone. The world isn't supposed to give you anything; you're supposed to take it for yourself, like I did.'

'You killed Mother!' said Joyce.

'Of course I didn't!' said Saul.

'I have someone here who would say otherwise,' said Johnny Wilde.

We all looked round, and there was the Wild Card, smiling easily. Standing beside him was a glamorous mature woman I'd never seen before, but I knew at once who she was. Who she had to be. Joyce took a step forward.

'Mother?'

Even as the Montressor family stared at Dana Montressor, returned from the grave, I suddenly realized that the crystal eye had sneaked out of my pocket and insinuated itself into my hand. The eye jumped up, carrying my hand with it, and forced itself in front of my face, insisting I needed to see something.

Lex, Miriam and Adelaide were standing inside Saul's vault. A massive steel-lined chamber that held none of the things we'd been expecting. No tables groaning under great piles of cash, no gold bullion or precious gems. No rare collector's items or works of art . . . Just a handful of open-topped packing crates. Lex moved slowly from crate to crate, peering at the contents and shaking his head.

'Where is everything?' said Adelaide. 'This was supposed to be Saul's treasure house.'

'I think this is all there is,' said Miriam. 'No wonder he didn't want anyone to get in and find out.'

'So there's no money?' said Adelaide.

'There is something,' said Lex. He gestured at the packing crate before him. 'There's a body.'

The crystal eye relaxed its hold on me, and I was able to lower my hand from my face. I glared at the eye.

'Once this is over, you and I are going to have a very intense discussion over which of us is in charge here.'

The eye had nothing to say, so I put it away and looked at the Montressors. They were still staring at the returned Dana, their faces full of all kinds of emotion. Johnny looked at Dana and smiled proudly.

'Isn't she amazing? My greatest triumph.'

As far as I knew, the Wild Card had never brought anyone else back from the dead. Perhaps after he brought himself back, it took him a while to figure out how it worked. But why would he start with Dana Montressor? And why bring her here? Well, when in doubt, ask.

I cleared my throat loudly, and Saul and his children turned quickly to glare at me, glad of an excuse to look away from the ghost at the feast: the woman who wasn't dead any more. I smiled easily at Saul.

'Can I just ask: what happened to all the money in your vault? Only my people are standing in it right now, and they're saying the cupboard is bare.'

Frank, Tony and Joyce forgot all about their returned mother and rounded on Saul.

'You used up all our money?' said Frank. 'When were you going to tell us?'

'It was none of your business,' said Saul.

'I have been working my ass off to keep the money coming in,' said Frank. 'So where has it all gone?'

Saul met his gaze unflinchingly. 'The masque cost me more than I expected. I'm still having to make payments. To the kind of people even I have to be wary of.'

'You threw all our money away on that stupid piece of junk?' said Tony.

'It wasn't your money!' said Saul.

'If there's no money,' said Joyce, 'how am I ever going to get away from you?'

And then Dana stepped forward and everyone turned to look at her. She moved stiffly, as though she hadn't needed to in a long time.

'You had me killed, Saul,' she said flatly. 'Was I really so much of an embarrassment that you could just throw me away after all our years together?'

Saul stared at her. Dana looked at Frank and Tony and Joyce.

'My poor children. Left alone in the ogre's clutches, with no one to defend you. What has he done to you? These aren't the lives I meant for my children.'

Frank and Tony didn't know what to say to her. In the end, Joyce was the only one who found the strength to speak.

'You can't stay, Mother. He'll only kill you again.'

'I never killed your mother!' It was the first time Saul had raised his voice, and it brought everyone's attention back to him. He glared defiantly at Dana. 'It isn't you. It can't be you.'

'I brought her here, just so she could come and talk to you,' said Johnny. 'Because I'm the Wild Card and I can do things like that.'

Dana ignored him, looking steadily at Saul. 'It's not too late to be a real father. Sell the masque. Sell the casino. Share the money with your children. Share their lives in the time you have left. Be proud of them, so they can be proud of you.'

Saul laughed at her. A harsh and vicious sound, full of spite and derision.

'I never wanted them. You were the one who insisted on having children. And I'll never give up what's mine while there's a breath left in my body.'

Frank went for Saul's throat with outstretched hands. Saul knocked them to one side and back-elbowed him in the side of the neck. Frank dropped to his knees. Tony threw a punch at Saul's face. Saul raised a shoulder to intercept the blow and barely staggered under the impact. He stepped in close and drove his fist into Tony's balls. Tony crashed to the floor, beside Frank. Joyce stayed where she was, frozen in place. Saul showed them all a death's-head smile of utter contempt.

'You never could fight worth a damn, though God knows I tried to show you how. I gave you jobs, I gave you money and opportunity, but that wasn't enough, was it? I never wanted you in my life, and it's not too late to disinherit all of you and be free at last.' He switched his glare to Dana. 'And whoever or whatever you are – I don't care!'

Saul broke off as Frank lurched forward and grabbed his legs, holding him in place. As Saul struggled to break free, Tony forced himself up on one knee and produced a gun. Security staff came racing forward to separate them. I turned to Sally.

'I think it's time we were leaving.'

'Couldn't agree more,' said Sally.

We slipped away unnoticed in all the chaos and confusion and headed out into the lobby. I quickly brought Sally up to speed on what I'd seen in the vault.

'No cash?' said Sally. 'None at all? Oh, poo. Big-time poo!'

'This heist was never about the cash,' I said sternly. 'It's always been all about getting the Masque of Ra for Judi.'

Sally glanced nervously back over her shoulder. 'You didn't tell me the little guy could bring the dead back to life!'

'It came as something of a surprise to me as well,' I said.

I took out the crystal eye and used it to send my voice down to the vault, telling all of them to come up to the lobby. Sally looked at me curiously as I put the eye away.

'I didn't know you could do that.'

'Neither did I,' I said. 'It's been a day of surprises.'

'Why didn't you just phone them?'

'Because you don't get good reception inside a steel-lined vault,' I said.

'Can I have that eye when we're finished with this? Pretty please?'

'Maybe,' I said. 'If you're good.'

She grinned. 'I'm always good, darling.'

When we finally reached the lobby, it was completely deserted. The security guards and the tourists were all inside, watching what was happening. I stood before the Masque of Ra, still hanging in place on its stone pillar. That ancient golden face, with its eyes fixed on forever.

'Security's attention will be fixed on the big family brawl,' I said. 'So go ahead, Sally; switch the masque.'

'I need to see the replica first,' she said quickly.

I slipped the golden cylinder out of my sleeve, tapped it once, and it sprang back into shape as the masque. Sally looked at it and then at the masque on the pillar; suddenly, the masque in my hand was far more solid and a lot heavier. And that was when the mummy of the Pharaoh Khuffu turned his bandaged head to look at us. The coins fell from his face, revealing dark gaps in the bandages where his eyes had once been. But he could still see us.

Sally screamed and backed away. 'It's alive!'

'Does nothing stay dead around here?' I said.

'It's moving!' said Sally. 'I told you . . . I can't stand mummies! Do something!'

She ducked quickly behind me so she could use me as a shield, peering over my shoulder at the mummy as he stepped out of his sarcophagus. He ignored Sally and me, his empty gaze concentrated on what I was holding. The only thing he still cared about, after so many centuries. His bandaged feet made dull thuds on the bare floor as he advanced on us. He didn't move like anything living; he was more like some primeval automaton set in motion by ancient commands. He held one arm out toward me, as though demanding I hand over the masque. Sally clutched my shoulder with a desperate grip.

'*Do something!*'

I turned and thrust the masque into her hands. The mummy immediately turned his blind head to follow it, while Sally stood frozen. I started forward, as though I was about to wrestle the mummy, and then I darted past him and ducked behind the empty sarcophagus.

'Don't just hide from it, you bastard!' said Sally. 'It's coming for me!'

She started to back away, and I stuck my head around the sarcophagus.

'Stay where you are!'

'Are you kidding?'

'Please, Sally, stay put,' I said urgently. 'I have a plan. Trust me.'

Sally stood her ground, shaking in every limb, but still clinging to the masque. The mummy advanced on her, one slow step at a time. I threw all my weight against the standing sarcophagus, straining until the blood pounded in my head, and finally the whole great weight of it toppled forward. The mummy must have sensed something because he stopped and looked back, just in time for the empty coffin to slam down on top of him. The massive weight drove the mummy to the floor and held him there. I went back to Sally, smiling easily.

'Told you I had a plan.'

And then we both froze as the sarcophagus shifted. It rose slowly up and was then thrown violently to one side. The mummy got to his feet again, while I thought quickly. How do you defeat something that has already defeated death and time? I frowned. Time . . . And just like that, I had a plan.

I took out my pen and moved quickly forward. The mummy turned to face me, and I hit the time pen's button just as I stabbed it into the mummy's chest. The same way I'd stabbed the photo in the Gallery of Ghosts. I snatched my hand away and quickly retreated. Time stopped for the mummy. Cut off from the ancient energies that sustained him, Khuffu collapsed into a pile of dust. I walked over, retrieved the deactivated pen from the dust, shook it fastidiously and then put it back in my pocket.

I turned to Sally, half expecting her to have run off with the masque while she had the chance, but she was still there. She met my gaze defiantly.

'I can't leave without Lex.'

Without even having to be asked, she thrust the Masque of Ra back into my hands. And then she smiled at me, dazzlingly.

'You saved me, darling.'

She threw her arms me and gave me a big resounding kiss. And then smiled at me again.

'Anyone can change, darling.'

'I've always believed that,' I said.

Fortunately for both of us, Sally released me just as Lex and Miriam came hurrying into the lobby, followed by Adelaide. Sally ran to Lex and hugged him tightly.

'Darling, it's been awful! The mummy came to life!'

'It's all right,' said Lex. 'I'm here now.' He looked around the lobby and then at me. 'What happened to the mummy?'

'I happened to it,' I said, and he just nodded.

Miriam came quickly over to join me, and I showed her the masque. She ran her fingertips lightly over the solid gold features as I told her I'd seen what they found in the vault. And then Adelaide raised her voice, and we all turned to look at her.

'That's the real masque, isn't it? I can't let you have it. Joyce and I are going to need that kind of money if we're to get away and have a life together. So give me the Masque of Ra, or I'll put my mask back on and look at you.'

Lex moved Sally gently to one side and put himself between Adelaide and the rest of us.

'You still think you can get past my armour?'

'You're not wearing your armour,' said Adelaide.

'And you're not wearing your mask with the Evil Eyes,' said Lex. He smiled. 'Want to race?'

And that was when Joyce came running into the lobby, calling out to Adelaide.

'You've got to do something! They're killing each other!'

'The guards won't let it get that far,' said Adelaide. 'Though if you want, I could go back in there and kill everybody.'

Joyce thought about it and then shook her head. 'No. I can't let that happen. Not in front of Mother.'

'I don't think that's really her,' said Miriam.

And then we all looked back at the main room, as a single shot rang out, followed quickly by several more. There was a long pause before Big Bill Buxton came strolling into the lobby, smiling broadly. He nodded easily to Joyce.

'I'm afraid Tony just killed your father. And then the security guards shot Tony. And Frank. Because I told them to.'

'Why would they follow your orders?' I said.

'Because I've been the real power behind the throne for ages.' Bill looked thoughtfully at Joyce. 'That makes you the last of the Montressors. So you have to die, too.'

He produced a gun and shot Adelaide. She was thrown backwards by the impact and collapsed to the floor, blood staining the front of her tuxedo. Joyce ran to Adelaide, knelt down and held the dying woman to her, sobbing loudly. Adelaide tried to say something and couldn't. Blood welled from her mouth and ran down her chin. Joyce stared wildly at Bill.

'Why? Why would you do that?'

'Always take out the most dangerous opponent first,' Bill said lightly. 'Saul taught me that.' He smiled at all of us. 'Everything that's happened has been my plan all along. From the moment

I first reached out to Judi Rifkin and set this scheme in motion, I've been the man in the background, pulling everyone's strings.

'You see, a long time ago, back when Saul and I were still very close because we had no one else, he made a will leaving me all his earthly possessions. And, what with one thing and another, not least because he couldn't stand anyone in his family, he never got around to changing it.

'I was happy enough to wait, while Saul played with his toys and put on a big show of being the man in charge, and, of course, I had my regular gig here. But once Saul found out what the masque could do, he moved heaven and earth to get his hands on it. And that changed everything. If Saul lived for ever, I was never going to inherit what I was already thinking of as mine.'

He took a step forward, covering us all with his gun. His eyes sparkled merrily.

'All those years of being closer than brothers, and in the end all he could think of was himself. So I arranged to have the masque stolen. And *I* killed your mother, Joyce. Oh yes, that was me. Not Saul. He honestly thought it was just a car accident. I had to do it, because Dana was threatening to tell Saul about our long-standing affair. I couldn't let her hurt him with that knowledge.'

He nodded to me. 'Once you and your crew turned up, I used you to spread rumours through the family and start all of this happening. Now Saul and Frank and Tony are dead . . . and I've had enough of playing games. It's been fun, but I'm afraid it's time for all of you to die. Because I can't have any loose ends hanging around, complicating matters. And yes, Lex, that does include you. You're going to stand there, without your armour, and let me kill you . . . because if you don't, I'll shoot Sally. Right in front of you.

'And when this is all done . . . I'll take the masque and find some way to make it work. And be young and strong and live for ever. Why not? I've earned it.'

I looked at Sally. 'Remember the power packs?'

She grinned broadly.

'I'll decide what's funny here,' said Bill. And he shot Joyce in the face.

Except when he pulled the trigger, nothing happened. Bill looked at his gun, shocked, and tried again. Still nothing. Sally opened her hand to show Bill the bullets she'd switched out of his gun. The same way she'd taken the power packs out of the energy guns on the Moonlight Express.

'Nasty little man . . .' said Sally.

She tossed the bullets on to the floor at Bill's feet. He dropped to one knee and scrambled for them. Lex strode forward and hit Bill once on the back of the neck, and the Khuffu Casino's resident funny man fell dead to the floor. Lex looked down at the body for a moment, and then turned to me.

'I really don't care for this town, Gideon. You can't trust anyone.'

'Funny you should say that,' said Johnny Wilde.

He came strolling into the lobby to join us, with Dana Montressor at his side. He looked at Adelaide and snapped his fingers, and Adelaide sat up suddenly. She clutched at her blood-stained chest and then ripped the shirt open to check where the bullet holes used to be. She wiped the blood off her mouth and smiled shakily at Joyce.

'I'm alive . . .'

Joyce hugged her and then helped her to her feet.

'Luckily, you still had a little life left in you,' said Johnny, 'or I couldn't have saved you. There are limits to what I can do.' He smiled happily round at all of us. 'Sorry I was a bit late; I got held up, persuading a whole bunch of security guards with guns to lie down and take a little nap. Hope I didn't miss anything important.'

Joyce looked at Dana. 'But . . . you brought my mother back to life.'

'No, he didn't,' said Miriam. 'When we were in the vault, we found a body in a packing crate, perfectly embalmed. Saul must have stolen his dead wife from the undertaker's and buried an empty coffin. Or perhaps he just bribed the man. This is Vegas, after all.'

'Why would he keep his dead wife in the vault?' said Sally.

'Because she was the one treasure he couldn't bear to give up,' I said.

Joyce looked at the woman with Dana Montressor's face. 'Then who's that?'

The woman's form seemed to blur and shake, and then was suddenly gone, replaced by a tall man in a grey suit with a flowery waistcoat and a terribly scarred face. He bowed briefly.

'Creighton Price, identity thief, at your service. I came to Vegas searching for some kind of penance, to make up for my many sins. Johnny found me and said he had a way. I hope I've been helpful.'

Lex looked at him and nodded briefly.

'If my work here is done . . .' Creighton looked to Johnny, who smiled cheerfully. Creighton bowed to him. 'Then I will leave you good people to your business, and I will be about mine.'

'Change your ways,' said Lex. 'And I won't have to come looking for you.'

'That is the plan,' said Creighton. He turned away and walked back into the main room.

'We can all change,' said Johnny. 'Some of us more than most.'

'Was it you who got rid of Saul's body?' said Lex.

Johnny grinned. 'I'm always having to clean up after you.'

I turned to Joyce. 'I suppose the casino is yours now.'

Joyce looked at Adelaide. 'We don't want it.'

Adelaide nodded to Lex. 'I never wanted to be the Enchanted Enforcer. Saul made me do it.'

She took the white silk mask out of her pocket and dropped it on the floor.

'I'm a singer.'

She put an arm round Joyce's shoulders, and they walked out of the casino. I held the Masque of Ra to me and smiled around at my crew.

'Let's go home.'

TWELVE

A Photo Finish

'How are we going to get home?' said Lex as I led the way out of the casino.

'How are we going to get out of Las Vegas?' said Sally. 'Far too many people know what we look like now.'

'You could always lose the monocle,' said Miriam.

I looked up and down the crowded street. The traffic was as

heavy as ever, and the sidewalks were packed with people. I tucked the Masque of Ra under my arm and fished in my pocket.

'We can't just hang around here, darling!' said Sally.

'She has a point,' said Lex.

'Does she?' Johnny said interestedly. 'Do you think she'd let me see it if I asked nicely?'

Lex looked at him, and Johnny stared innocently back.

'Gideon, tell me you have a plan to get us out of here,' said Miriam.

'Of course,' I said. 'We're going home on the Moonlight Express.'

Lex looked at me dubiously. 'How are we supposed to find it this time?'

'The Conductor left a little keepsake,' I said. 'I found it tucked away in one of my pockets.'

I brought out an old-fashioned steel whistle and displayed it solemnly to my crew. They didn't seem particularly impressed.

'Why would he give you that?' said Lex.

'Never question a gift from the gods,' Johnny said wisely.

'The Conductor isn't a god, darling!' said Sally.

Johnny looked at her. 'Isn't he?'

'Perhaps he thought he owed me something,' I said. I put out a hand to Lex. 'Give me all the cash you have on you.'

'What?' said Lex.

'I need all your winnings from the roulette wheel,' I said patiently. I turned to Miriam. 'And everything you won at cards. We're going to have to pay for our tickets this time.'

'I don't have any cash on me,' said Lex. He gave Sally a significant look, and she slumped sulkily.

'Oh, poo. I just knew I wouldn't get to keep it.'

Under the pressure of Lex's gaze, Sally reluctantly produced wads of cash from several places about her person and slapped them into his waiting hand. Miriam was already digging money out of her designer bag.

'Easy come, easy go,' I said encouragingly.

'That's easy for you to say,' said Miriam. 'I had to bluff with a pair of tens to get most of this.'

Sally glared at Lex. 'So much for all your worldly goods . . .'

'Judi Rifkin promised us five million in cash,' said Lex.

'She never had any intention of paying!' said Miriam. 'Judi

will have us all killed the moment she gets her hands on the masque!'

'She can try,' said Lex.

'If anyone has a weapon that could get past your armour, it would be Judi,' said Miriam.

Sally stirred uneasily. 'We need to insist on some kind of neutral ground, darlings – somewhere we can make the exchange safely.'

'Judi would never agree to that,' I said. 'She won't pay up unless we place the masque in her hands, and she never leaves her mansion.'

'So we're just going to walk into the lioness's den?' said Lex.

'Trust me,' I said. 'I know what I'm doing.'

Sally sniffed loudly. 'Is he's saying he's got a plan?'

Miriam sighed. 'He's always got a plan.'

'It's what I do,' I said.

'I used to do plans,' Johnny said wistfully, 'but they always got away from me. I think they did it on purpose.' He stopped and frowned. 'You're ignoring me, aren't you?'

'Only in self-defence,' I said.

I took the money from Sally and Miriam, and then raised the steel whistle to my mouth.

'Hold it,' said Lex. 'You're going to summon a steam engine into the middle of Las Vegas?'

'The Moonlight Express is a law unto itself,' I said.

The whistle produced a sweet and piercing note that seemed to hang on the air over and above the roar of passing cars. And then I watched, fascinated, as the two streams of traffic seemed to just drift apart without any of the drivers noticing, until a wide gap had opened up between them.

The sky was suddenly dark, just for us, and a great beam of moonlight stretched across the starry night, before bending sharply down to touch the Earth. It shot along the street, a shimmering moonbeam hanging a foot above the ground, like a line drawn across the world. And from out of the darkness came a wild and exuberant cry: the triumphant steam whistle of the Moonlight Express. The engine appeared first, a big black beast of a train thundering along the moonlit trail, followed quickly by the old-fashioned carriages in their brown-and-cream livery. There was a great screeching of brakes and much venting of steam, and the Moonlight Express slammed to a halt right in front of us. A door in the front carriage swung open, and the Conductor's top-hatted head emerged. He looked at us for a long moment and then fixed me with a cold appraising stare.

'I trust you are planning to pay for your tickets this time?'

I held up Lex's and Miriam's winnings, and the Conductor shook his head slowly, as though even that much money was barely sufficient to justify stopping his train. But he kicked out the collapsible wooden steps and disappeared back into the carriage, so we could enter. I led my crew on board, doing my best to look as though it had never even occurred to me that he would do anything else.

The Moonlight Express rode the moonbeam trail across the roof of the world, covering the distance between Las Vegas and London in hardly any time at all. There were no dangerous passengers to disrupt our journey this time. They all looked human enough and made a point of keeping to their seats and not even glancing in our direction. I assumed the Conductor had put a quiet word in their ears.

Lex and Sally propped up the bar. Miriam and I found seats together and studied the star-speckled view. And Johnny practised sitting on his seat, as opposed to above or near it. In his own way, he was trying to be good.

The train dropped out of the night sky and deposited us outside the front door of Judi Rifkin's isolated mansion. The moment we'd all disembarked, the carriage door slammed shut and the Moonlight Express disappeared in a blast of steam.

It was still dark, still night. The mansion's exterior security lights snapped on, so that we seemed to be standing in one big spotlight. What I could see of the grounds were still completely deserted, and there wasn't a sound to be heard anywhere. Miriam moved in close beside me.

'Shouldn't a whole bunch of alarms be deafening us by now?'

'Don't worry,' I said. 'I'm sure someone knows we're here.'

'Judi is supposed to have her own private army of guards, darlings,' Sally said nervously, sticking very close to Lex. 'Big, brawny types, with low foreheads and guns that make really big holes in you.'

'As long as I'm here, they'd have to get past Heaven and Hell to get to you,' said Lex.

'And you've got me!' Johnny said cheerfully. 'What could possibly go wrong?'

'Do you want me to write out a list?' said Sally.

'If you like,' said Johnny.

'We're perfectly safe,' I said firmly. 'As long as we have the masque. Miriam, why are you scowling?'

Miriam sniffed loudly. 'I can't believe the Conductor took every bit of cash we had, just for five tickets.'

'Yes . . . I thought that was a bit much,' said Johnny. 'So I quietly transferred it back into your pockets when the Conductor wasn't looking.'

I shook my head. 'Just when I thought we were finally on good terms . . .'

Sally and Miriam ignored me, making loud, happy noises as they dug into their pockets and produced handfuls of cash. Lex looked thoughtfully at the Wild Card.

'You're being very practical these days, Johnny.'

He nodded solemnly. 'I know. I fight against it, but what can you do?'

Miriam put her money away and scowled at the front door. 'She's going to kill us.'

'Don't worry,' I said. 'She might have a plan, but I've got a better one.'

'How many plans have you got?' said Sally.

'It's all been the same one,' I said. 'Right from the beginning. And we are finally approaching the endgame.'

'That's what worries me,' said Miriam.

I headed for the front door, and my crew quickly fell into place behind me. I was quietly proud that they trusted me to know what I was doing. I knocked loudly, and there was barely a pause before the door was yanked open and a whole bunch of very upset guards stared out at us. It was a moment before they remembered they had weapons and pointed them at us.

I smiled easily at the guards, not even glancing at the guns.

'Gideon Sable and crew. I think you'll find we're expected.'

'How the hell did you get this close to the mansion without setting off all the landmines and bear traps?' said the senior guard.

'Trade secret,' I said briskly. 'Now, take us to Judi. We have something she wants.'

I held up the Masque of Ra, and the guards looked at the man in charge for instructions. He nodded reluctantly, and they lowered their guns and fell back. Once we were inside, the door was slammed shut and locked, and several bolts were slammed into place. Just to make it clear we weren't going anywhere. The senior guard stuck his scowling face into mine.

'You hand that thing over to me for safe keeping, and then I'll go find out whether Ms Rifkin feels like seeing you.'

I just smiled and shook my head. 'I have strict instructions from Judi to deliver the masque to her and no one else.'

The guards looked at each other. It was obvious from their faces that they had experience of what happened to people who didn't follow Judi's instructions exactly. The senior guard gestured brusquely for us to follow him, and led us quickly through familiar corridors full of expensive art and impressive statues. I had to wonder how much it must cost to keep everything dusted. Sally made squeaky little *Ooh!* and *Aah!* noises, but kept her hands to herself. It probably helped that Lex had a firm grip on her arm. We finally reached the door to Judi's private chamber, and the senior guard gestured to his men. They quickly moved to cover us with their guns. The senior guard smiled at me in a very unpleasant way.

'You can go in with me, but the others stay out here to ensure your good behaviour. One wrong move and you can listen to them scream.'

'Now that's just rude,' I said. 'Lex, teach them some manners.'

The light and dark armour swept over him in a moment, and the guards cried out in shock and horror. The Damned was in and among them with inhuman speed, striking men down before anyone could get off a shot. He was like a force of nature, or an act of God, and the guards never stood a chance.

Part of me wanted to get involved, if only for my pride's sake, but it was all over before I could think of anything to do. I consoled myself with the thought that I was a thief, not a fighter, and that the truly dangerous business was still to come.

Judi Rifkin was waiting for us behind that closed door, like a black widow spider sitting in the middle of her web of money and power. And all I had was a plan.

Unconscious guards lay scattered over the rich carpeting. The Damned dismissed his armour and studied his work with calm satisfaction. I could remember when he wouldn't have left a single man alive. Sally kicked one of the guards in the face. Lex looked at her.

'He was going for his gun, darling! And he was looking at my arse all the way here!'

'I believe you,' said Lex.

'You do?' said Sally. She hugged him fiercely and then beamed at the rest of us. 'Isn't he a sweetie?'

The Damned had been called many things in his time, some of them by me, but I was pretty sure that sweetie wasn't one of them. I turned to the closed door and kicked it open. Start as you mean to go on. I strode into Judi's private chamber with the Masque of Ra under my arm and my crew behind me, to find her sitting on her elevated throne, deep in conversation with Old Harry.

Judi started to yell for her guards, but broke off when I held out the Masque of Ra. She stared at the gleaming golden face as though she'd never seen anything more precious.

'Bring it to me,' she said, her voice hoarse with emotion.

I walked over to the throne and placed the masque carefully into her withered hands. She leaned back so she could balance the masque on her lap, and stared into the impassive golden features as though they contained all the wisdom in the world. After a moment, I cleared my throat meaningfully. When that didn't work, I raised my voice.

'You promised us five million pounds, Judi, once the Masque of Ra was in your hands.'

She didn't even look at me. 'Now I will be young and strong and immortal, just like Fredric,' she said in a slow, gloating voice. 'And I will persecute him for all eternity.'

Miriam fixed Harry with her coldest stare. 'What are you doing here?'

'Talking shop,' he said calmly.

'I thought you were going out of business?' said Miriam.

'Never too late for one last deal.'

Miriam scowled at him, and I felt like ducking. This was Old Harry we were dealing with.

'All the way through this heist, your name kept coming up,' said Miriam. 'Why have you been working with Judi?'

'Just taking care of some unfinished business before I have to leave,' said Harry. 'Fredric Hammer might not be the threat he once was, but Judi seems intent on moving into the territory he used to occupy. She has collected all kinds of things that are far too powerful to be left in unsafe hands.'

'Including the Masque of Ra?' said Miriam.

Harry smiled. 'I've never had any interest in acquiring that particular item. I just used it to bring all the right players together.'

I turned to Sally. 'All right, switch it back.'

She looked at me innocently. 'What's that, darling?'

'Back in the casino lobby, you grabbed the replica of the masque while we were all distracted by Creighton Price,' I said. 'And while we were travelling on the Moonlight Express, you switched the replica for the real thing. Did you really think I wouldn't notice the difference in weight?'

'I don't know what you're talking about, darling.'

'Give him the masque,' said Lex.

She stared at him disbelievingly. 'You'd take his word over mine?'

'Gideon knows who you used to be,' Lex said steadily. 'I have put my faith in the woman you could be.'

'Are you asking me to choose between you and the masque?' said Sally.

'No,' said Lex. 'Between your old life and your new.'

Sally shot a quick glare at Judi, so immersed in her treasure that she wasn't paying any attention to us. Sally lowered her voice anyway.

'Why should that old witch have the masque? We could be immortal together, darling! You'd never have to worry about Hell because you'd never die, and I'd never have to worry about growing old and losing my looks. Think of all the things we could do!'

'The masque only makes its owner immortal,' said Lex. 'And then only for as long as they hold on to it. I could be immortal, or you, but not both. Make your choice, Sally.'

'This isn't fair,' said Sally.

'The things that matter rarely are,' said Lex.

'Oh, poo,' said Sally.

The masque was suddenly in her hands, shining brightly in the cool, unemotional light of Judi's private chamber.

'Where have you been hiding that?' said Miriam.

'Trade secret,' said Sally.

'I know!' Johnny said brightly, and then Sally looked at him and he stopped talking.

Sally switched the masque for its replica. Judi looked startled as the masque in her hands was suddenly heavier and more solid.

Lex nodded to Sally. 'You can't have it all.'

'I can have a damned good try,' said Sally. And then she tucked the replica up her sleeve and smiled at him dazzlingly. 'But what the hell – you're worth it, darling.'

'What is going on here?' Judi said querulously. 'Why does the masque feel different? Are you trying to cheat me, Gideon?'

'A lot of people want the Masque of Ra,' I said smoothly. 'Its unique energies make it easy to track down, and the masque can't help but react. Might I suggest we move it to a more secure setting? Some place better protected from outside influences?'

Judi nodded slowly. 'I have a special vault, underneath the house. Something I learned from my ex.' She gave me a stern look. 'Don't try any of your tricks. My vault's protections are specially prepared to deal with you and your toys.'

'The masque will be safe there,' I said. 'And we will be free to discuss the fee you promised.'

Judi smiled. 'Trust me, Gideon; you'll get everything that's coming to you.'

She started to get up from her throne, clutching the masque to her, but she was so frail that Harry and I had to step forward and take an arm each to help her. Once she was on her feet, she shrugged our hands away, angry at us for our effrontery, and at her own infirmities for making it necessary. She made her way over to a stretch of blank wall and slapped one palm against it. I could just make out a series of faint electronic sounds as a hidden sensor recognized her palm print, and then a whole section of the wall slid sideways, revealing a dark opening.

I carefully kept any hint of a smile off my face. I knew Judi had to have a secret vault somewhere, because Judi couldn't bear for Fredric to have something she didn't, but I hadn't been sure how to persuade her to give me access. But there's always room for improvisation in every plan. I exchanged a glance with

Miriam, and she nodded to confirm she'd also picked up on the electronic noises and was ready to charm and shut down all security systems as necessary. Judi entered the dark opening, clutching the Masque of Ra to her, and a whole bunch of lights came on. We followed her in.

Judi rode a stairlift down the steep incline, into the depths under her house. The rest of us had to walk down a long flight of bare stone steps. We finally ended up before a massive steel door that reminded me of the entrance to Saul's vault, only this one was traditionally rectangular. Harry and I had to help Judi out of her chair again. She waved us away irritably and announced her name to the steel door. There was a long pause as the security systems thought about it, and then the door swung slowly back.

Judi's vault was just a great stone chamber. No furnishings or fittings, not even any shelves. But it was still a collector's paradise, packed full of the expensively odd and outrageously unique. A suit of medieval armour, twelve feet tall and fashioned from leaf-green jade, standing over a longsword thrust though a blacksmith's anvil. A sheep in a bottle, which looked at us sadly as we passed. And a stuffed and mounted pterodactyl, its outstretched leathery wings pinned to a massive display board like the world's biggest and ugliest butterfly. There were priceless works of art, lost historical treasures and all the wonderous flotsam and jetsam of the hidden world. Along with piles of gold bullion and precious jewels, and everything that should have been in Saul's casino vault, but wasn't. None of Judi's treasures had ever been properly set out or displayed, just dumped wherever she put them. Because all that mattered to Judi was that she owned it, and her hated ex-husband didn't.

'My fingers are itching, darlings,' murmured Sally.

'Behave yourself,' I said quietly. 'We are not at home to Ms Impulse.'

Judi swung round and glared at Sally, catching all of us by surprise. We hadn't realized she was paying attention.

'Don't get ideas above your station, young lady. You even look like touching one of my precious things, and you'll end up as a new exhibit. After you've been properly stuffed and mounted, of course, and someone has done all the invisible mending to hide the bullet holes in your clothes.'

She laughed happily, her good humour restored at the prospect, and she looked quickly around to make sure we were all properly impressed. The moment her eyes were off me, I looked to Miriam, and she smiled quickly to reassure me that she'd charmed all the security systems.

'You've got the masque now,' I said to Judi. 'You have immortality and revenge on your ex. Everything you ever wanted. Why don't I take a photo, to commemorate the occasion?'

I took out my mobile phone, slowly and carefully, and showed it to Judi so she could be sure that was all it was. She smiled regally and struck a pose with the Masque of Ra. I took her photo, and Judi disappeared. A moment later a photo appeared on the nearest wall: a portrait of Judi Rifkin holding the Masque of Ra. She looked perfectly happy.

'What the hell just happened?' said Sally.

I smiled and held up the phone. 'Allow me to present the Camera of Doctor Caligari.'

'But that was invented at the beginning of the last century!' said Miriam.

'The original camera fell apart long ago,' I said. 'This is the latest update. I lifted it from Sebastian's pocket, back in the Gallery of Ghosts. I had a feeling it might come in handy.'

'And that is what I'm here for,' said Harry. 'The last item on my list, before I head off into the wild dark yonder. Because some things are just too dangerous to leave behind.'

I nodded and handed him the phone.

'You're just giving it to him?' said Miriam.

'It's not my phone,' I said casually.

Harry smiled at all of us. 'The game is over. You are safe from a woman who would never have stopped trying to kill you, I have the Camera of Doctor Caligari, and this little collection is no longer in a psychopath's hands. I can leave the world behind with a clear conscience.' He nodded at the photo of Judi with her masque. 'A kind enough fate. Captured in her happiest moment, for ever. She did say she wanted to be immortal . . .'

'But we've lost the masque!' said Sally. 'After everything we went through to get it!'

'It doesn't matter,' I said. 'The Masque of Ra is a fake – nothing more than an ancient Egyptian legend. That's why Saul could never find a way to make it work. I discovered it was nothing but an old funeral mask when I first tried to steal it, years ago.'

Miriam looked sharply at Harry. 'That's why you were never interested in owning it.'

Lex stared at me. 'Why didn't you tell us this before?'

'It was important that all of you believed in it,' I said. 'So you could convince everyone else it was real. I needed Saul to concentrate on the masque, so he'd never see me coming.'

'Are you happy now he's dead?' said Miriam.

'Happy now that there's one less burden on my conscience,' I said. 'I was the one who persuaded Robert and Doug to get out of the con game and invest their savings in a casino.'

'They wouldn't have blamed you for what happened,' said Miriam.

'Probably not,' I said. 'But I did.'

Lex nodded. 'I know how that works.'

I turned to Harry. 'Miriam and I will take over your shop.' I gestured at all the marvellous items surrounding us. 'And I think I've found our first stock.'

'That is what I had in mind,' said Harry.

'Does everyone around here have a plan?' said Miriam.

'It does feel that way sometimes,' I said.

'How are we going to get all of this past the guards?' said Miriam.

'With Judi gone, there's no one left to pay their wages,' I said. 'But since this house and all its contents belong to us now, by right of conquest, I think they'll be happy to work for us.'

'So,' said Sally, 'no Masque of Ra and no five million pounds?'

'That was never going to happen,' I said. 'But I will buy out your share of the house. Eventually.'

'Oh, poo,' said Sally.

'In the meantime, we still have my roulette winnings,' said Lex.

Sally beamed at him. 'Seed money! Oh, I have such marvellous plans, darling!'

'Of course you do,' said Lex. He nodded to me. 'Now the heist is over, it's time we were on our way.'

'Where will you go?' said Miriam.

Sally took Lex's arm possessively. 'Anywhere we want.

Nobody has to be damned, as long as one person is ready to forgive them.'

'It took me a long time to realize that,' said Lex.

'You just needed a little push, darling,' said Sally.

Lex turned to Johnny. 'I don't like the idea of leaving you on your own.'

'You don't need me,' said Johnny. 'My little boy is all grown up . . . And since the crew clearly doesn't need me, because I hardly had to do anything this time, I think I'll walk behind the curtains of the world and take a really good look at what's going on there.'

'Will you be coming back?' said Lex.

'Would you?' said Johnny.

I put my arm around Miriam and grinned at everyone. 'That old gang of mine is breaking up. And I couldn't be happier.'